T0148671

Applying her Manhattan fashion sense to the sensibilities of a Long Island clientele, Kelly Quinn is setting new trends with second-hand name brand apparel—and finding killers with a deadly sense of style . . .

The fortunes of Kelly's Lucky Cove Resale Boutique are sinking fast—literally, as the weathered roof of her grandmother's old consignment shop springs a new leak with every rain. She hopes her latest client, overnight fitness and social media sensation Tawny Nicole, has enough valued and wanted items she can sell fast enough to keep her roof from crumbling down.

When Kelly arrives at Tawny's home to appraise her attire, she's stunned to find Serena Dawson, "the Dragonista of Seventh Avenue," there. The last time she saw her ex-boss was when Serena humiliatingly and publicly fired her from her New York City job. Now Tawny is married to Serena's ex-husband and is caught in the crossfire of some unfinished divorce settlements.

But when Kelly returns to Tawny's the following day, she discovers her dead body—and Serena standing over it. Her former employer may be nasty and unrepentant, but she's no killer—prompting Kelly to pick up the threads to try and find the real culprit . . .

By Debra Sennefelder

Food Blogger Mysteries
THE UNINVITED CORPSE
THE HIDDEN CORPSE
THREE WIDOWS AND A CORPSE
THE CORPSE WHO KNEW TOO MUCH

Resale Boutique Mysteries
MURDER WEARS A LITTLE BLACK DRESS
SILENCED IN SEQUINS
WHAT NOT TO WEAR TO A GRAVEYARD
HOW TO FRAME A FASHIONISTA

How to Frame a Fashionista

Debra Sennefelder

LYRICAL UNDERGROUND
Kensington Publishing Corp.
www.kensingtonbooks.com

LYRICAL UNDERGROUND BOOKS are published by
Kensington Publishing Corp.
119 West 40th Street
New York, NY 10018

First Electronic Edition: December 2020
ISBN-13: 978-1-5161-0895-4 (ebook)
ISBN-10: 1-5161-0895-7 (ebook)

First Print Edition: December 2020
ISBN-13: 978-1-5161-0898-5
ISBN-10: 1-5161-0898-1

Printed in the United States of America

For my niece, Sarah Kuhlmann.

Chapter 1

Holy Manolos!

Kelly Quinn's eyes widened as she stared at her watch. She'd fallen back to sleep. For a whole hour.

"No, no, no, no." She tossed off the covers and swung her legs over the side of her bed. "Not this morning." She stood, ignoring her Ugg slippers and her cashmere robe, both indulgences bought while she'd had a discount at the high-end department store where she once worked.

She jogged on bare feet across the carpet into the bathroom. She brushed her teeth, turned on the shower, and applied a mud mask to her face in record time before stepping into the teeny stall to let the water spray down on her.

Lathered up and rinsed off, she stepped out of the shower. A quick blow dry and the minimalist amount of makeup was applied to make her look refreshed and awake.

Time-crunched, she didn't have the leisure of sorting through her closet to find the perfect outfit of the day or hashtag OTTD when she posted on Instagram. With her late start, there'd be no selfie, filter selection, or posting that morning. Hashtag Notimesleepyhead. No, what she needed was something to wear ASAP. She reached in for the easiest, yet fashionable, garment from her closet. Darn. She wanted to look extra chic and pulled together when she met with Tawny Fallow.

Then why did I fall back to sleep?

Kelly let out a sigh. Another late night of uploading garments she sold on a resale website and finishing up an article for BudgetChic.com. She recently landed her own weekly column on the website all about affordable fashion. These days without her beloved employee discount and access to in-the-know sample sales, she was the target reader for Budget Chic. A yawn escaped her glossed lips as she pulled out a cap-sleeved, black, faux-wrap maxi dress. The lightweight poly-blend dress was a good choice for working a full day in the boutique and meeting her newest consignment customer.

After she slipped the dress over her head, she stepped into a pair of snakeskin booties with a cone heel, swept her hair up into a messy bun, and added a pair of silver hoops.

After a final head-to-toe look over in the full-length mirror, she dashed out of the bedroom, and Howard, her orange cat, greeted her.

His loud meow and cool stare made it crystal clear that no matter how late she was running, he would be fed breakfast. When she claimed her inheritance of the boutique, she believed the business end of things would be the most challenging.

She was wrong.

The cat was the most challenging part of her new life. He had multiple personalities—lovable, playful, demanding, and *I'll kill you in your sleep*—and she never knew which one she would encounter.

She glanced at her watch. Fifteen minutes until the *Open* sign needed to be flipped over and the front door of the boutique unlocked. Luckily her commute was only one flight of stairs.

Last fall, after her beloved granny passed away, she took over the Lucky Cove Resale Boutique. Since then, she worked 24/7 to turn the business around. At this point, it was now eking out a profit. If she hadn't been a hawk with her spreadsheets, she might have missed it. Yeah, it was that small. Regardless, it was better than the red the boutique was in previously.

She pressed her lips together. "You don't think you could skip a meal just one time? How about brunch?"

Meeooow.

"Okay, fine, you win. Breakfast, it is." She walked past Howard, and he followed on her heels to the kitchen.

After Christmas, with the help of her friends, she gave the small yet efficient space a budget-friendly makeover. Now all she needed was to learn to cook.

Tucked in the corner on the counter sat a pressure cooker that was gifted to her by her friend, Ariel Barnes. She made a few meals in it and hadn't blown the place up—unlike her cookie baking attempt in December that left the apartment filled with smoke. It seemed she was making progress.

"Would you like tuna and shrimp this morning?" She pulled out a small can from a cupboard, and Howard rubbed against her leg. "I'll take that as a yes."

As she emptied the minced food into Howard's bowl, her frazzled mood, the result of her late start, faded away and was replaced by excitement.

Every time she landed a new consignment client, she was elated. During their conversation, Tawny said she had a sizable amount of clothing to consign and a tight schedule, so bringing all of the items to the boutique was impossible. Kelly assured her it was not a problem to drive over to the house to look through the clothing.

Kelly had done her first in-home estimate when an over-scheduled, exhausted housewife made the request. Not wanting to lose sales or repeat business, Kelly jumped at the chance to land some impressive designer labels, only to find that the woman had done a bait-and-switch. Kelly fell for the drop of designer names, only to find a rack full of shopping channel clothing.

Luckily, a few items from higher-end shops helped round out the merchandise. Kelly left with a bunch of clothing and information about the death of a local resident.

Kelly not only made a huge career change when she moved back to her hometown of Lucky Cove, but she also found herself doing a little amateur sleuthing on the side.

Though it was a new year, and so far she'd stayed out of any murder investigations. See, sometimes New Year's resolutions work.

She glanced at her watch again. Time to hustle. She set the filled bowl on the floor for Howard and filled his water bowl.

"See you later, little guy." She walked out of the kitchen toward the door. Before she reached for the knob, she snatched her Louis Vuitton six-key holder from the tray on the console table. Outside on the small landing, her brightening mood vanished. Poof. Just like that.

A puddle of water could do that to a gal.

She gazed upward and spotted a big wet circle on the ceiling. Her mouth gaped as she watched water drip from above.

Apparently the roof patch she'd done in October failed.

"No, no, no, no. Not today."

Drip.

Kelly balled her hands into fists and muttered a few words her granny would have disapproved of.

Drip.

She spun around, opened her apartment door, and hurried through the apartment to the kitchen to get a bucket.

Howard gave her a quick look and then went back to feasting on his breakfast. At least one of them was having an excellent start to their day.

She opened the cabinet beneath the sink and pulled out a bucket. She dashed back to the hallway and positioned the bucket to catch the water and then took a deep breath.

The house was old, so a leak here or there didn't seem unreasonable. It would stop leaking at some point. Right?

With the bucket in place, Kelly descended the stairs, glancing back one too many times causing a misstep that had her almost tumbling down the stairs. She'd love a do-over for her morning—one that didn't include a leak.

Downstairs in the boutique's staffroom, aka the office, storage area, and breakroom, Kelly made a pot of coffee. It brewed while she opened the cash register and did a quick walk-thru of the boutique. Back in the staffroom and sipping her first cup of liquid gold, she checked her phone's calendar to confirm the appointment time with Tawny.

Next, she made sure the contact info for her roofer was still on the phone. You know, just in case the leak upstairs became something more significant.

The back door opened, and the lyrical sound of birds chirping filtered in as Breena Collins entered. The music was a sure sign spring was on its way.

Breena had a bounce in her step, and excitement sparkled in her amber eyes. Someone was in a good mood.

Kelly slipped her phone into her purse. Tawny's house was a short drive away, so it wouldn't take long to get there. Maybe she had time for a second cup of coffee.

"Good morning. It's a beautiful day, isn't it? Even if I'm stuck here while you get to meet Tawny. I'm so jealous. I've been dying to meet her. You'd think, in a town the size of Lucky Cove, we'd have run into each other at some point. Guess we don't move in the same social circles." Breena shrugged out of her jacket and set her lunch tote in the refrigerator.

Kelly pressed her lips together. Breena was a huge fan of Tawny. While it would have been nice to take her sales associate with her to the appointment, it was always important to present a professional image. The last thing she needed was for Breena to go all fangirl over the new client.

Until Kelly received the call for consignment, she hadn't heard of Tawny or her online fitness business. She'd been too busy, and now with a regular fashion column, she doubted there would be much free downtime in her near future. Last night over dinner with her best friend, Liv Moretti, she reviewed her plan for bringing in extra money. By the time they got to the brownies Liv baked, Kelly was sure she'd have no social life for the next ten years. That might have been the reason she had seconds of the brownies. Okay, she had three of them, and she was feeling the guilt and bloating. Another reason wearing the maxi dress was the perfect choice.

"I don't think you not running into her has anything to do with social circles. Between your two jobs, college courses, and raising Tori, you stay busy. And probably Tawny's business keeps her busy too." It looked like Kelly wasn't alone in the too-much-to-do phase of life. At least she didn't have a child to take care of. Only a cat. She shrugged into her black wool coat. Her second cup of coffee would wait until she got got back.

Breena grabbed her Break A Leg mug off the drainboard. After high school, she headed straight to NYC to pursue an acting career. Things hadn't worked out as she expected, and she returned to Lucky Cove. Settled back into her parents' home, she enrolled in college and found more stable work. Kelly thought back to her high school days and tried to recall what Breena's parents thought of their daughter's big dream to be an actress. She couldn't. As for most of her life, her thoughts were mostly about herself. She frowned. That wasn't a character trait she was proud of.

"I guess you're right."

"So, what exactly is her business?"

Breena's frown quickly shifted into a smile. "It's a workout and diet program called Personalized Body Fit or PBF for short. It's all over social media. She has her own video channel where she uploads short workouts that complement the program."

"How did you find PBF?" Kelly moved from the coat rack and over to the desk. There she gathered her key ring holder and slipped it into her purse along with her phone and lipstick.

"I found her video channel. Remember, in January, when I was home because Tori was sick?"

"You were looking for a workout for Tori?"

Breena laughed as she added cream to her coffee and then walked to the table where the boutique's staff of three ate meals and had meetings. She dropped onto a chair. "No, silly. I was looking for kids' videos, and somehow I came across Tawny Nicole."

"Tawny Nicole?"

Breena nodded. "That's what she goes by online. Tawny Nicole Fitness. TNF."

Kelly shook her head. PBF. TNF. Too many acronyms.

"Anyway, I started with her free videos, and I followed her everywhere online," Breena said.

Kelly understood that was how social media worked, but it sounded too much like stalking to her. Though, what she wouldn't give to have such committed stalkers on the boutique's social media platforms.

Breena continued. "And then I found out about PBF, and I had to try. I don't have time or money to go to a gym."

Kelly cringed at the comment. She wanted to pay Breena more, but there wasn't any extra money in the budget for pay raises for her or her two employees. Another reason she was staying up late in the evening to work on freelance assignments and marketing for the boutique.

"Why? You look great." Kelly wished she had Breena's hour-glass figure. Her long-time friend always seemed to have a healthy self-image. What changed?

Redness tinged Breena's cheeks, and she tucked a lock of auburn curls behind her ear. "Thanks to Tawny. Like you said, I'm way busy, and I slacked on exercise. I've also been making poor food choices. Since starting PBF, I've lost ten pounds. It's all customized for your body. She's a genius."

Genius? Kelly considered trying PBF. She glanced at her mid-section. Not that bad, but maybe a little too soft. Her infrequent morning runs weren't cutting it like they used to. A flash of panic set through her. Everyone was right. By the time she hit thirty, she'd have the makings of middle age spread. *Whoa*! She had a few years to go, so she had time for a course correction. Besides, thirty wasn't anywhere near middle age.

"You should try it."

Kelly gave Breena a questioning look.

"Oh, no, I didn't mean it that way. You're in good shape. PBF is designed to meet your goals. Mine is to lose about twenty pounds. Yours would be to build more muscle so you can keep your lean frame easier." Breena jumped up and dashed over to Kelly, pulling her phone from her jean's back pocket.

Nice save. But the fact Kelly's employee used the word *good* instead of *great* to describe her shape gave Kelly a reason to consider the program seriously.

"Look, here's Tawny's Instagram account." Breena swiped through Tawny's feed.

Kelly's eyes nearly popped out of their sockets when she saw how many followers Tawny had. It was official. Her new client was a social media star.

She was also uber-fit.

"Oh, my goodness." Kelly took the phone and studied the photographs of Tawny. Fit would be an understatement. She bared her midriff in every other photo. Taut, sculpted, and flat. Everything a gal wanted in a mid-section. Sprinkled in between the bare midriff pics were close-ups of Tawny's makeup-free face. She looked healthy and approachable. Someone Kelly would feel comfortable working with. There were some motivational quotes. *Stop wishing. Start doing.* Kelly scrolled past them and came to video clips.

Kelly tapped on a video and watched Tawny do a burpee. She agreed that it was a challenging exercise for working several parts of the body at once, but burpees were also evil. She hated them. Watching Tawny do them so easily, and the fact that she was at least ten years older than Kelly, irritated her.

"She's amazing, right?" Breena asked.

"She certainly is." Kelly handed the phone back to Breena.

"It would be so much fun if we were doing PBF together!"

"I don't think burpees are fun. Look, I have to leave now and I won't be long. After my appointment with Tawny, we can go over the marketing plan for summer." Even though they were only weeks from the start of spring, retail was always at least a season ahead.

Breena beamed with excitement. "Great! I saw the printout for the items we sold online. I'll pack them up now and dash out to the post office after our meeting. Okay?"

"Sounds good." Kelly picked up her purse from the desk. She'd broken out her no-label, black, faux crocodile shoulder bag for today's appointment. It was simple yet elegant, and even though it didn't have a designer label, it was pricey because of its quality. A definite splurge, but a smart investment.

"Oh, I want to hear everything about your meeting with Tawny. All the details." Kelly nodded, then turned and walked to the back door. She sucked in her three-brownie-bloated stomach and squared her shoulders. Surely that was enough to make her look ten pounds thinner.

Kelly parked her Jeep in the driveway of the Fallow house, a stately two-floor Colonial with an intricately patterned walkway that led to the elegant front door. The home was located on a quiet street not too far from Main Street. It would have been a pleasant walk if she had been sure she'd be leaving without merchandise.

When she spoke with Tawny, she was instructed to come to the cottage situated behind the main house. Kelly grabbed her purse and stepped out of the Jeep. Gently curved garden beds flowed along the property and around the house. She imagined, in a few weeks, bursts of color would bloom, nudging out all the drabness leftover from a harsh winter. Not a gardener by any stretch of the imagination, Kelly could only guess at how those garden beds would transform.

She walked around the front of her Jeep and took notice of the sleek silver Mercedes parked next to her vehicle. She glimpsed into the passenger window as she walked past the car. Not too shabby. And neither was the Louis Vuitton duffel bag on the passenger seat. Her heartbeat did a pitter-patter at the sight. She barely scraped together enough money to buy her key holder. The duffel would have to wait for many more years, possibly decades.

Kelly walked away from the luxury car and the duffel bag before she started drooling. She followed the stone path that veered off the main walkway.

The sun was out in full glory, melting the fallen snow, just what her roof didn't need. She pushed aside those thoughts. They were counterproductive to what she needed to do—land a new client obsessed with clothes. They always made the best consigners.

* * * *

Continuing along the path, she sidestepped some puddles. The cottage came into view. It had petite windows framed with shutters and window boxes that must overflow with pretty flowers in the warmer months. As she got closer, she heard raised voices coming through the open front door.

One voice sounded oddly familiar to her.

OMG. Was it *her*?

Nah. Not possible.

There was no way in heck the Dragonista of Seventh Avenue would be in Lucky Cove.

A few footsteps closer, and Kelly couldn't shake the fact that the voice belonged to her former boss.

"This is none of your business!" That voice sounded like the one she heard on the phone when she talked to Tawny.

"It's between Jason and me." That was definitely *her* voice.

All at once, Kelly's chest tightened, her vision blurred, and she became lightheaded. It was a familiar feeling that she hadn't experienced since her last day at Bishop's Department store.

She froze as her eyes focused on the figure clad in a faux leopard coat blocking the doorway of the cottage. Same height, same frame.

"Of course, it's my business. He's my husband!" Tawny said.

"Only because he was desperate and vulnerable when you paraded into his life in your knockoff Lululemon."

Yep. There was no doubt in Kelly's mind now. But what was *she* doing in Lucky Cove?

"How dare you! Get off my property."

"You're forgetting who I am."

Oh, boy. Kelly, still frozen in place, had to figure out what to do. Interrupt? From her experience, that was never a good idea. Turn and run? Then she'd miss her appointment with Tawny, and she needed clothing to sell.

Buck up. I don't work for her any longer.

Kelly squared her shoulders, not to shave a few pounds from her appearance this time, but to fortify herself. She was about to have a very awkward encounter with the woman who fired her in front of the whole office staff.

Kelly put one foot in front of the other and continued forward until she reached the cottage's entry. She cleared her throat loudly and caught both women's attention.

The unwelcome visitor slowly turned her head to look over her shoulder. Her trademark tortoiseshell sunglasses covered a good portion of her face. Her plump lips, thanks to injectables, were pursed, and her raven-colored hair was still chin length with wispy bangs.

"Kelly Quinn? Well, wonders never cease." Serena Dawson's voice was icy and

haughty, as much of a trademark as her sunglasses. She lowered her glasses and gave Kelly a thorough once-over, then readjusted them on the bridge of her slender nose. "What on earth are you doing here?"

Chapter 2

"I could ask you the same thing." Kelly stood firm. She wasn't about to let Serena see that her legs were wobbly or get a hint of the fact her heart was racing a mile a minute. No. She wasn't the assistant fashion buyer that never could do anything that pleased the grand dame of retail fashion. She was a business owner and an up and coming fashion writer.

Serena waved her gloved hand. "It's none of your business why I'm here. Run along now. Tawny and I are in the middle of a conversation."

It appeared that time hadn't mellowed Serena or improved her manners. Kelly shouldn't have been surprised by the dismissal but she was. They were now in her hometown, her territory. Serena may have ruled Seventh Avenue but Lucky Cove was Kelly's.

Before Kelly could say something, Tawny stepped forward, wagging a finger at Serena.

"The almighty Serena Dawson never ceases to amaze me. Just when I think your behavior couldn't possibly get any worse it does. Not that it's any of your business, but I've asked Kelly to come here. She's welcome. You're not!" Tawny's tone left no doubt in Kelly's mind she wasn't messing around. While she didn't have big, bulging muscles, her biceps were defined, and she looked like she could easily toss Serena, who was stick-thin thanks to her mastery of a lifelong strict diet. And maybe a few tweaks here and there at a clinic that was referred to as a spa.

Serena's mouth formed an "o". Clearly, she was shocked by Tawny's sass. Well, that was the only way her former boss could possibly look shocked. Regular appointments with her dermatologist for injectables kept Serena's face neutral of expression. That's why Serena firing her had come as such a shock to Kelly. Had she seen Serena approaching with just a hint of anger or disappointment or any flicker of emotion on her face, Kelly would have been prepared for the unpleasant news. But, no, she was blindsided thanks to modern medicine.

"As I recall, this isn't your house. It belongs to Jason," Serena spat out.

Jason? Kelly searched her brain for intel. Jason? Who…Oh! Jason was Tawny's husband. Wait…was it possible that…no. No. Maybe?

"You just won't stop, will you? Not until you destroy my marriage like you destroyed yours. How many husbands have you been through?" Tawny's nostrils flared and her fists balled tightly.

Kelly's mouth dropped open. Jason was Serena's ex. How did she not know that?

"What in the world is going on here?" A man rushed by Kelly, jolting her out of her stupor before inserting himself between Tawny and Serena. "I thought I told you to leave, Serena?"

"I told you we weren't finished. Nothing has changed. You never listen to me, Jason." Serena lifted her chin and glared at him. "We need to settle this once and for all."

"We did a few minutes ago," he said, with an irritated twist to his lips.

"Clearly, she didn't like the answer, so she's going to continue to harass us until she gets what she wants. Isn't that right, Serena?" Tawny propped a balled fist on her hip and glared.

"No, she's not. She's leaving now and going back to the city." Jason cupped Serena's elbow and jostled her away from the door frame. "Leave, Serena."

Serena huffed as she yanked back her arm. "Do not touch me."

"Stop being so dramatic. There are no paparazzi." Tawny rolled her eyes as she dropped her hand from her hip.

Serena raised her hand and pointed a finger at Jason and then Tawny. "We're not finished. I'll be back." She turned, her coat swinging dramatically, and marched away.

Kelly's gaze followed and she chided herself for her thoughts. While her ex-boss and her newest client were in the middle of a domestic squabble, she was lusting after the coat. *Bad Kelly.*

"I'm so sorry you had to witness that, Kelly. I thought she'd be gone by the time you came, or else I would have rescheduled." Tawny looked annoyed, and that unhappiness was laser-focused on Jason.

"Yes, well, she's gone now. I don't expect she'll be back." Jason sounded confident, but Kelly knew Serena, and the tough-as-nails executive didn't give up easily. No, she was like a hungry, high-strung little dog with a bone clenched between her capped teeth. She'd not go away quietly.

"Oh, I'm so sorry for my manners. Kelly, this is my husband, Jason. Honey, this is Kelly. She's going to help me clean out my closet."

Jason extended his hand to Kelly, and his expression softened. Gone was the cold glare he'd given Serena.

"Well, you do have your work cut out for you." He chuckled. A little humor to help lighten the mood was welcome.

"It's nice to meet you." Kelly took back her hand. He appeared to be at least ten years older than Tawny. His salt and pepper hair was thick and styled with a bit too much gel. The collar of a plaid shirt collar peeked out from a pale blue crew neck sweater, which matched his eyes. His chinos were wrinkled, and his loafers were scuffed. He must have been enjoying a relaxing day at home until Serena showed up. Kelly knew from personal experience; Serena could ruin any day easily.

"I have to apologize for my ex-wife's behavior." Jason shoved his hands into his pants pockets and offered a weak smile.

"She seems to know you, Kelly." Tawny tucked a few strands of her hair behind her ear.

Oh, she knows me all right.

"I worked at Bishop's as an assistant fashion buyer." Kelly opted to leave out the part about Serena publicly firing her. No need to dwell on the past. She was too busy focusing on the here and now to fret about how she lost the job she loved thanks to a string of mistakes that really weren't her fault.

Both Jason and Tawny nodded.

Kelly recognized the nod. She had seen it often when she'd worked at Bishop's. Serena's thinness, sunglasses, and temperament were well known by everyone in fashion. Along with the nod came sympathy, and if she was in a bar, her next drink was usually free.

What followed was an uncomfortable silence that made Kelly wonder if the visit and consignment were doomed.

"Well, I should leave you two ladies to your business. It was nice meeting you, Kelly." Jason turned and walked away. He eventually disappeared around a curve.

"He's right. We should get started. I have a coaching call in an hour. Come on inside." Tawny pivoted and walked into the cottage.

"I'm excited to see what you have for consignment." Kelly inhaled a cleansing breath. With any luck, Serena was heading to the Long Island Expressway never to be seen again in Lucky Cove.

She entered the cottage. Of all the places she never expected to see her former boss…no, she had to let it go. A quick mental shake forced her to release the unpleasant encounter with the Dragonista. After all, she was there to do a job and under no circumstances was she going to allow Serena to take up residence any longer in her brain. Nope. Not going to happen.

The cottage packed a lot into its small square footage. Kelly's gaze flitted around the open layout, which had clearly defined spaces. There was a comfy seating area with a glass coffee table, a tidy office area and a filming studio, but it was the garment rack filled with clothes that drew her farther into the cottage.

"Wow. You have a lot here." Kelly didn't waste any time. She began fingering through the items, all neatly organized by type and by color. She'd found a kindred spirit. The maxi dresses caught her eye. They'd look great on a mannequin, and she knew they'd sell in a heartbeat. She discreetly glanced at Tawny, who was checking her phone. Why on earth would a woman with a body like hers want to cover it up with those long dresses?

Kelly sucked in her tummy. Bikini season was just weeks away, she reminded herself.

"Sorry. I needed to check my direct messages. I get so many every day." Tawny set her phone down on the desk and picked up her bottled water. The label said it was "smartwater." Was there really such a thing? Kelly thought water was water. Tawny must have noticed Kelly's curious stare. "Hydration is important to our overall health. This brand adds in vitamins and minerals. It's a win-win for busy women like us." She flashed a smile.

Kelly was impressed but tap water was more in her budget these days. The last thing she needed to do was add yet another expense to her life. "These dresses are lovely." She swiped the hangers to the side and counted. There were nine of them.

"Thank you. I'm not really into fashion. That's more Serena's thing. So I have no explanation to why I have so many clothes." Tawny took a swig of her water.

Kelly wasn't looking for an explanation. Rather, she wanted to encourage Tawny's shopping habits because she had good taste and she wanted to consign.

"Yes, Serena lives and breathes fashion." Kelly was certain the woman came out of the womb fully accessorized. The image made her grimace. There was no way Serena was ever a baby.

"Well, when I had my closet mishap last week, I realized I was getting carried away with shopping. It was time to clear out my clothes."

"Rods fell down?" Kelly moved from the maxi dresses to the collection of casual tops. Definitely Tawny's style. Fitted and neutral colors.

Tawny's green eyes widened. "How did you know?"

Kelly laughed. "Been there. And a lot of my clients have the same story to tell when they come into the boutique. So, know you're not alone."

Tawny let out a relieved breath. "Thank goodness!" Her mood shifted, and she seemed more relaxed.

"Which is why consigning is a great option. You earn a little extra cash when you declutter."

"I'm really sorry about you having to run into Serena."

"No worries. I guess sometimes the past rears its ugly head." Kelly pressed her lips together. Shoot. "I didn't mean that like it sounded."

"I know. Don't worry about it. I just wish we didn't have to deal with her any more. You'd think after all this time she'd be out of our lives for good." Tawny set her water bottle on the desk. She swept her shoulder-length, ash blond hair up into a ponytail and secured it with a hair tie she pulled off her wrist. The lady was so low-maintenance compared to her husband's ex-wife. With her hair up, she joined Kelly at the clothing rack.

Kelly dipped her head to avoid eye contact with Tawny. She was chewing on her lip, trying to decide what to say next. She knew she should guide Tawny back to their task at hand—evaluating the clothing. But, she really did want to know what the deal was with Serena and the Fallows.

"If you don't mind me asking, if she and Jason are divorced, why is she still in your lives?" And there she went sticking her nose where it didn't belong. Ehh. It wasn't like the last few times she'd given into her curiosity—*there was no dead body.*

"Jason and Serena have been battling over a piece of property they own up in the Poconos."

"How long have they been divorced?"

"Over ten years. They bought the property while they were married planning on using it as a weekend getaway."

Kelly arched a brow. She couldn't imagine Serena trekking up to the Poconos for a weekend. No, she was more the hop-on-the-plane-to-Paris for a quick shopping spree and a café allonge, sipped while being seen.

Suddenly, she had a craving for an espresso.

"When they divorced it didn't make financial sense to sell it. Now it does. But Serena doesn't want to sell. There's a really good offer on the table, and Jason thinks they should take it. The fighting has gotten uglier the past few months."

"I'm sorry to hear that. Disputes over property can get nasty." Kelly had firsthand experience thanks to her inheritance. Although the disagreement between her and her uncle hadn't risen to the level that Tawny was speaking of.

"Thank you." Tawny clapped her hands together and gave off a chilled vibe. She looked as if she'd had enough of Serena and her antics. "You're here for clothes not to listen to the details of the dispute between my husband and his ex-wife. Talk about boring."

Oh, contraire.

Kelly was anything but bored. As much as she wanted to behave professionally, she was dying to know all the details Tawny was willing, yet hesitant to share. Was there a tactful way to get Tawny to spill the family secrets? *No, there isn't.*

"I guess we all have our family issues. I definitely have my share." Aside from her greedy uncle, Kelly was rebuilding her relationship with her sister. Their strained relationship had gotten to the point that they'd barely said a word to each other at their grandmother's funeral. Luckily, that was changing. They were not only talking on a regular basis, but also getting together for dinners and the occasional Sunday brunch. "Perhaps we should get back to why you asked me here today."

Kelly turned her attention back to the garments, and for the next fifteen minutes she studied each item. All of the clothing was in good shape, recently purchased, and a mix of spring and summer seasons, which was great because they'd probably get full asking price. She pulled a calculator from her purse and did a quick estimate of how much money Tawny could earn by selling through the boutique.

She showed Tawny the number. "It's only an estimate. I can't guarantee you'll earn this much, but I promise that I will do my best to get it for you."

Tawny smiled as she patted Kelly on the arm. "I'm sure you will. I don't think I mentioned it earlier, but I knew your grandmother. She was a nice lady. Everyone adored her."

Kelly lowered the calculator. While she loved hearing people talk about her granny, it was painful. The rawness of Martha's death still cut through her. She had no idea how long it would last and reminded herself the kind words of people who'd known Martha was a comfort she should embrace.

"She was a remarkable woman." Not only had Martha declared her independence after becoming a widow by opening her business, she'd stood by Kelly during the darkest period in her life.

"And I'm sure her granddaughter is also." Tawny walked past Kelly toward the desk. She bent over and pulled out a dust bag from beneath the desk.

Kelly couldn't believe what she was seeing. Her heart did a pitter-patter when she saw the dust cloth. Was it really a Fendi?

"I have one more thing to consign."

She held her breath as Tawny opened the dust cloth and revealed the designer's iconic Peekaboo bag.

Is she really going to consign it?

"I don't think I need to tell you what this is," Tawny said.

Kelly shook her head. "No, you don't. It's beautiful." She stepped closer to the purse and she swore she heard angels singing. Okay, not really. But there should have been. The bag was gorgeous. She'd been in the presence of a Peekaboo before. Her uncle's third wife, Summer, had one and carried it often, though hers was a small.

"It's a beautiful bag, isn't it?"

Kelly nodded. The purse combined elegance with casualness in a simple trapezoid structure that allowed it to go from dressy to everyday wear with a simple outfit change. Its top handle was classic, while its shoulder strap was a must-have for the modern woman.

"Yes, it is a beauty. It's a medium?"

"Good eye." Tawny lifted the purse from the dust bag. "I bought it on a whim."

"Impulse purchase? Ouch." Buying a Peekaboo purse on impulse wasn't like buying a handbag at TJ Maxx. No, that on a whim purchase set Tawny back four figures, but hopefully it would fetch Kelly a nice commission.

"Tell me about it. It's been sitting in my closet all this time. I think there's someone out there who would actually use it. I tried carrying it the other day and realized it just doesn't fit my lifestyle. I'm more of a casual crossbody kind of gal."

Kelly wanted to raise her hand and volunteer to give the Peekaboo a good home, but there was no way she could afford or justify such a splurge. Instead, she took the bag from Tawny and gave it a once-over.

"I'm sure there is. And you'll get a good price for it since it's in such good condition. However, I don't sell this type of merchandise in my boutique." *Not yet.* "I have an account on a resale website that does. I've had success with a lot of high-end dresses, like a Gucci dress not too long ago. Although, I'll have to get this authenticated first."

It looked like the real deal to Kelly, but she couldn't risk her boutique's reputation if the item were indeed a fake. And fakes were getting harder and harder to spot.

Tawny took back the purse and placed it in the dust bag. "I understand. Get it authenticated and let me know what price you'll be selling it for."

Kelly was surprised that Tawny was letting her leave with the bag. "Are you sure? I can come back for the bag when I have the appointment set up."

Tawny waved away Kelly's suggestion. "Don't be silly. You're Martha Blake's granddaughter. I trust you." Her cell phone rang again, and she frowned when she looked at the caller ID. Kelly also saw the name. Chase. "Excuse me." She gave a faint smile as she snatched the device up and turned away with the phone by her ear. She then stepped away from the desk.

"What do you want? I don't have time to talk now…I said, I'm busy." She ended the call and lowered the phone to the desk. "Do you need help to get all this stuff out to your vehicle?"

"I hope everything is okay." Kelly picked up the Fendi purse.

Tawny shrugged. "It's just business. Expansion has a downside." Her tone definitely changed from a few moments ago. Then again, Kelly knew firsthand how business stuff could change her mood in a blink of an eye.

"I don't need any help. It'll take me just a few minutes, and then I'll be on my way." Kelly crossed the room back to the garment rack. She wanted to pinch herself just to make sure she wasn't dreaming. She had a high-end designer bag to sell.

"Good. Thank you for coming over today." Tawny pulled out her desk chair and sat. She opened her planner and made a notation. "And again, I apologize for Serena's behavior. The woman can be unbearable. But trust me. It ends now."

* * * *

When Kelly returned from Tawny's house, she did a quick inspection of the boutique for new leaks. It looked like her prayers had been heard because there were none.

Heaving a sigh of relief because she didn't have to scramble for more buckets or cover merchandise, she got to work on the window display. Thirty minutes later she was done.

Flowy sundresses and sandals didn't feel right in the window this time of the year, but she needed to get the women who passed by to think about what their clothing needs would be in a few weeks. She hoped spring weather would arrive soon. With the temperature fluctuating between below freezing, snow, and mild temperatures in the 60s, it was challenging to draw customers in to shop for their spring wardrobes.

Last month she found an old lamppost at a flea market and negotiated an affordable price. When she brought the post home, Kelly gave it a makeover. She took care of the rust, primed, and painted the post yellow.

Its wiring was bad, but she wasn't planning to use it for light, so she left the wiring alone.

The new coat of paint made the lamppost pop, but it still lacked something. While browsing another flea market, she found old street signs and knew they'd be perfect for the post. With the help of her friend, Gabe Donovan, she cleaned them up and attached them to the post.

Now, there were signs for Fifth Ave and Broadway along with three One Way signs. Finally, the lamppost looked perfect for display.

Wrangling the clunky display item was no easy task, but Kelly positioned it right where she thought it should be. She set two mannequins on either side of it. She used the time, pulling merchandise and dressing the mannequins, to sort out her unexpected run-in with Serena.

When she woke that morning, she had no idea she'd come face-to-face with her past. Nevertheless, there it was, all fashionable in a faux fur coat and Prada sunglasses. Serena represented more than a job loss. Kelly hadn't just lost *a job* but her *dream job*. She was labeled an outcast, as well, in the industry she'd spent most of her life working to break into.

After a tragic accident left her friend, Ariel Barnes, paralyzed, her family and friends blamed her. For a long time she couldn't fault them for it. The only reasons she kept getting out of bed in the morning were her classes at fashion school and her desire to rise to the top of her class. Had it not been for that dream, she doubted she would have graduated. She did graduate, and she worked her butt off when Bishop's hired her, only to be tossed out by Serena.

Kelly stepped outside the boutique and stood back from the window, scanning the display from a different angle. She'd dressed the first mannequin in a khaki trench coat, perfect for this time of the year, and added a red tote bag. On the other mannequin, she put a pair of skinny chinos and a black and white striped sweater. She tilted her head. The trench coat mannequin needed to be moved a smidge. Just a smidge.

"You can't hide from me!"

Chapter 3

Kelly's head turned in the direction of the loud voice coming from up the street.

The woman storming out of Courtney's Treasures, a quaint gift shop, was unfamiliar to her. But she knew the woman she was humiliating. It was Tawny.

"Everyone knows what you've done!" the woman shouted as she followed Tawny, who picked up her pace and headed right for Kelly.

"Hey, Tawny, what's going on?" Kelly dropped her hands to her sides as she walked toward Tawny. She hoped aligning herself next to her new client would force the other woman to back off.

"You'll pay for what you did!" The angry woman stopped advancing. She pointed a finger and scowled at Tawny before pivoting and rushing away. Eventually she was out of sight.

"I'm so embarrassed. First, you witness the altercation with Serena and now this. Talk about a heck of a morning." Tawny shook her head. The expression on her face confirmed she was indeed embarrassed.

"Who is she? What was she talking about?" Shouting threats wasn't common on Lucky Cove's Main Street. She was more accustomed to them in the city, where it always seemed someone was yelling at someone else.

Tawny waved away the question. True to her word earlier of not being a fashionista, she wore yoga pants, a hoodie, and a black nylon bag slung across her body.

"It doesn't matter, really. Since I started uploading my workouts online, I've learned everyone isn't going to be happy with me."

"I'm guessing she's one of those people."

Tawny broke eye contact with Kelly and looked at the window. "New display?"

The shift in conversation wasn't subtle but Kelly understood why Tawny didn't want to discuss the scene. As she said, it was embarrassing, not only for her, but also Kelly. The stranger's raging outburst was an uncomfortable thing to see.

"It's a work in progress."

"Looks pretty good to me. I love the trench coat." Tawny stole a glance over her shoulder.

Kelly suspected she was checking to see if the woman had returned. "You should call the police and report what happened. I heard her threaten you."

"No, I don't want to escalate the situation. She'll calm down. Besides, my business partner is dealing with the matter. It's really a big misunderstanding. She'll see." Tawny inhaled deeply and exhaled. "I think I need some yoga."

"Restorative?" Kelly enjoyed a few of those yoga workouts when she worked at Bishop's. While most days were non-stop from the moment she stepped from the elevator onto the ninth floor business offices, certain days hit her like a tsunami. Restorative yoga sessions helped her relax and soothe her frazzled nerves.

Tawny smiled. "You know your yoga."

"I've taken a few classes. Though, not recently."

"Let's change that. Come over to my place tomorrow. I like to do a yoga session early in the day. Join me."

Kelly chewed on her lower lip. She'd love to do a workout with Tawny, and she certainly needed to relax a little.

"Thanks, but I don't want to intrude on your practice."

"Nonsense. I'd love the company. I'll text you later with the time." Tawny hurried away along the sidewalk while Kelly headed to the boutique's door and grabbed the handle. Tawny continued along Main Street, finally disappearing inside the gourmet cheese shop. It was nice to see a fitness pro like Tawny wasn't afraid of dairy.

"Hey, Kell!"

Now there was a familiar and friendly voice that Kelly gladly stopped for. She let go of the door and walked toward her approaching friend, Ariel Barnes.

"What's up? Day off from the library?"

Running into Ariel on Main Street wasn't something Kelly ever thought she'd be doing. Given what happened, she'd expected if they ever passed by each other on the street, they'd simply nod and continue walking.

Her granny used to say God had plans they knew nothing about. Never in a million years did she think He planned for her and Ariel to reunite and rebuild their friendship, especially after ten years of silence.

They were at a summer party when Kelly slipped away with her on-and-off boyfriend and left Ariel on her own. Ariel wanted to leave but couldn't find Kelly, her ride, so she got into the car with Melanie Carlisle, who was drunk. On the drive home, there was an accident. Ariel was paralyzed, and Melanie was arrested. The fallout continued in Kelly's family. She'd been flighty, acting before thinking her whole life, and the incident at the party was yet another example of this unpopular character trait. Her parents made sure she knew her impulsive behavior needed correction.

Ariel navigated her wheelchair to a halt. Her pale pink faux shearling denim jacket brightened her face. The white button-down shirt and dark jeans were her day-to-day uniform when she worked at the library. Lucky for her, the head librarian was a fan of Friday casual every day of the week. Ariel's chestnut brown hair skimmed the collar of the jacket. Her bangs were finally getting longer. Kelly warned Ariel of bangs, often regretted and took forever to grow out.

"No. I went in for an early shift." Ariel worked part-time at the library and the rest of the time as a freelance writer. She'd been landing magazine articles and recently finished a corporate project she'd tried to get for months. Her hard work and long hours were paying off.

"Nice day to be outside. What are you up to?"

"I was just at the post office. I ordered one of the DNA tests, and it arrived." Ariel's face lit up when she gestured to her Mary Poppins sized tote.

"Good Lord, that thing is ginormous. What else is in there? A body?"

Ariel laughed. "No, silly. I have things I need. Like my notebooks, reference books, and my makeup bag."

"Oh, well, that explains it." Kelly grinned.

"Don't judge. I can't imagine not having my honey melon lip balm or my midnight black mascara with me at all times."

"Or any of the hundreds of other beauty products you own."

"I said don't judge." Ariel winked.

Kelly held her hands up in surrender. "Not judging. Only stating facts. So, what prompted you to do a DNA test?"

Ariel shrugged. "I don't know. I guess I'm curious about where I come from."

"Lucky Cove."

"Haha. You know what I mean. Also, it's a great way to connect with distant relatives. It's probably the researcher in me. My mom isn't thrilled. She says I'm wasting my money. She says both her parents came from Galway, Ireland. And my dad's family is from a village in Scotland."

"I get it. Maybe Caroline and I should do one of those tests one day."

"Sisterly bonding?"

"Well, we need all the bonding we can get." After the car accident, Kelly's sister blamed her for Ariel's injuries. She made it clear she wanted nothing to do with Kelly. They limited all their communication to only what was necessary. Looking back, the fact that Caroline was in her senior year of high school was a blessing. Life became more bearable when she moved out to her dorm. Kelly no longer had to live 24/7 in a Cold War situation. Now that Kelly was back in Lucky Cove, she and Caroline were talking and visiting each other. For the first time in a decade, Kelly felt there was hope they'd be friends again.

"How did your appointment with Tawny go? Did she have a lot to consign? I mean, when I see her around town, she's in her athleisure wear."

"Surprisingly, she did have a bunch of clothes, and I'm sure they'll all sell fast. She even has a Fendi purse she wants to sell."

"No!"

Kelly nodded. "Wait. There's more."

"What?"

"It turns out Tawny is married to Serena Dawson's ex-husband."

Ariel's forehead furrowed, she was trying to place the name, and then her eyes widened. "Serena as in your ex-boss?"

"The one and only."

"How do you know? Did Tawny tell you?"

"Nope. Serena was at the house when I got there."

"No! What did you do?" Ariel's cell phone rang. It was her dad's ringtone. "Oh, sorry. I gotta take this. I'm supposed to meet him for coffee. Call me later. I want to hear everything!"

After Kelly promised, Ariel steered her wheelchair along the sidewalk toward the Gull Café. It was for the best. She wasn't eager to relive the encounter with Serena even though she mentioned it.

* * * *

Kelly returned to the boutique and spent the rest of the day on the sales floor. The nice weather brought customers who were eager to get a head start on updating their spring wardrobes. She glanced at her watch. She had fifteen minutes to go before locking the door, turning off the lights, and going upstairs to collapse on her sofa. It had been a roller coaster of a day, and all she wanted were her comfy clothes and a glass of wine. She looked at her watch again.

Fourteen minutes.

The last customer left a few minutes earlier, and Kelly tidied up and reviewed her schedule for tomorrow. She could stare at her watch for the next thirteen minutes, or she could get a sneak peek at what was in store for her tomorrow when she joined Tawny for yoga.

She pulled out her phone and found Tawny's video channel.

There were dozens of workout videos to choose from, and they all were free. It looked like there was a variety to choose from, and not having to pay for the videos was a bonus. Kelly clicked on the first video, and Tawny started talking. She welcomed her viewers and gave them an overview of the twenty-minute workout they were about to start. Dressed in green leggings with lace inserts and a floral sports bra, Tawny began marching in place and encouraged her viewers to join in.

Kelly looked; the boutique was still empty, no last-minute shoppers popping in. Breena and Pepper had left hours ago. She took a step back from the sales counter and marched in place, pumping her arms by her sides as Tawny instructed.

Tawny then added bigger moves to get the whole body prepped for the workout, but Kelly continued with the marching. As Tawny slowed down to grab a pair of hand weights, Kelly stopped marching in place and scrolled down the screen, reading the comments.

"Great workout."

"Still scamming people with your workouts? Have you no shame?"

"Hey, can you do a workout for toning up the bra hang area?"

"Seriously, PBF? Personalized Body Fitness more like Pure Bull Fraud."

"How do you sleep at night?"

"Love this workout!"

Kelly clicked the video, and it stopped. She drew back from her phone. "Talk about a mixed bag of comments. Seeing those negative comments can't be easy," she said to herself. The time display on the phone showed her it was close enough to closing time. Finally.

All in all, it was a good day but exhausting.

Kelly was getting used to being on her feet for extended periods. Before inheriting the boutique, it'd been a long time since she worked on a sales floor.

She glanced at her booties and smiled. They had good support, and she needed more shoes like them. Twenty-six and needing supportive shoes. How life had changed for her.

At the front door, she turned over the *Open* sign to *Closed* and turned the lock. Before she stepped away from the door, she took a sweeping glance at Main Street. A handful of businesses were still open, but most of them were dark.

There definitely wasn't a lot of nightlife in Lucky Cove. Her evenings were a lot different from what they were when she was a single gal living in the big city.

Back in the city, she'd leave work like she was now. But she wouldn't have been heading up to her apartment to change into her favorite pair of fleece pants and snuggling her tired feet into her Ugg slippers. She'd be meeting friends for drinks and a quick bite.

Oh, times had changed.

Just as she was about to pull away from the door, a figure across the street caught her eye.

Kelly couldn't make out the woman's face clearly, because she was out of the streetlamp's pool of light. However, the woman's leopard print coat was unmistakable.

So, Serena hadn't left town.

Well, she was never one to be told what to do.

Kelly wasn't sure why Serena was standing in front of the Gull Café. Maybe the grand dame of Seventh Avenue was waiting to be picked up by her car.

An unexpected thought flashed through Kelly's head. Maybe she should check on Serena. Make sure she's okay. Yeah, that was a silly thought. When was Serena not okay? Besides, Kelly didn't feel like being insulted, belittled, or dismissed. She just wanted to make something quick for dinner and go to bed.

But, what if there's something wrong?

What could be wrong?

Kelly's internal struggle ceased when a man approached. She stepped closer to the door. All she could really see was his salt and pepper hair. Well, mostly the salted part. She squinted. It looked like Jason.

Serena checked her watch. No doubt, she was admonishing him for being late. But late for what?

He gestured to the restaurant, and Serena turned and walked toward the entry.

Kelly shrugged. Maybe they agreed to meet to work on a peace treaty. After what she witnessed earlier, the divorced couple needed one. Desperately.

They went inside the restaurant, ending Kelly's surveillance. She walked away from the door and through the boutique to the stairwell.

As she climbed the steps, her thoughts shifted from the divorced couple to the fabulous faux leopard coat. Somehow, Serena inspired an idea for Kelly's column on Budget Chic. Ten tips for working animal prints into a spring wardrobe. Serena finally inspired something other than a gory tell-all of Surviving the Dragonista.

Before her article, dinner, or wine, she needed to check on the leak. Or leaks. As she reached the landing, she gave herself a stern talking to. She ignored the leak, and it was irresponsible. In fact, it was a shadow of the old Kelly, and that couldn't happen again.

No, before her yoga session with Tawny, she needed to contact the roofer. That sounded like a good plan. Deal with the stressful task and then indulge in an hour of yoga bliss.

Yes, she was looking forward to her workout with Tawny. Even though there was a chance Tawny would twist her into all shapes and break her, the visit couldn't be any worse than it was today.

Chapter 4

The next morning, Kelly arrived downstairs, ready to get to work. She prioritized her tasks because all were urgent and she had to complete them before opening.

The cash register and computer system needed to be turned on, and the cash drawer needed to be filled.

The front door had to be unlocked, and the *Closed* sign flipped around, so passersby and customers knew the boutique was open.

Pray to the roof gods to be kind and forgiving to her aging roof and to her checking account.

Call the roofer and get him there ASAP because it was not only the responsible thing to do, but there was another leak in the hall upstairs.

Tasks one to three were done in the blink of an eye. Her prayer was short and sweet. She guessed this time of year the roof gods were busy. Task four was done quickly. After all, it was only a message. Still, she was near hyperventilation after she ended the call that threatened to derail her. As she was explaining the problem upstairs, she remembered the mid-five-digit estimate she'd gotten last fall, and her head spun. How on earth would she pay for a new roof?

Get a grip, Kell.

She took a deep breath and another. It was too soon to panic. For all she knew, another patch could be the solution. And a patch would fit into her budget.

One more deep breath steadied her nerves and gave her enough clarity to head into the staff room to brew a pot of coffee. If there was ever a morning she needed coffee, this was that morning.

It only took a few minutes to get the coffee brewing and her mug from the upper cabinet. She leaned against the counter, closed her eyes, and willed her mind to settle.

The coffee pot beeped. And the freshly brewed smell of the coffee wafted in the air, brightening her mood. She picked up her mug, ready to pour a full cup.

Drip.

She froze. She had to be hearing things. Yes, that's what it was.

Drip.

She sighed. She wasn't hearing things. There was another leak.

Kelly set down her mug and turned around, looking upward for a stain on the ceiling, and there it was. In the room's corner. The muddy brown color streaked the white paint, and she held her breath as she watched another drip land on the floor.

Drip.

She pressed her lips together and silently cursed. Then her gaze drew back upward.

Her first plea to the roof gods hadn't worked. Maybe she needed to strike a deal. Perhaps offer something in return for not having to replace the whole roof.

Drip.

No, she didn't need to make a deal. What she needed was a bucket. Quickly, she searched the lower cabinets and found one. After she positioned it under the leak, she returned to the coffee machine and filled her mug. Two more leaks weren't the end of the world. She could handle two leaks, she told herself before taking a grateful drink of her coffee.

Kelly heard the back door open, and a moment later, Pepper Donovan appeared, shrugging out of her lightweight jacket. She was not only the boutique's employee but also a lifelong friend. Pepper began working at the boutique over twenty years ago with Kelly's granny. Until last fall, she was the only employee. When Kelly took over the business, she made drastic changes, many of which Pepper opposed. The two she welcomed were hiring another salesperson and closing the boutique on Sundays during the winter months. Yes, those changes had Pepper's blessing from the get-go.

Pepper's gaze landed on the bucket. Nothing ever got past the woman, as Kelly learned over the past few months.

"What's going on?" Pepper walked to the table and dropped her purse along with the jacket she'd shrugged off.

"New leaks." Kelly pointed up.

Pepper surveyed the situation. "Guess I'm not surprised. The roof is old, ancient. And we're experiencing a thaw. It was almost fifty degrees yesterday."

"Yeah, just a couple of days before we had a snowstorm."

Pepper nodded. "The melting snow has to go somewhere."

"But does it have to go there?" Kelly pointed to the bucket.

Pepper frowned. "Oh, my goodness. Did you call Buck? I heard he's planning on retiring soon, so you better get him out here."

Now it was Kelly's turn to frown. Buck was sympathetic to her financial struggles because he had known her granny. He discounted the patch he did in October. Would another roofer extend the courtesy? Pepper was right, she had to get him out here ASAP.

"Already left him a message. Waiting to hear back." Kelly sipped her coffee. She needed something stronger.

"It's also supposed to be warm today and plunge again tomorrow." Pepper joined Kelly at the counter and poured a cup of coffee. "Don't worry. It'll be okay, you'll see."

Kelly nodded. She could easily spin out of control, think of the worst-case scenario, and host her own pity party. But she had a business to run, clothing to sell, and a yoga session with Tawny. No, there was no time for self-pity.

Drip.

Kelly and Pepper's gazes drifted to the other corner of the room, near the filing cabinet. There was the smallest of stains on the ceiling and another drip.

"I'm going to have to inspect every room," Kelly said.

"I'll call Clive and ask him to go to the hardware store to get more buckets. We might need them. There's one in the mudroom you can use for that leak."

An hour later, Kelly had spread out more buckets and Clive showed up with six buckets after his wife's SOS call. Luckily, although Kelly never thought she'd associate that word with roof leaks, the spots that needed the buckets were in areas not seen by customers. So, yes, in that regard, she was lucky. She also felt fortunate because soon she'd be lying on a mat, quieting her mind, while flowing from movement to movement. It would relax her frazzled nerves.

She was a little relieved that business had been slow so far. It gave her time to catch her breath and let her mind race with all of her doomsday scenarios without an audience. Seated on a stool behind the sales counter, Kelly stared at the boutique's online banking statement.

Anemic.

But much better than when she'd taken over the business.

Still, not enough money to replace the entire roof. She shut her eyes and prayed for a minor roof repair. There were buckets scattered throughout the first floor and up in the hallway. They didn't indicate a small roof repair.

Her eyes opened at the jingling bell over the front door, and a familiar woman entered the boutique. Kelly had seen her a few times around town while running errands but didn't know her. She closed out of the bank's website and stood, while forcing her mood to shift to perky, upbeat boutique owner.

"Good morning." She came from behind the counter and toward the customer, extending her hand. "I'm Kelly, the owner."

"So nice to finally meet you." The woman, several inches taller than Kelly with slim features, shook Kelly's hand. Her grasp and pump were firm. "It's been a while since I've been in this shop. It's lovely."

A flush of heat warmed Kelly's cheeks. She'd done as much work as she could with limited funds to revamp the once tired, old consignment shop into a trendy resale boutique. There was still a lot of work needed, like a roof. *Whoa, don't go there!*

"Thank you. It's a work in progress." Kelly glanced around the boutique. It was a never-ending, costly, remodel project she never thought she'd be responsible for. But there she was. Back in her hometown, putting her degree in fashion merchandising to work in a secondhand shop and rebuilding relationships she'd thought were beyond repair. Okay, so the boutique wasn't the only work in progress.

"The last time I was in here, there wasn't anything that interested me, but that trench coat in the window? Oh, my goodness. I really like it. And something I could definitely wear to work."

Kelly's heart swelled with pride. She interned one summer at Bishop's in the visual merchandising department while in fashion school, and there she'd learned many tricks of the trade. When she began making changes in the boutique, the things she changed first were the window displays. They lacked pizzazz, oomph, that *gotta look at me* quality that would stop a passerby and make her want to come into the boutique.

"And so is that suit." The woman pointed to a mannequin displayed by the door.

"Would you like to try it on?" The suit was a consignment from an up-and-coming PR executive. She loved the look of Chanel but couldn't afford the designer label, so she faked it until she made it by wearing dupes that gave off the high-end vibe. Kelly paired the multi-color tweed crop jacket and the matching skirt with a bright floral print blouse. The combination definitely had a *gotta look at me* quality.

"If it's not too much trouble."

"Good morning, Liza," Pepper called out as she entered the room from the back hall. She'd been tidying up the changing rooms and on bucket duty. "What brings you by today?"

"The trench coat in the window, and I'm glad it did. I'm loving this very Coco suit," Liza said as Kelly made her way to the mannequin. "I hope it's within my budget."

"It'll take me a moment to undress the mannequin. Would you like to try on the blouse?" Kelly dismantled the arm and then carefully removed the jacket.

"Oh, I don't think so. It's a little too much for me." Liza sounded like she wanted to try the whole look but was too timid. Kelly knew the type all too well. Liza played it safe in her buttoned-up navy coat and sleek bun, and needed to be nudged out of her comfort zone.

"Well, why don't you at least try it since you're here?" Kelly handed over the three garments.

Liza looked apprehensively at the blouse, and a slow smile crept onto her pale pink lips.

"Okay, since I'm here. Where are the changing rooms?"

"Right back there." Pepper guided Liza around and pointed to the doorway. "They're both empty."

Liza nodded and walked toward the doorway, disappearing around the corner.

Kelly moved the mannequin to the sales counter. Either she'd re-dress it with the suit or she'd have to find another garment to display. There was a floral, three-quarter length sleeve dress that was just consigned. She could dress the mannequin in that.

"How do you know her?" Kelly asked.

"She's the office manager at the Congregational Church. You know, you should come on Sunday to service with Clive and me." Pepper stepped behind the sales counter. "I'm surprised she's trying on the blouse. It's not really her. Actually, the whole suit isn't her."

"Well, our styles change. Look at yours." Kelly gestured to the short, tartan plaid skirt Pepper wore with a graphic sweater depicting a rearing stallion. The look was edgy yet sophisticated as it was paired with wedge pumps and black tights.

Pepper glanced at her outfit of the day. "I guess you're right."

Kelly locked her gaze on Pepper and arched a brow.

"Okay, you're right. Our styles do evolve."

"Could you say the part about me being right again?" Kelly laughed.

"Don't push it." The smile on Pepper's face betrayed the firmness in her voice. She'd been a rock for Kelly since her granny's death and the source of unconditional kindness. She'd loaned Kelly a Jeep, helped her move into the apartment upstairs, and made a pot of tea and sat with Kelly on what would have been Martha's birthday in January.

"I can't help it. I love hearing I'm right."

"Well, I hate to be a buzzkill. I came out here to tell you there's another leak in the bathroom ceiling."

Kelly groaned. It was looking more and more as if she didn't have a simple roof repair but a massive project with an equally huge price tag.

"I'm worried about the inventory. So far, there aren't any leaks here or in the accessories room."

Not too long ago, Kelly's granny expanded the business by adding a room to the back of the building. She'd used the new space to sell home accessories. What Kelly found on her first official walk-thru was a space filled with old knickknacks and lackluster sales for its substantial square footage.

Her number one task was to clear out the room, give it a good cleaning and a new coat of paint. Next, she'd found close-out deals online for display items and did a few DIY projects to add a little panache to the space.

Now fashion accessories and shoes filled the room, and sales were up. Every inch of square footage needed to earn the boutique money. The last thing she needed was merchandise being ruined by water leaking from the ceiling.

She made a mental note to check her insurance policy.

"Well, you were right, Kelly. I love the blouse with the suit. I'll take all three items." Liza joined Kelly and Pepper at the sales counter.

"I'm so glad you love the whole outfit. What about the trench coat?" Kelly asked.

Liza looked over her shoulder at the mannequin in the window. She returned her gaze to Kelly. She had that all-too-familiar look of a woman torn between wanting a new outfit and her budget.

"Maybe next pay period. I'll say an extra prayer that it hasn't sold by then." Liza winked.

"Hopefully He's listening. If not, I'm sure we'll have something similar." Kelly folded the garments while Pepper rang up the sale.

"Wait until Reverend Will sees you in your new outfit," Pepper said as she processed the credit card payment.

"He's going to be surprised, that's for sure. I typically stay with neutrals. But I think it's time to break out and change things up." Liza returned her credit card to her wallet.

"Well, I hope you'll come back and look for some more outfits. And don't forget, if you have anything you want to sell, let me know." Kelly handed the shopping bag to Liza.

"I have to be honest I never gave much thought to consigning, but I can now see it's a good idea. I can't wait to wear this new-to-me outfit. Thank you! Have a nice day." Liza hurried out of the boutique with her shopping bag.

"She seems nice," Kelly said to Pepper.

"She is. She's very reserved usually. It was nice to see her a little more…I don't know, happy."

Kelly nodded. "Clothes can do that for a gal."

"Yes, they can. Now, I noticed on the calendar you have another appointment with Tawny. She has more clothing to consign?"

"No. It's a private yoga session. I'm a little terrified. She's in amazing shape."

"She most certainly is. Don't go getting yourself hurt. We need you in one piece. I'm going to rearrange those silk scarves." Pepper stepped away from the counter and walked toward the accessories department.

The bell jingled again, drawing Kelly's attention to the front door.

"So sorry I'm late." Breena rushed into the boutique carrying a coffee tray, her auburn curls bouncing as her feet nimbly crossed the sales floor to the counter.

"Only by a few minutes."

"Half of Lucky Cove must have insomnia because it was crazy at Doug's. I don't think I've ever seen so many people ordering coffees before." Breena set the tray on the sales counter, careful not to disturb Pepper's decorations of little pots of gold and a shamrock spray centerpiece.

Pepper had a tradition of making the counter festive year-round. While it wasn't part of Kelly's vision for the boutique, she left the displays alone. She knew the small contribution to the boutique was important to Pepper, and who knows? Maybe having the pots of gold there would be good luck. Maybe that's why she got the Peekaboo purse to consign.

Kelly eyed the three medium coffees. One had a "TO" written on the side.

"Is that a Top o' the Morning for me?" Doug's was known for its seasonal coffee, and this time of the year, it was an Irish Crème flavored brew. Kelly didn't wait for Breena to answer; she snatched the cup out of the tray and then took a sip. "All's forgiven."

Breena giggled. "Thank you." She pulled out her coffee cup and took a sip. "Is the roof still leaking?"

Kelly heaved a sigh. "Yes. In more spots now."

Breena made a face. And it was precisely how Kelly felt.

"Tell me about it." Kelly took another drink of her coffee. "Pepper is back in the accessories department, why don't you take her a coffee to her? I have to schedule an appointment to get the Fendi authenticated."

"I wish I could afford it. But there are a couple of items she consigned that I might be able to swing." There Breena went again, looking at the bright side of things. Kelly wished the optimism would rub off on her. Actually, what she hoped for was the permanent removal of the dark cloud that seemed to hang over her.

Since October, she'd had a few glimpses of sunshine. The handful of moments where she felt like she was making headway and finding her balance. Like her freelance writing and now, she had a regular column. Like meeting Mark Lambert and now having a steady boyfriend. Like landing a client who had superb taste in clothes and a ridiculously expensive purse to sell.

"I'll be going out after I make the call. While I'm gone, can you dress her?" Kelly gestured to the mannequin she undressed moments ago.

"Sure. Anything in particular in mind?"

Kelly opened her mouth and was about to describe the floral dress but instead said, "Why don't you pick out the outfit?"

"Really?" Breena clasped her hands together, and her amber eyes lit up.

"Really. I know you'll do a good job." With her coffee in hand, Kelly walked out from behind the counter and headed to the stairs.

Leaving Breena to dress the mannequin was difficult for Kelly, who was a bit of a control freak when it came to displays. But it lessened the guilt she felt for not telling her friend where she was going.

Breena would jump at the chance to work out with her favorite fitness guru. No doubt she'd be bummed that she wasn't going to have the opportunity that Kelly was. Now Kelly had to change her clothes and duck out without being seen in her workout leggings.

* * * *

Kelly flicked on her turn signal and turned onto Tawny's street. She navigated around potholes and puddles. There was going to be a lot of roadwork come spring. She arrived at the house and drove into the driveway.

Before she changed into her Lululemon knock-off tights and tank top, she called the authenticator who was in Southampton, the summer playground of the rich and famous. She set an appointment, and was eager to confirm the purse was the real deal. She also hoped to learn a few tips on how to spot fakes because they were bound to come into the boutique.

While the trend of re-purposing and upcycling was taking off, websites selling designer goods were popping up all over the internet. Some were legit, like the site where Kelly sold her items. Others weren't. They sold fakes because either they didn't care about authentication or they intended to sell replicas to rip people off.

Kelly knew it was only a matter of time before unwitting customers came into the boutique with what they thought were real designer bags and expecting a big payout.

She parked her Jeep next to a familiar silver Mercedes. It was there yesterday when she first arrived. Oh, boy. Was Serena back?

Her hand hovered over the ignition. Maybe she should turn the car on, back out of the driveway, and head back to the boutique.

On second thought, maybe Serena was there, and was dealing with Jason since Tawny was preparing for her morning workout.

Thinking positively, she grabbed her yoga mat and water bottle before closing the driver side door. She walked along the path to the carriage house and pushed all thoughts of Serena out of her mind. All she wanted to think about was Zen stuff. Maybe she'd get to try meditation.

The cottage came into view, and the door was open. Just like the day before. But unlike the day before, there was no yelling. Maybe all the hatred and fighting finally had ended. Serena and Jason must have brokered a peace treaty over dinner last night.

Kelly continued, hopeful the next hour would be the relaxation she craved. A little OM and Namaste were good for the soul. When she reached the entry, she rapped her knuckles on the door rather than just barging in because Tawny could be meditating. When there was no reply, she peered in.

Her eyes bulged, and shock hit her like a hard slap. Her yoga mat fell to the floor as a scream rose in her throat but never made it out of her mouth.

She was wrong about Tawny meditating. Instead, she found Tawny's body draped on top of the now shattered glass coffee table. Blood puddled beneath her head.

Kelly's gaze landed on a pair of pink suede pumps and traveled upward. It took a moment for her brain to register she was looking at Serena standing over the body.

"She's dead!" Serena blurted out.

Chapter 5

Kelly's pulse kicked into overdrive, and the onslaught of questions that popped into her head dizzied her. So, she started with the most logical one first.

"What happened?" Instinctively, she made a move forward. While her head whirled with questions, her heart screamed to her to go to Tawny, to help, to prove Serena's declaration was wrong. Though she knew from binge-watching *Law and Order,* as well as her own experience with crime scenes, it was best to stay put. And the apparently lifeless body told Kelly her ex-boss was indeed correct.

Tawny was dead.

"I said, what happened?" Kelly locked her gaze on Serena, who, for the first time, looked confused and uncertain. She would not lie; it wasn't a good look on the powerhouse of fashion.

"I…I…don't know." Serena broke eye contact and looked down at Tawny. "I found her like this. I came to finally put an end to this ridiculous argument…"

"By killing her?"

"No! I told you she was like this when I came in. The door was open, and I walked in, expecting…"

"Expecting what?"

Serena threw up her hands in a dramatic gesture. Her face was flushed, and her usually sleek hair was mussed.

"An argument, a scene, like always. But I found her on the floor. I checked her pulse. There's none."

"Did you call the police?" Kelly reached into her cross body purse for her phone. "Did you call the police?" she asked again, only that time louder.

Serena jerked, apparently startled by Kelly's raised volume. "No. No, I didn't. I didn't have time." She clumsily dug into her Prada top handle tote.

"Never mind." Kelly willed herself to keep it together. Her head buzzed, and her stomach flip-flopped. She surveyed the room. Not much difference from the day before, except that it looked like there had been a struggle.

Shards of broken flowerpots and spilled soil covered the floor. The rug beneath the now smashed coffee table was bunched up and skewed. And there was the coffee table—wrecked with a body through it.

How did it happened?

Was Tawny pushed, forcing her fall through the coffee table?

Pushed by Serena?

Kelly took a couple of steps back to put more distance between her and her former boss.

Or, had Tawny simply lost her balance because of a medical condition? Or, maybe she tripped? It would have to have been a heck of a trip backward to crash through the table.

"I know how this looks. But you believe me, don't you?" The curtness and disregard she directed at Kelly yesterday was gone. Now, worry, doubt, and fear filled her voice. Yet Kelly remained firm, even though her insides were taking a roller coaster ride. She wasn't the same person she'd been when Serena had marched to her desk and ripped her a new one before firing her. She would not be intimidated any longer.

"You had a huge fight with Tawny yesterday, and now she's dead, and I found you standing over her...body."

"9-1-1, where is your emergency?" a voice asked on the other end of the telephone line.

"I had no reason to kill her! Unlike him!" Serena pointed over Kelly's shoulder.

As Kelly relayed information to the emergency dispatcher, she looked behind her and saw Jason coming up.

He rushed past Kelly, much like he had the day before. He came to a sudden stop and gasped when he saw his wife's body. His shoulders sagged, and his body wavered.

"You did this!" He went to lunge forward, but Kelly grabbed his arm, earning her a harsh look. "Let go of me."

"No, you can't disturb the scene." She ended her call with the emergency dispatcher, and after shoving her phone back into her purse, she used her free hand to guide Jason back from the door.

"Who do you think you are? She's my wife!"

"I know it's difficult, but we want to make sure we don't tamper with evidence unintentionally."

"What evidence? We know who did it. Her." He tossed an accusing look at Serena.

Serena recoiled, but then looked like she was ready to spring forward and attack. "How dare you accuse me. What reason would I have to harm Tawny?"

"You're a vindictive witch, and you never needed much provocation to attack before." Jason wrangled free of Kelly's grip. He was stronger than she was, so it wasn't much of a struggle. He slumped forward, gripping his hand on the doorjamb. "She's really dead?"

Kelly rested a hand on his shoulder and whispered, "I'm so sorry for your loss."

Jason buried his face in his hands. He tried to hide his tears, but his sobs were painstakingly audible, breaking Kelly's heart.

Sirens wailed from a distance and finally closed in on the property. Car doors slammed, and footsteps rushed toward them. Kelly was grateful she could hand Jason and Serena off to the officials.

The first officer to come up the path was Gabe Donovan.

A mixture of relief and dread coursed through Kelly's body. Having him there was no doubt a comfort, but she was pretty sure he'd have something to say about her ending up at another crime scene.

"Not again, Kelly," Gabe said in a low voice when he reached her while the other officer went to Tawny. In uniform, he barely looked like the boy she climbed trees and rode bicycles with on summer days until dark. When had they grown up?

"What happened?"

Kelly shrugged and looked at Tawny. "I found Serena over her, and then I called for help."

"Serena? As in Serena Dawson from Bishop's?"

"The one and only. She's his ex-wife." Kelly pointed to Jason. "This wouldn't happen to be Detective Wolman's day off, would it?"

Gabe gave her a sympathetic look and shook his head. "You know the drill. We have to separate the three of you."

Kelly knew the drill all right. She also knew Wolman would not be happy to see her at another crime scene.

Gabe led Kelly into the kitchen after depositing Jason and Serena in other rooms on the first floor of the house. He instructed the three of them to stay off their phones while they waited for Detective Wolman to interview them.

The kitchen was a modest-sized room and had a French countryside vibe. There was a cozy breakfast nook with a painted petite chandelier overhead. On the counter beside the sink, Kelly spotted the super-duper blender. That's where Tawny whipped up her protein shakes.

While finishing up her work last night, Kelly checked out more of Tawny's videos. She was sucked into watching a marathon of What I Eat In A Day videos. There were dozens of them. It amazed Kelly people were interested in what other people ate. In her videos, the fitness expert shared her favorite recipes along with her positive affirmations. Kelly wondered if Tawny had said her affirmations that morning.

* * * *

"You should be okay in here," Gabe said standing in the doorway. His hands were propped on his hips. He'd assumed his official police stance.

"It's a nice room. I wonder who the cook was. Tawny or Jason." Kelly dropped her purse on the table and pulled out a chair. It really didn't matter who the cook in the family was, now that half the family was gone. But a little small talk would take the edge off jagged nerves.

"You okay?"

Kelly shrugged as she sat. "It's not like it's the first dead body I've found." And yet, the same sensation she felt the first time she came upon a crime scene buzzed through her when she'd discovered Tawny.

"No, it's not. You can't keep doing this."

Kelly rubbed her neck. "It's not like I plan for these things to happen."

"Good to know." Detective Wolman appeared in the doorway and already looked annoyed with Kelly. Dressed in her usual black pantsuit, she wasn't much of a fashion risk taker. She projected seriousness and competency. Perhaps that's why she chose the outfit. Her dark hair was swept back, letting her large eyes become the focus. Her thick lashes fringed them, and a swipe of eyeshadow had been applied. There was also a sweep of blush on her checks and a tint of pink on her lips.

Kelly cringed at the sound of the detective's voice.

"Good morning, Detective." Even though Kelly was dating the detective's brother, she wasn't comfortable calling her Marcy. Maybe that would come when they had a meet-the-family-dinner—when she and the detective would chat and find common ground. It was a long shot, but anything was possible.

"Not quite when there's a murder." Wolman dismissed Gabe and entered the kitchen. She gave the room a quick scan. Kelly figured she was assessing what was in the room and what wasn't. This forced Kelly to give the room another glance. Had she missed something? She was struck by the lovely décor, but what if there was a clue to who had killed Tawny?

"I have a few questions. You're familiar with this process, aren't you?" Wolman seated herself across from Kelly. She set her notepad and pen on the table.

"I am familiar with the process." Which meant there was no need to prolong their conversation for any longer than necessary. "I came by today to do a yoga workout with Tawny. She'd invited me yesterday."

"You and Mrs. Fallow were friends?" Wolman opened her notepad.

"No. Not really. She's a…she was a consignment customer." Kelly crossed her arms over her body and leaned back.

Wolman jotted something down.

"Do you know Ms. Dawson?"

"I do. She's the vice-president of merchandise at Bishop's department store."

Wolman lifted her head. "You worked there, didn't you?" After Kelly nodded, the detective continued. "How well did the deceased know Ms. Dawson?"

"I honestly don't know. As I said, we weren't friends. But their relationship was intense. When I came by yesterday to do an estimate for Tawny's clothing, I found them arguing."

"What exactly did they say?"

Kelly unfolded her arms and leaned forward. A twinge of guilt pricked at her. For some odd reason, she felt loyalty to Serena. Surely, that loyalty was misplaced on Serena, and she needed to figure out why she had it. She could do that later, now she had to tell Wolman everything she heard yesterday.

"How well do you know Mr. Fallow?" Wolman was jotting down notes as Kelly spoke, recounting her visit there yesterday and this morning.

"I don't. I only met him yesterday. He seemed upset because I guess Serena was supposed to have left, but she didn't. He looked a lot calmer last night when he met Serena at the Gull Café."

Wolman set her pen down and cocked her head sideways. "How do you know they met?"

"I saw them out the window when I was closing up the boutique."

"Why am I not surprised?"

"I wasn't snooping."

"Of course not. You're just a concerned citizen who keeps popping up at my murder scenes." Wolman closed her notepad and clicked her pen. "I know I've said this before, and I hope this time you actually do as I say. I do not want you interfering in this investigation. Am I clear?"

Kelly leaned back. "Perfectly." Considering who was involved in the investigation, she preferred not to be a part of it. Thank you very much.

Wolman had a few more questions, ones she'd already asked, but now phrased differently. Kelly guessed it was a way for the detective to catch an inconsistency. There were no inconsistencies in her answers. Just an urgency. She wanted to be the one to tell Breena that her fitness idol was dead.

Chapter 6

When Wolman wrapped up her interview questions and allowed Kelly to leave, she darted out of the house. Her intention was not to look back. But she did.

Halfway between the house and her car, she stopped and stared at the surreal scene. The crime scene unit was busy at work, moving efficiently and methodically to process all the evidence.

All the evidence of Tawny's death. Just yesterday, she was alive, getting ready for a coaching call, espousing the virtues of smartwater. Now she was dead.

All the smartwater in the world hadn't mattered. Nor had Tawny's hours of exercise or all of her hard work in building her business. She was gone.

Kelly gave herself a sharp mental shake, forcing herself to climb out of that dark tunnel.

Tawny led a life she loved, pursued her passion, and was making a living from it. Rather than viewing all of that as a waste of time, it should be an inspiration. Live life with no apologies or regrets. If you want to spend all your money on smartwater, then so be it.

She stared at the scene for one more long moment before returning to her Jeep. How long the morning's events would replay in her mind was uncertain. What was certain was that the image of Serena standing over Tawny's body wouldn't be leaving her soon.

On her drive back to the boutique, Kelly decided she'd be gentle but straight forward, no hedging when she told Breena what happened. Just rip the Band-Aid off and tell her. With her plan set, she knew what she had to do. Take Breena aside, give her the facts, and then hand her a box of tissues. Breena was an emotional person. Perhaps the actress in her allowed her to be so tapped into her emotions. She wasn't shy about crying in front of others, while Kelly preferred to keep her weeping to private moments. After all, who wanted to see her ugly cries?

For an added dose of fortification to break the news, Kelly stopped at Doug's. She found a parking space and dashed inside. It took only a few minutes to get three large coffees, and just as she reached her car, she heard her name called out. She looked over her shoulder and found her best friend, Liv Moretti, standing in the open door of her family's bakery. Tall and lanky, Liv was dressed in her usual work uniform of dark jeans and a T-shirt with a bright pink apron tied at her waist. Her dark auburn hair was styled into a pixie cut, and her brown eyes were warm and friendly.

"Are you okay?" Liv shuffled from the doorway to Kelly's side. She rested her hand on Kelly's arm and gently squeezed. She was forever the mother hen of the two of them. When Kelly was sick, she brought homemade chicken soup. When Kelly was heartbroken, she brought wine. When Kelly was grief-stricken, she brought cannoli and tissues.

"You heard?" Kelly knew that news traveled quickly in town, especially along Main Street retailers. She wondered how much information was shared. And how accurate it was.

"Of course, I did. Was Tawny really killed by Serena?" Liv slid her hands into her apron's pockets.

"I don't know. All I know is that I found Serena standing over Tawny's body. She claimed she found Tawny dead when she arrived."

"What was Serena doing there?"

"Good question. She had some excuse, but I'm not sure." Kelly wasn't sure how much she could share about what they'd said at the crime scene. While Liv didn't intentionally spread gossip, she would tell her mother and sisters, and they would pass it along to customers. Before you knew it, an innocent comment made was turned into a full-fledged scandal, and it would bring Wolman's wrath down on her. So, tightlipped it would be.

"It's a shame. Tawny was really nice. Once a week, she popped in to pick up a blueberry muffin for Jason. She didn't eat baked goods, but she liked to treat her husband."

"When was the last time she was here?"

"Last week to get the muffin. Like clockwork. I better get inside. Call me later." Liv pivoted and darted back to the bakery. She disappeared inside.

When Kelly arrived back at the boutique, it appeared she had nothing to worry about when it came to breaking the news to Breena. Yep, she'd been worried for nothing.

"We just heard! It can't be true. Tawny can't be dead." Breena dropped the handful of blouses on the sales counter and rushed to Kelly as she entered the boutique.

Kelly looked to Pepper, who was walking toward the sales counter from what used to be the dining room and now held mostly outerwear and evening apparel. She held a roll of paper towels and a spray bottle.

"So, it's true?" Pepper asked.

"I'm afraid it is." Kelly walked to the sales counter. She set down her purse and the coffee tray. "I'm sorry, Breena. I know you were a fan."

Tears welled up in Breena's eyes, and her shoulders sagged. "I can't believe it. You just saw her yesterday."

"What I can't believe is that you have found another body." Pepper set the spray bottle on the countertop. Her precise enunciation got Kelly's attention and the unspoken message that had just been relayed to her—don't go sticking your nose into the murder.

"It's not like I went looking for one." Kelly heard the defensiveness in her voice and regretted it. Any lectures, verbal or telepathic, from Pepper, came from a place of love and concern. "What I can't believe is that I found Serena standing over the body."

"No way! We didn't hear that." Breena dashed to the counter. She leaned her elbow on the glass top and dropped her chin to her palm. Her tears had dried up, and now she was curious to hear more.

"Did she kill Tawny?" Pepper asked.

"I know she can be overbearing, rude, condescending, and icy. I mean, she makes Cruella de Vil look warm and fuzzy." Kelly plucked a coffee from the tray and took a sip.

Breena stepped back from the counter and dramatically extended her arms outward. She then pulled them back to her body, wrapping them around her chest, as if she was closing a coat. She lifted her chin, batted her lashes, and channeled an unfamiliar voice.

"Where are the puppies? Bring me the puppies!"

Breena's impersonation of Cruella had them laughing, something Kelly desperately needed and welcomed.

"And end scene," Breena said with a curtsy.

"Oh, my gosh, I almost spit out my coffee," Kelly said.

"She's one of my favorite villains. Do you think Serena could be such a villain?" Breena asked.

"I honestly don't know. I never thought of her as a killer. Although she's killed a lot of careers." *Like mine*. "No, she's not a murderer."

"Don't be too sure. We don't always know a person like we think we do." Pepper patted the counter twice for emphasis before taking a coffee and heading into the accessories department.

"I better go check changing room one. Mrs. Parsons is back, and she's trying on a boatload of stuff. Cha-Ching." Breena giggled as she broke away from the counter next.

Changing room one. It made the small stall with a hanging curtain for privacy sound so official. Like there was a bank of them when, in reality, there were only two. But Breena had the right idea. It was time to get to work. The police had everything under control with Tawny's murder, and she had a business to run. Her smartwatch vibrated, reminding her of her appointment with Buck to inspect the roof. She could use a little *Cha-Ching* to help pay for the repair. She called out to Pepper as she walked through to the staff room. He should arrive at any moment.

She hustled out to the parking lot, and as she closed the door behind her, she spotted Buck's pickup truck. It was parked next to her Jeep, but there was no sign of him.

"Up here, Kelly!"

Her head swung upward, and she shielded her eyes with her hand. Buck Phillips was standing confidently on the roof. Propped up against the exterior of the building was a ladder. He wasn't expecting her to join him up there, was he?

"Be right down."

Phew. She stepped forward to the ladder as the roofer made his way down with practiced ease. She wondered how many times over the years he'd been up and down a ladder.

"How bad is it?" she asked when Buck set foot back on the pavement.

"I've seen worse. But it's pretty bad."

She groaned. There wasn't a budget for *pretty bad.* "Bad enough to require a new roof?"

"This winter was a rough one, and now with all this thawing and re-freezing, ice dams are forming. I have three more appointments after I leave here. Anyway, add to the fact that the roof has outlived its expectancy… yeah, Kelly, you'll have to replace it. 'Fraid it's going to include taking off the two roofs already up there and possibly removing the sheathing if we find damage."

Kelly groaned again.

"I'm sorry I can't recommend a patch job like last time. The roof's only getting worse. You will have to bite the bullet at some point. If you don't do it now, you're risking damage to the building."

"Any chance that it's not going to cost more than your estimate from last fall?"

When she'd seen the five-digit number last year in his email, she gasped in horror. She didn't have that kind of money then, and certainly didn't have it now.

Buck removed his baseball cap; he was a die-hard Yankees fan and faithfully wore the team's apparel often. He dragged his fingers through his thin hair. Unlike Jason's hair, which was a refined shade of salt and pepper, Buck's hair was a dull color of gray with strands of pure white at his temples. His weathered face and calloused hands resulted from decades spent up on hot roofs.

"Your granny and I went way back, so I'll do my best to keep the cost down."

"Thank you." Even with his offer, she still didn't know where she'd get the money to pay him. She expected he'd want some money upfront.

"I appreciate whatever you can do." Kelly turned away, trying to figure which of her Stuart Weitzman boots to sell on the Mine Now Yours, the luxe resale website she loved. Selling one pair of over-the-knee boots wouldn't put a dent in the money she needed for the new roof. But maybe two. And a few other items. Every bit would help.

Buck cleared his throat in a way that made it clear he wasn't finished with her. Great. More bad news? She slowly turned back around. What else could be wrong?

"Is it true you found Tawny Fallow dead this morning?"

"Yes. Let's just say this morning has been a bad one."

"Yeah, I would say so. You know, we did some work on their house last summer." Buck went to his truck and pulled opened the driver's side door. He reached in and pulled out a clipboard.

"A roof?"

Buck nodded. "Nothing was wrong with the roof they had on, but the mister wanted a better…what did he call it? Aesthetic. Gotta love these rich city people who move out here." He closed the truck door.

Kelly echoed his sentiment. Jason Fallow had enough money to put on a new roof while his old one was perfectly fine, and there she was struggling to replace her roof—not for aesthetics but for function.

"Yeah, the whole exterior was redone with new siding and new windows. Man, you should have seen the plans for the landscaping. I saw the drawings and the costs. In my next life, I'm coming back as a gardener."

"Too bad Tawny won't be around to see the finished landscaping."

"Oh, there's no landscaping. The mister pulled the plug on the project and canceled all the interior work just after I put on the new roof."

"Do you know why?"

Buck shrugged. "Nah. But I see it all the time. These homeowners overextend themselves, and then at some point, reality sets in after they keep writing those big checks. The landscaping job alone was six figures."

"Holy Cow!"

"And here I am balancing on rooftops in the blazing sun most days. Yeah, next time I'm going to be planting flowers and raking out mulch. Look, don't worry. I'll take care of everything. When I'm done, you'll have peace of mind for the next thirty years." He patted Kelly on the arm as he passed by her and climbed up the ladder again.

With him safely up on the pitched roof, finishing his assessment of the job, she walked around to the front of the building. She'd do her best not to think about the estimate. Keeping nimble on her feet to avoid the minefield of puddles, she followed the narrow strip of walkway along the side of the building to the sidewalk.

Mr. Tillerman passed by with Abigail, his Jack Russell terrier. The retired economist walked every morning from his home on Sandy Drive to Main Street. He always waved, and Abigail gave a friendly bark.

Passing the pair on her way to the curb, she gave the dog a quick pat on the head. Abigail responded with another yip. They continued with their walk while Kelly stared up at the roof of her building. She raised a hand to shield her eyes from the sun.

From a novice's point of view, the roof looked just fine, confirming the old saying—looks were deceiving.

"Good morning." An unfamiliar voice dragged Kelly's attention from the roof to a petite redhead approaching her. "You're Kelly Quinn, right?"

Kelly dropped her hand and moved away from the curb toward the woman. "I am. And you are?" Her wish was a new customer who needed to revamp her entire wardrobe on a budget or who needed to empty out a closet full of clothes. Either was good with Kelly.

"Ella Marshall. I'm a reporter for the *Lucky Cove Weekly*." She looked to be around Kelly's age. She was smartly dressed in a dove gray sweater, slim black pants, and black patent loafers. Kelly appreciated the effortless chicness of the reporter's outfit. Especially the pearlized buttons on the sweater and the simple coin necklace that filled the sweater's V-neck. Slung over her shoulder was a black tote.

The *Weekly* was a staple in town for decades. Kelly's mother read the paper every Friday morning at the kitchen table while she drank her tea. And there was always a stack of the newspaper each week at Doug's Variety Store. When Kelly re-opened the boutique with its new name and new image, the *Weekly* covered the event. It helped bring in business, so she was eager to learn why Ella was there, and then it hit her. The reporter wanted to interview her about Tawny's murder.

"It's nice to meet you. Would you like to come into the boutique?" Kelly was preparing for her 'no comment' comment. She wanted to be firm yet graceful. There was no need to offend the reporter; she was just doing her job.

"I'd love to interview you…"

She knew it. Kelly opened her mouth to give her firm "no comment" comment.

"About your boutique. Women are seeking alternatives to fast fashion. Shops like yours are becoming trendy."

Kelly closed her mouth. She'd been hasty, quick to judgment.

"I applaud you for being a part of this nationwide, if not, global movement."

She was a part of a movement? Who knew? Well, Kelly had been doing research since taking over the boutique. She found there had been an uptick in women who wanted to recycle clothing, not only in her age bracket, but women in older age groups. Fast-fashion's surge seemed to have hit its peak, and women were realizing the true cost of dropping tens and twenties on a whim—poor quality, overspending, and tons of waste. Consigning was a way combat those problems, but still buy affordable clothing.

Ella pulled out a business card from her tote and handed it to Kelly. "Give me a call, and we can set up a time for the interview."

While Ella's angle on the interview would be about the broader landscape and social and economic impact of the consignment industry, Kelly saw the interview as a chance to promote the boutique. She could show case the newer merchandise for that in-between season, the one between winter and spring. Over one too many glasses of wine and lamenting about those few weeks where it was cold one day and hot the next, she'd dubbed it *wring*. With a clearer head the following day, she realized her bright idea was a dud. *Wring* would never take hold. A marketing genius she wasn't.

Anyway, she had several lighter weight jackets in neutral and bright colors along with a few classic trench coats. One was a perfect dupe for Burberry. Oh, what she'd give to get her hands on a real Burberry. But the dupe was pretty close and would be snatched up quickly. There was also a bunch of cotton blend sweaters from consignors and from a boutique not too far away that was going out of business. The only downside to getting inventory from another boutique was that she had to lay out the money and hope to sell the garments; otherwise, she'd be out the investment.

"Also, I'd love to talk to you about Tawny Fallow's death. Would you mind giving a quote about her? According to the police report, you were one of the persons on the scene. As was your former boss, Serena Dawson."

And there it was. Ella's real reason for being there. How could Kelly have been so naïve?

"Unfortunately, since it's an ongoing investigation, I'm not at liberty to make a statement. I will take you up on your offer for an interview about the surge of resale shops like mine." Kelly waved the business card in her hand and then pushed off for the boutique's front door.

"Surely you're at liberty to talk about your relationship with both women. I'm not looking to jeopardize the police investigation. Or get you in trouble." Ella followed.

Kelly swung around. "I'm not going to comment on those relationships or what happened to Tawny. I'd love to talk to you about the boutique and about the newfound interest in my industry. Have a nice day, Miss Marshall." She turned back toward the door and yanked it open. She stepped inside; the bell jingled, and she left the pesky reporter out on the street.

The door closed behind her, and she debated what to do next.

A to-do list was sitting on her desk, but it was written up before she found Tawny's body. One of the actionable items on the to-do list was to steam Tawny's garments and get them ready to sell.

She walked through the boutique to the photo studio, AKA storage room, where she photographed garments to sell online. The rolling rack was full of Tawny's clothes. She wondered what to do with them. She doubted Jason would want them back, but she had to make sure. Some people tended to be litigious. Better to be safe than sorry and on the receiving end of a subpoena. *Been there, done that.*

She walked out of the photo studio and into the staff room. At the desk, she dropped onto the chair and stared at her to-do list. So much for making plans for the day. She set the list aside, and that's when it hit her.

The Fendi purse.

With everything that had happened, she'd forgotten about the Peekaboo. It was still in her Jeep. Not exactly the best place for it. She had to bring it inside and keep it some place safe until she spoke to Jason. Before she headed out to get the purse, she browsed through her emails and responded to a few. Then after the purse was safely inside, she joined Breena out on the sales floor and worked there until closing. Much of the hushed conversations among customers who came in were about Tawny's death.

No one could believe there was another murder in Lucky Cove.

The only upside to this was the fact that no one asked her for specifics. Maybe they didn't know she was on the scene and called 9-1-1. By this time tomorrow, everyone would know she found Tawny's body.

Kelly was almost done closing the boutique when a weather alert came up on her phone. Another snowstorm was on its way, and according to the new data, it would pack a doozy of a punch, her very unofficial term, when it arrived on Long Island.

Another powerful storm was the last thing her hanging-by-a-thread roof needed.

The next alert that followed turned her frown upside down, and she giggled at her girlish behavior. A text from Mark. He was confirming their dinner date at Gio's Restaurant. The smiley face and heart emojis had her smiling and racing through the boutique to finish performing the end of day tasks. She was done in record time and on her way upstairs with the Fendi purse.

Howard greeted her at the door. He made his usual slinky move along her legs, and he let out a loud meow.

"I know what you want. You really don't cut a gal a break, do you?"

She tucked the purse into the coat closet and then went to the kitchen. Howard followed closely and then leaped onto the trashcan. From the perch, he could monitor her to make sure she didn't dilly-dally.

She dished out his food and set the bowl on the floor. He jumped off the trashcan and hurried to his food mat. While he chowed down, she refilled his water bowl. Then, with her cat's belly full, Kelly dashed into the bedroom to get ready for her date with Mark.

Standing in front of her closet, she eyed a few outfits that had potential. Mark mentioned something about going to a movie after they ate. If they were indeed going to the movies, she wanted to be comfortable as well as cute. She pulled out a pair of harem pants with an elastic waistband and a long-sleeved t-shirt. Add a pair of flats and hoop earrings, and she was all set to go.

Chapter 7

Mark held the door open for Kelly, and when they entered Gio's, the hostess showed them to a table. As they made their way through the dining room, Kelly felt the stares. It looked like news that she found Tawny's body had spread.

Her cheeks heated, and her pace quickened, though the hostess seemed to enjoy the excruciating trek from door to table.

"Kelly!" Liza popped up from a table for one and wended through the tables to intercept Kelly and Mark. "I heard about Tawny. It's such a shock. She was so young and vital. What a waste." Her eyes teared up.

"I'm so sorry; I didn't realize you and Tawny were friends." Kelly offered a weak smile and hoped Liza wouldn't break down there in the middle of the restaurant.

Liza sniffled. "She and Jason are members of the church. Such good people. They always volunteered. She was just helping out the other day." She took in a ragged breath.

"Would you like to join us?" Mark offered.

Liza shook her head and dabbed at her watery eyes. "Oh, how sweet of you. No, I'm almost finished with my meal. My one treat every now and again when my budget allows. Kelly, I'll let you know when the service for Tawny is."

Kelly murmured a thank you and then Liza returned to her dinner as the hostess caught their attention. "Sorry." Kelly dipped her head and continued following the hostess.

The other diners either had curious looks on their faces or whispered to their companions as Kelly passed by. Beads of sweat pooled at her temples, and her gaze bounced around the room. All of this reminded her of the weeks following Ariel's accident. Back then, the comments were in the lowest of low tones because they were harsh and cruel about Kelly. She swallowed hard and shook off the unpleasant memory.

After the hostess handed them their menus, she told them their waitress would be with them shortly.

"You've created quite a stir." Mark opened his menu. The past week he'd been putting in long hours on a case, forcing him to postpone their date night more than once.

Kelly looked over her shoulder. "Believe me, it wasn't my intention."

"I spoke with Marcy earlier. She caught the case, huh?" Mark closed his menu and set it down.

Kelly didn't have much of an appetite but refused to cancel because they hadn't had a date night in ages. Okay, that was an exaggeration. But it felt like an eternity. Now, with the subject of his sister brought up, what little appetite she had vanished.

"She most certainly did. She wasn't pleased to see me there." Kelly closed her menu.

"Shocker." Mark flashed his sexy McHottie Lawyer grin. When they first met, he was representing a customer who wanted to sue her for an outlandish reason. Mark realized the lawsuit would have been a waste of his client's time and money, so he worked out a more than reasonable settlement.

Kelly laughed. "I'm serious. I hadn't planned to walk in on a murder scene. I was there for a yoga session. Some Zen time. Maybe even a little meditation.

"You meditate? Since when?"

"I don't, but maybe I should start. Between the roof and the murder—"

"Good evening, I'm Jessie, your server tonight. Are you ready to order?"

Kelly recognized Jessie as the owner's granddaughter. Still in high school, she had a freckled nose and rosy cheeks with long strawberry hair pulled back into a high ponytail.

"Would you like to hear the specials?"

Kelly and Mark both shook their heads no.

"I'll have the spaghetti and meatballs." Kelly handed her menu to Jessie. Whatever she didn't eat, she'd take home for leftovers tomorrow.

"I'd like a lasagna. And two glasses of red wine." Mark handed his menu to Jessie and listened as she recited the wine options. Before Kelly could make her choice, he selected for them.

"I'll bring out your salads right away." Jessie began to turn away but stopped. She leaned toward Kelly. "I heard you found Tawny Fallow's body earlier today. That must have been awful." Interest filled her hazel eyes.

"Yes, it was—" Kelly began to say.

"Since it's an open investigation, she's not at liberty to discuss the details," Mark said as he covered Kelly's hand with his.

Kelly didn't appreciate being cut off, but he made a valid point. The same point she made when she'd refused to give Ella a comment.

Jessie nodded curtly and spun around. She marched away.

Kelly had a new worry to obsess over. Was her food going to be safe?

"I could have told her myself that I didn't want to discuss the matter." Kelly pulled back her hand and unfolded her napkin.

"Of course, you could have." Mark reached for his water glass and took a sip.

Kelly kept her gaze on her lap. She hadn't meant to snap at Mark. Maybe going out had been a mistake. Perhaps she should have stayed home and made an early night of it.

"You've had a long day, and I was only trying to help. So how are you doing?" He set his glass down.

Kelly shrugged. "It's not like this was the first time I found a dead body." After she said it, she regretted it. She knew she shouldn't be glib, because a woman was dead, but she barely knew Tawny. "Sorry. It was a shock finding Tawny and seeing Serena standing over her. I'm sure your sister considers her a suspect, but I don't think she's capable of such a thing." Kelly stopped talking when their salads arrived. She lifted her fork and pierced a cherry tomato. "Besides, she didn't look disheveled."

Mark finished chewing his forkful of salad. "I don't understand. What does how she looked have to do with anything? Are you saying she didn't look like she killed someone?"

"Exactly. While I was at the cottage, I got a quick look around. It looked like there had been a struggle before Tawny died. Serena looked too pulled together, even though her hair was a little messy but not too messy. Trust me, there wasn't any sign she murdered someone."

"From what you told me about their relationship, it sounded contentious, and you did find Serena beside the body."

"I see your point. It's probably the point your sister is taking with her investigation." Kelly continued to eat her salad. Her appetite was returning, and they changed the topic of conversation while they enjoyed their main course. Once the subject of murder was off the table, they relaxed, and shared ideas for a quick weekend getaway before summer got into full swing. It would be Kelly's first summer as a merchant on Main Street, so she didn't want to take vacation time then.

Their main course was served and over tossing around ideas for getaway locations, they ate. Kelly surprised herself by finishing her meal. Boy, her appetite had returned in a big way.

Mark pushed away his plate and wiped his mouth with the linen napkin. He smiled, lighting up his dark-as-charcoal eyes, and leaned forward. "How many lawyer jokes are in existence?"

Kelly rolled her eyes. "Not another lawyer joke?"

Mark liked to poke fun at his chosen profession with random jokes. She was always tempted to remind him that, while he wasn't an ambulance chaser, they'd met because one of his clients thought a piece of furniture she bought at the boutique was haunted. "Okay, how many are there?"

"Only three. All the rest are true stories." He laughed and then gestured to their waitress for their check.

Kelly giggled. "Good one." Her jovial mood and laughter came to a skidding halt when her uncle's current wife appeared at their table.

Summer Blake pulled out a chair and sat without so much as a hello or an invitation.

"Good evening, Summer." Kelly set her fork down.

"No, it's not. Tawny is dead. I'm heartbroken. Devastated." Summer's exquisitely made-up face didn't show an ounce of sadness. Nor did her perfectly styled bleached blond hair or her burgundy wrap dress. Apparently, former-models-turned-Pilates-instructors grieved differently than regular folks.

"You and Tawny were friends?" Kelly didn't know whom Summer socialized with. They hardly spent time together and when they did it was usually at a family dinner. This meant Kelly wasn't privy to Summer's circles of friends, and she'd prefer to keep it that way. Since moving back to Lucky Cove, Kelly tried to strike up a friendship with her uncle's wife. For the record, she refused to call Summer her aunt. They were only a few years apart in age, and it felt weird adding the word aunt in front of Summer's name. Her attempts at friendship always seemed to end with Summer criticizing her posture, her career choice, or her bad luck of being dragged into murder cases.

She hadn't thought it would be so hard, since they both shared a love for fashion. Their one and only bond. She soon found out that Summer preferred the friendship of women who could help her climb the social ladder. Kelly couldn't help her with that because she was busy climbing the ladder of retail fashion for a weekly paycheck. And then, gasp, taking over a used clothing store. Yeah, there was no bonding on that topic.

Summer nodded as she set her clutch purse on the table. “We met for runs. We had a lot in common.”

Kelly thought about it, and Summer was right. Both women were in the fitness industry building their own businesses, and both were married to older, wealthier men.

“I’m sorry for your loss.” Mark handed his credit card to the waitress.

“I want to make sure the person responsible for my friend’s death is sent to prison for a lifetime. I heard your former boss is a suspect. You found her standing over the body. Why didn’t you call me? Why did I have to learn about this through my clients at the studio?”

Kelly drained the last of the wine in her glass before answering Summer. A refill would have been good right about then.

“Until right now, I didn’t know about your friendship with Tawny. And, yes, Serena has been asked to stay in Lucky Cove for the time being. I don’t know anything more.” Although, she wouldn’t mind knowing why Serena and Jason met last night at the Gull Café.

“Well, I hope you’ll stay clear of the case because I want nothing to jeopardize the police investigation.” Summer leaned back and stared at Kelly.

Kelly looked to her wine glass and was sad it hadn’t magically refilled. “I feel the same way. However, you don’t get to tell me what to do. With that said, I can assure you, I have no intention of interfering with the police.”

Summer scoffed. “Oh, please, you really expect me to believe that?”

“Well, there’s always a first time for everything,” Mark added.

Kelly lifted the napkin from her lap and dropped it on the table. Her lovely dinner was over. She heard a hint of sarcasm in Mark’s tone, and like his cutting her off earlier, she didn’t appreciate it. Nor did she appreciate Summer sweeping in and telling her what to do.

“There you are, dear.” Ralph Blake approached the table with his arm extended. When he reached his wife’s side, he leaned in for a kiss. Kelly lowered her gaze; she didn’t want to see any PDA between her uncle and his wife.

Ralph was in his mid-fifties and had a peppering of distinguishing gray at his temples and a year-round tan thanks to his in-home tanning bed. He was particular about his appearance and what it conveyed. There was little wonder that all his wives had been former models. Every detail in his life was calculated and weighed on how it would appear. As a real estate developer, he spent countless hours networking, wheeling, and dealing. Successful people wanted to do business with other successful people.

“Good evening, Kelly, Mark. Dear, our table is ready.”

Summer stood. “We were discussing what happened to Tawny.”

"Quite a mess you've gotten yourself into again, wouldn't you say, Kelly?" Ralph's eyes fixed on his niece, and it almost made her squirm, but she wouldn't give him the satisfaction.

Since she'd come back to Lucky Cove, he hadn't been shy about voicing his displeasure regarding Kelly. From inheriting his mother's house and business to her involvement in three past murder investigations, he made it no secret he was unhappy with her.

"No. Actually, I wouldn't—"

"I hear they have a suspect. A woman from the city," Ralph said.

"Kelly used to work for her. Can you imagine? I'm still trying to wrap my head around Tawny being cut down in the prime of her life. Her business was taking off." Summer's green eyes watered as she snuggled in closer to her husband for comfort.

"Speaking of taking off…" Kelly hoped her hint wasn't too overt but then again, not too subtle.

"We should get to our table. Have a nice evening," Summer said with a wave as she and Ralph walked away arm and arm.

Kelly leaned forward, propped her elbows on the table and rested her chin in her palms. "I'm beat."

"You look tired. Come on, I'll walk you home." Mark stood, and being the gentleman he was, he pulled out Kelly's chair.

"I need to use the restroom. I'll be just a minute."

"No need to rush." He kissed her on the cheek before heading to the hostess station to wait for her.

She made a beeline to the back of the restaurant and pushed the swinging door to the restroom. Like the rest of the establishment, it was classy and clean with bright lights and a double vanity. Both stall doors were closed, and the ladies were chatting. Kelly caught something about the Gull Café as she moved to the sink.

While she waited, she inspected her eyes. She'd gotten a new tube of mascara a week ago, and it came with a boatload of promises to thicken, lengthen, and nourish her lashes. What she really wanted was a mascara that didn't give her raccoon eyes.

She leaned toward the mirror for a closer look. So far, so good.

Well, at least where her makeup was concerned. Staring at her reflection, she couldn't help but reflect on the latest turn of events.

How had she landed in the middle of another murder? Was this now her thing? Her new lot in life?

In the previous cases she'd been drawn into, she'd helped to solve the cases. Whether or not it was due to luck, she wasn't sure. She just seemed good at it. Maybe she had a knack for amateur sleuthing.

"My sister waited on their table last night. The woman he was with wasn't his wife," the woman in stall one said.

Kelly was pulled from her thoughts and into the conversation happening a few feet from her. Who were they talking about? She rolled her eyes. Duh. They had to be talking about Jason and Serena. Apparently, the only topic of conversation in Lucky Cove. They'd met at the Gull Café last night. Kelly looked over her shoulder at the stalls.

"Seriously? He sounds like a suspect to me," the other woman said. Her voice was accusatory.

"My sister said they were holding hands."

"Wow! And his wife is dead now. You don't have to be a math genius to put two and two together and get a cheating husband murders his wife."

"Exactly!"

Kelly returned her gaze to the mirror. Serena and Jason were holding hands?

A toilet flushed.

She didn't want to be caught eavesdropping, so she swung around and darted out of the restroom. She was moving so fast, she skidded to a stop so she wouldn't collide with a server carrying a tray full of dirty dishes. Murmuring an apology, she continued through to the hostess area where she found Mark waiting for her.

"Everything okay?" His forehead was creased, and he looked confused.

"Yeah, everything is fine. Ready?"

"After you." He guided her out of the restaurant. With their arms linked, they walked along Main Street. There were a few passersby who Kelly knew, and they nodded. The walk was short, so she made the most of it by burrowing closer to Mark.

"Be sure to lock up tonight, okay?" Mark said when they reached the back door of the boutique.

"I will. Call me tomorrow?"

"Of course." He leaned in for a goodnight kiss, and Kelly happily obliged. "Sleep tight."

Kelly nodded and then unlocked the door and stepped inside, flicking on an interior light. She locked the door and made her way through the boutique to the staircase up to her apartment.

The conversation she overheard in the ladies' room repeated in her head as she was greeted by Howard and kicked off her shoes. Howard continued to slink his lean body around her legs and then wandered off to the bedroom. Going to bed was a fantastic idea, so she followed her feline.

She pulled out a new pair of pajamas from the dresser and undressed, her mind drifting back to last night when she saw Serena and Jason meet and then enter the Gull Café. She guessed they were trying to workout out a deal about their shared property. Now, hearing they held hands made her doubt her initial thought.

After brushing her teeth and quickly wiping off her makeup, she snuggled in bed with Howard and her phone. He lasted a whole two minutes before he pulled away and curled up at the foot of the bed. She learned not to take it personally. Clearly, he liked his space.

She tapped on her phone and searched the internet for anything on Tawny and Jason. Dozens of results came up. The couple had been active in their church, like Liza said. Jason's advertising agency had recently celebrated its fifth anniversary, and Tawny was planning a destination retreat for her clients.

All in all, the Fallows seemed like a successful, happily married couple. She lowered the phone, pressing it against her chest. It's exactly how she envisioned her future with Mark. Minus the murder and possible cheating thing. She'd been resistant to think too far out into the future, but she and Mark seemed to be getting serious. Maybe letting herself dream a little of what could be wasn't such a bad idea.

A text message popped up. She lifted the phone and saw it was from Mark.

Sweet dreams. XOXO

She quickly replied.

You too. XOXO

So corny, but she didn't care. She was falling in love and wanted to enjoy every minute. Sure, he irritated her earlier, but wasn't that a part of loving someone? Tolerating their quirks? Hopefully, he felt the same way about her quirks. What was she thinking? Of course, he did. How could he not?

Chapter 8

The next morning, a new coating of snow greeted Kelly when she pulled open the back door. She did her best to look on the bright side. The storm hadn't packed the punch the meteorologist forecasted. Keeping with the whole bright side thing, she gratefully accepted shoveling the walkway and the sidewalk as a replacement to her morning run. In fact, shoveling provided her both cardio and toning. If she wasn't so busy moving snow, she'd pat herself on the back for being so optimistic.

The task of clearing the snow didn't take too long. With her shoveling AKA workout session over, she sprinted inside to change into work-appropriate clothing. She chose a pair of bootleg pants and a blouse. On the way out of her apartment, she slipped into a pair of mid-heel pumps. Back downstairs, she opened the boutique on time. Another accomplishment so early in the morning.

At the sales counter with her laptop computer open, she heard the jingle of the bell over the front door. When she looked up to welcome her first customer of the day, all that bright side thinking slid to the wayside.

"What on earth is Serena doing in my boutique?" was Kelly's first thought. Her second thought was about Serena's footwear. Were those the boots that set the fashion world abuzz last year?

The fashion icon dared to pack only one pair of shoes for fashion month. Dark brown tall boots. She'd paired those boots with countless outfits for fashion shows in Paris, London, Milan, and New York. Serena was photographed coming and going and looking effortlessly chic without trudging a suitcase full of shoes all over the world.

While Kelly applauded the risky fashion move, she now realized she'd have no excuse for over-packing shoes on her next trip. Darn.

Kelly stood and stepped out from behind the counter. "I wasn't expecting to see you…here."

"That makes two of us." Serena removed her sunglasses. She had forgone her faux leopard coat for a pale blush wool coat draped over her shoulders. Her midi-length geometric print dress skimmed her body, and a large chunky necklace filled in the neckline.

"Then, why are you here?"

Serena advanced farther and gave an appraising gaze of the boutique. "It seems you've used your time at Bishop's wisely. The window display is striking." She glanced over her shoulder. "However, you need to do something with the empty space. You're telling a story in the window, and utilizing the empty space can help with that."

Kelly was stunned. She'd received an honest-to-goodness compliment from the Dragonista. She honestly didn't know how to react. It never happened before.

Serena snapped her fingers. "What's with the look? Did I confuse you?"

Kelly was now back in familiar territory. But she wouldn't take the bait.

"I appreciate your suggestion about the window display. But I don't think that's why you're here." No, Serena wasn't known for visiting boutiques and offering free advice to increase sales.

"I wanted to stop by before I to go back to the city."

"The police are allowing you to leave town?" Whoa. Right there, she sounded like a bad cop show.

Serena browsed the circular rack of blouses. She flitted through the hangers at warp speed. "Not too shabby. Tory Burch? Not one of her better prints. You probably should mark this one down." She shoved the blouse into Kelly's arms.

"Thank you, I'll keep it in mind."

"As I was saying, I thought I should stop by to express my appreciation to you."

Another kudos? Kelly needed to sit, but she remained standing and was positive there was a dumbstruck look on her face. Again.

"Yesterday was a difficult day. I've never found someone murdered before, and you were kind to me. Offering me tea when we were in the house waiting to be interviewed by that boringly dressed detective." Serena lowered her eyelids and shook her head as if she pitied Wolman's poor fashion lot in life.

Kelly hadn't thought a cup of tea would earn Serena's gratitude. Now, looking back at the time after finding Tawny's body, she was thankful Wolman allowed her to make a pot of tea before she left the house. It was a small gesture and it was intended for Jason, primarily. He was in shock and grieving. A cup of tea was the least she could do for him. But to hear the simple act had touched Serena made Kelly wonder when the last time somebody had done something kind for her. A pang of sadness for Serena struck her heart.

"Again? You have nothing to say? Do you have a speech problem I'm not aware of?"

And just like that, the moment passed. Kelly discarded the blouse. It didn't need to be marked down.

"I appreciate you stopping by. But do you think you should leave? I thought the police asked you to remain in town."

Serena patted Kelly's arm and smiled in her condescending way. "I think you've been out of the city for far too long. I'm Serena Dawson, and no one dictates to me. Especially the Lucky Cove Police Department. Trust me, they're no match for the top law firm that represents me. My driver is waiting for me." She pivoted and headed for the door but stopped. She looked over her shoulder. "It looks like you've done nicely for yourself since your last day at Bishop's."

Three compliments? It wasn't possible. Was it? Or was Kelly dreaming all of this?

"Even though this is a used clothing shop." Her words dripped with the snobbery and judgment she was known for.

Nope. It wasn't a dream.

The front door opened. The jingle of the bell faded as Kelly's gaze locked on her visitor. Detective Wolman. Behind her was Gabe.

Kelly's body tensed, her mouth suddenly dry.

The grim expressions on both of their faces told her that Serena wasn't going anywhere anytime soon.

"Ms. Dawson, you need to come with us." Wolman approached Serena as she removed a pair of handcuffs from a pouch on her belt.

"What? I have to do no such thing." Serena looked at the handcuffs with disdain and then shot a look at Kelly, which she couldn't read. "This is absurd."

"Ma'am, please. It'll be easier if you cooperate." Gabe stood next to Wolman with his hands set on his utility belt, and he held a hard stare on Serena. Was he expecting her to make a run for it? Was he trying to intimidate her? Kelly wanted to tell her friend Serena didn't run, nor did she cower. He'd have to take his glare up a couple of notches just to get Serena's attention.

Serena huffed. "Again, since you seem to have difficulty understanding me, I'll repeat it. I don't have to go with you. I've done nothing wrong."

Wolman's facial expression grew direr. "We understood you the first time. Now it's your turn to use your ears and listen. You do have to come with us because I'm placing you under arrest for the murder of Tawny Fallow." In one swift motion, Wolman had Serena turned around and was applying handcuffs while reciting the Miranda warning.

"I didn't kill her. I demand to know on what grounds you're basing this arrest," Serena said once she was face-to-face with Wolman and Gabe again.

"Maybe it's better for you not to say anything without your lawyer." Kelly's suggestion earned her a scathing look from Serena. So much for trying to be helpful.

"We've uncovered hostile, threatening text messages between you and the victim. You were heard threatening to kill Tawny, and you were found standing over the body," Wolman said.

Serena huffed again, that time with much more indignation. "Do you even hear yourself? Tawny and I have been arguing for years, so why would I suddenly kill her? Besides, Kelly was at the scene also. She could have been there earlier."

Kelly gasped. What on earth was Serena thinking? Trying to blame her for the murder?

"You know, Serena, comments like that really don't help your cause." *Or, mine, for that matter.* Kelly glanced at Wolman, who maintained a neutral expression so she couldn't tell if the detective was buying what Serena was trying to sell.

Serena rolled her eyes. "I'll have your badge, Wolfman."

Kelly cringed at the slight. She knew Serena well enough to know it was intentional.

Wolman handed Serena off to Gabe, who escorted the suspect out of the boutique. Kelly hadn't expected Serena to come into her boutique only to be arrested right in front of her. Talk about a heck of a way to start the day.

"I'm honestly shocked." Kelly walked back to the sales counter and lifted her travel mug to take a sip of her coffee. "I don't think she's guilty. She's not a murderer."

Wolman pursed her lips. "I appreciate a fashion girl's opinion on my murder case. But there's no need to be concerned because I know what I'm doing. You just need to stay out of this one." She turned and left the boutique.

"Sure, no problem, Wolfman." Kelly took another drink of her coffee. It seemed all too convenient that Serena just happened to be at the cottage, but then if she was set up, no one knew Kelly would find Serena there with

Tawny's body. Maybe the plan was for Jason to discover his dead wife, and perhaps he was the one who was supposed to be set up. Or maybe, he killed his wife and lured Serena to the cottage to frame her.

It took all of Kelly's power of concentration to get through the morning without dwelling on Serena being arrested right in front of her. How on earth had that gone down right there in the boutique? If Serena hadn't behaved out of character, her arrest would have happened somewhere else. Maybe a high-speed chase on the Long Island Expressway? Kelly shook her head. She doubted Serena's driver would have engaged in such an illegal and dangerous activity. But then again, he'd have Serena leaning over the front seat, telling him to lose the police. Okay, now she was thinking crazy thoughts. Serena wouldn't dare lean over the seat and take part in a conversation with her help. Then again, Kelly hadn't expected Serena to come in, thank her, and give her not one but three compliments.

People changed. Maybe Serena had softened a little since the last time Kelly saw her at Bishop's. She didn't have much time to dwell on Serena because a steady stream of customers came in to either buy or sell and that kept Kelly busy.

* * * *

"Thank you for coming in today. The blouses look lovely on you." Kelly handed the shopping bag to her customer, who smiled before turning away to head for the front door.

Kelly glanced around the now quiet shop and took in a deep breath. Her mind started to wander back to Serena's arrest, but she quickly stopped the thought in its tracks. She had new merchandise to log into the inventory system and an article to write. She didn't have time for Serena's drama or a problem of her own making. Serena may not have murdered Tawny, but her actions led her to become a prime suspect. She got herself into this mess; she could get herself out of it.

And yet, Kelly sent a text to Ariel.

She was at a loss to explain why she asked Ariel to do some research on Tawny and her online business.

Ariel was a research ninja. Between her job at the library and her freelance writing, she'd honed amazing researching skills, which meant she could quickly and effectively dig into someone's past at warp speed. And the way things were moving in Tawny's murder case, warp speed was needed.

Mid-day, Kelly was able to break away from the boutique, leaving Pepper and Breena to handle things while she made a quick trip to the library. She found her friend at the reference desk finishing up with a patron.

The older gentleman nodded as his gaze followed to where Ariel was pointing. After a thank you, he was off toward the history section while she smiled. Kelly knew Ariel loved helping people. She volunteered at the hospital and senior center before the accident. After the life-altering event, she seemed more determined to help others. Over dinner one night, she explained it was because she received so much love and support from her family, friends, and strangers after the accident. She had a choice back then. Either she could be bitter about the hand she was dealt, or she could be thankful she had survived and not take anything for granted. Not only had Kelly gotten a delicious meal of mac and cheese, but she'd also gotten a life lesson that night.

"Hey there. I didn't expect to see you until later." Ariel's hair was swept off her face by a headband, leaving a fringe of bangs over her brows. She grabbed a notepad and then navigated her wheelchair from behind the counter. She led Kelly toward a wooden table.

"I hope you have a few minutes to talk. I was getting antsy." Kelly hated waiting.

Maybe that's why she'd been so impulsive over the years. Leaping without looking had been her MO through most of her life. She set her purse on the table and was eager to hear what Ariel found.

"I have a few minutes. First, are you sure you're okay?" Ariel's head tilted sideways and she looked concerned.

"I am. I admit, finding Tawny dead was a shock. She seemed like a really nice person. It's why I want to make sure her killer is caught. So, tell me what you found. I know you found something. You always do."

Ariel beamed. "I did. Actually, I found a lot. Tawny started her online business two years ago after marrying Jason and moving to Lucky Cove. Before that, she was a waitress and spinning instructor."

"Seriously? Her bio on her website made it sound like she'd been a personal trainer and nutrition coach for years. Maybe over a decade."

"You can't believe everything you read on the internet." Ariel laughed softly. "It's like overnight she went from living on tips and teaching classes six times a week to a virtual fitness/wellness guru, complete with a flashy website and a personalized fitness plan."

"Wow. So much happened in a short period of time. It doesn't sound like she was qualified to do what she was doing."

"Oh, no. She was qualified. She had all the required certifications from legitimate fitness organizations. I think her business partner had something to do with her overnight success. His name is Adrian Chase."

"Chase?"

"Do you know him?"

"No. But when I was at Tawny's doing the estimate, she got a phone call from someone named Chase. It must have been him. She didn't look happy to take the call. Their conversation seemed tense, at least on Tawny's end. Did you find out anything about him?"

Ariel shook her head. "No, but I will. Anyway, I also found that for an online program to be successful, there needs to be a lot of advertising, especially on social media, and there needs to be cash to pay for it. It appears Chase gave an infusion of money."

"Why didn't Jason invest in his wife's business?"

"Maybe he didn't have enough to invest? Or, maybe they kept their personal life separate from their businesses."

"That would be the smart thing to do, huh?"

Ariel nodded. "I think so. Now I found something very interesting." She flipped a page on the notepad. "Five months ago, a woman from Nebraska complained via an online video that Tawny's personalized program..."

"PBF."

"Yes. She complained that PBF was a sham. Then another woman came forward, and three weeks ago, someone from Oregon sued Tawny's company."

Kelly leaned back. "A sham? I doubt it. Tawny didn't seem like the type of person who would do that." She chewed on her lip. "Or, would she?"

Ariel pushed aside her notepad. "Sometimes, people mean well at the beginning. It appears her business took off so fast, maybe everything wasn't set up the way it was supposed to be. There could be a lot of things that caused those women to complain and sue."

"You're right. Breena seems pleased with PBF. She's lost ten pounds so far."

"Awesome. But I don't know why she feels like she needs to lose weight." Ariel glanced at her watch. "I need to get back to work. I'll do more research and see what I can find about Adrian Chase."

"I appreciate your help." Kelly stood and slipped her purse on her shoulder. "It would take me days to find all this info."

Ariel blushed. "Lucky for you, I have finely tuned research skills." She grabbed her notepad from the table and navigated her wheelchair back to the reference desk. "I'll call you later."

The day had warmed up to nearly forty degrees, making for a pleasant walk back to the boutique, until Kelly realized the warm weather would wreak more havoc with her roof. Thawing and refreezing wasn't the best scenario for a roof on its last leg.

As she got closer to the boutique, she saw a familiar person lurking outside the building.

What was she doing back there?

"Good afternoon, Kelly," Ella said. She had her recorder out and pointed at Kelly. "Serena Dawson was arrested for Tawny Fallow's murder. As a former employee of Serena's, would you like to make a comment? Is she as horrible as reports say she is? Do you think she's capable of murder?"

Kelly walked past Ella and grabbed hold of the door handle. "I have no comment."

Ella placed a hand on her hip. "Come on, I'm just doing my job. Can't you give me something?"

Kelly let go of the door handle. "I get you're doing your job, but I don't want to be dragged into any more of this case than I already am. Can you understand that?"

Ella didn't look like she understood. "Well, if you won't talk to me, then I'll move on to the next person on my interview list. Breena Collins. She was a member of Tawny's PBF program, which is accused of being a scam. Two lawsuits have been filed against it."

"Two lawsuits? I heard there was only one." Kelly asked.

"The second one was filed a few days ago. I don't think it's stopping with those two. There are a lot more customers who feel cheated. She was charging hundreds of dollars for what was supposed to be customized to each participant's own body and goals. Turns out, she was sending the same program to everyone. To make it even worse, when they used the instant message coaching portion of the program, they received generic replies. They were promised one-on-one, individualized coaching."

"That's horrible." Kelly hadn't known about the coaching part of the program. Now she worried that Breena had sunk a good chunk of money into a program that was indeed a scam. But Breena seemed to be having success. Maybe it was beginner's luck. It's easy to lose a few pounds at the start of a weight loss program because you're excited, motivated, and determined. Then, after a few weeks, all those things could easily slip away. If Tawny's program wasn't providing what it promised, then it was a scam.

"I'm not trying to ruin Tawny's reputation. I'm just trying to get to the truth. There's a chance she might not have known about her program's problems, and if she knew, she might have been working to fix them. I'm keeping an open mind. With the problems of the program aside, Tawny was a nice person."

"You knew her?"

Ella nodded. "I met her through my aunt, who is a parishioner at the Congregational Church."

Out of the corner of Kelly's eye, she saw Liza approaching with a shopping bag.

"Good afternoon, Kelly. I have some clothes to consign." Liza glanced at the overflowing bag.

Before Kelly could say anything, Ella swooped in.

"Aren't you, Liza Farley? You're the office manager at the Congregational Church, where Tawny Fallow was a parishioner."

Liza looked confused. "I am. And you are?"

"Ella Marshall with the *Lucky Cove Weekly*. Did you know Tawny?"

"Oh, yes, I did. We were friends since she married Jason and started coming to church. I can't believe she's gone. I miss her terribly." Liza got teary-eyed, and she reached into her purse for a tissue.

"I'm very sorry for your loss," Ella said. "I'm sure you've heard the police have arrested Serena Dawson in connection to the murder," Ella said.

"I did. It's about time. You don't need to be a rocket scientist to have figured it out." Liza wiped her eyes dry.

"What do you mean?" Ella asked.

"Well, Tawny had told me in confidence only a few days ago that she was afraid of Serena. She said the woman was a force of nature and as unpredictable."

Kelly couldn't believe Liza was throwing Serena under the bus with such ease. She could only imagine how Ella's article would read. The reporter wouldn't miss the opportunity to paint Serena as some vindictive, jealous ex-wife. Which she likely was, but that didn't mean she was a murderer.

"It's probably best if we all keep in mind Serena is innocent until proven guilty." Kelly's not too subtle reminder earned her an unpleasant look from Ella, which didn't bother her in the least. Even though Serena was unlikable, demanding, and self-absorbed, she shouldn't have been presumed guilty because of her character flaws.

Liza offered an apologetic smile. "You're right. However, the facts remain that Tawny felt threatened by Jason's ex-wife."

"During the police investigation, I'm sure more facts will come out. Now, Liza, do you want to come inside, and we can get those clothes ready for consignment?" Kelly grabbed the door handle.

Liza nodded and entered once Kelly opened the door.

"I have a few more questions," Ella said as Kelly followed Liza inside.

"Not in my boutique, you don't." Kelly let the door close behind her and guided Liza to the counter.

She probably just kissed goodbye her chance to be featured in Ella's article about the boom in the consignment industry, but she couldn't fret over that. She couldn't allow a reporter to hound a customer in the boutique. Although, Liza didn't look like she was bothered by Ella's questions.

"I'm sorry. I shouldn't have said anything to the reporter." Liza emptied out the shopping bag on the sales counter. She had an assortment of blouses, slacks, and skirts.

"It may be wiser not to speak to the press. Our words can be taken out of context sometimes. And, whoever is responsible for Tawny's death is entitled to a fair trial."

"You are friends with Serena Dawson, aren't you?"

"No, we're not friends. I worked at Bishop's, where she's the VP of Merchandising. But it sounds like you were very close to Tawny for her to confide in you her concerns about Serena."

Kelly inspected each garment. The clothes were a mix of fast fashion, inexpensive and low quality, but all were used gently, so they had a few more wears in them. And, at a low price point, they would sell quickly.

"Yes. We were. It's still hard for me to wrap my head around all this. You know, she mentioned there was a Fendi bag she wanted to consign. I saw it once. Simply. Gorgeous. Did she consign it before she died?" Liza folded the empty shopping bag.

"Yes, she did. It's a fabulous bag." Kelly pulled out the boutique's consignment contract. There were many things she had to revamp, upgrade, or replace when she took over the business, but the contract wasn't one of them. Her granny crafted a solid agreement with clearly laid out terms for consigners.

Liza leaned forward and dropped her voice. "I'd love to see it again. I know I can't afford it right now."

"It's in safekeeping. I need to get it authenticated before I can put it up for sale. I think you're going to earn some quick cash." Kelly patted the pile of clothes. She set the clothing in a bin and then grabbed a pen from a drawer. "I just need you to read this contract and sign it." She offered Liza the pen.

"So formal." Liza reviewed the one-page document while tapping the pen on the counter.

Kelly shrugged. "It protects us both."

While the document was well thought out, her granny rarely used it. When she did, she hadn't followed the policies it detailed, such as when merchandise gets marked down and to what percentage. That was one of the first things Kelly changed when she took over. Kelly followed the contract to the letter.

* * * *

"I'm curious, since you and Tawny were friends, did she ever talk to you about her fitness program?"

Liza looked up from the contract. "Sure. She was very proud of it. It took her months to develop the program and then implement it."

"Well, I've heard some disturbing things about the program."

"Like what?"

"She was being sued by two customers who felt the program wasn't personalized."

"Nonsense. They were just nuisance lawsuits." Liza signed the contract and pushed it toward Kelly.

"I see. Tawny was a spinning instructor before she started her online business. It's a pretty impressive leap to go from spinning to coaching women in weight loss through a pricey program."

"She'd been certified as a personal trainer and wellness coach for over a decade. Those women who filed the lawsuits clearly didn't follow the program. She always said the hardest part of losing weight and maintaining the weight loss was doing the work."

"You're probably right. I'll get these items out on the sales floor so you can earn some cash soon." Kelly took the contract and dropped it into a file folder. She'd scan the document into the computer system later.

"Great! You've inspired me to upgrade my wardrobe. Time to get some new clothes and not worry about the price tags for once. Have a nice day, Kelly." Liza turned and walked out of the boutique.

The boutique's landline phone rang. Kelly answered the call and happily provided information about the hours and directions to Lucky Cove. It looked like customers beyond her little town were hearing about the boutique and wanted to pay a visit.

Drip.

Kelly's good mood was momentary.

Drip.

She looked to the direction she thought the leak was coming from and then looked up to the ceiling. There was a streak of muddy brown by the front door. She hurried to get a bucket and then placed it under the leak.

It was time to do some number crunching. And some praying to the finance gods.

Chapter 9

Over a quick dinner of greens and chicken tenders last night, Kelly contemplated what Ariel and Ella told her about the lawsuits filed against Tawny's business. Since Breena was a member of PBF, luckily a happy one, there could be other members not only in Lucky Cove but elsewhere on Long Island. Maybe one was angry enough to confront Tawny, and then the situation deteriorated, and the person lashed out, killing Tawny.

Now, getting ready for a new day and applying a final coat of mascara to her lashes, the thought still lingered in Kelly's mind.

She pulled back from the mirror over the bathroom sink and frowned. There was one person who could help her understand the nuances of the fitness business.

Summer.

She'd bite the bullet, pull up her big girl panties, and pop into Summer's studio before the boutique opened. Minutes later, she arrived at the studio and pulled open the glass door of the Pilates studio.

She entered the sleek and serene cocoon of strong cores, firm legs, and perfect posture. A perky receptionist with cropped blond hair, a bright smile, and zero body fat greeted her. She had the ever-present look of hopefulness all front-desk personnel had—of getting a commission from signing every new person who entered the studio to a fitness package.

Kelly was almost sorry to disappoint the barely twenty-something, but she got over it quickly.

Kelly approached the desk. Its surface was clear except for a computer and telephone. "Good morning, I'm here to see Summer."

Behind the reception desk were four fitness rooms enclosed with glass walls. They used the three larger rooms for classes, apparatus, and mat work. The fourth was used for private one-on-one sessions.

"And you are?" The receptionist's perkiness vanished. Guess she saved it for paying clients.

Before Kelly could answer, she spotted Summer approaching from the employee-only area. She'd forgone her usual coiffed hairstyle for a ponytail. The casual style was flattering and appropriate for working with clients all day. She still wore a full-face of makeup. Kelly would never dream of doing a workout, sweaty or not, in false lashes.

"Good morning, Kelly. What brings you by?" Summer reached the reception desk. She wore a lightweight, long-sleeve, black top tied at the waist with a pair of plum-colored leggings and rose gold sneakers. Even her workout wardrobe was pricey. Those sneakers alone cost three digits. "Carly, let's give my niece a pass for a class."

Kelly raised her hand in objection. "Thank you for the offer, but I can't today." She would have loved to take Pilates classes again. When she lived in the city, she took them when her budget allowed. But the classes in Lucky Cove would come with Summer. She'd stick to her runs, thank you very much.

Summer came out from behind the desk. Even in sneakers, she was several inches taller than Kelly. Then again, in her former life, Summer was a model. Summer rested a hand on Kelly's shoulder and one on her mid-back, applying gentle pressure she said, "Keep your shoulders squared, and your chin lifted. Pilates would correct your posture, and you'd look ten years younger."

"Thanks. I think." Kelly did as Summer instructed even though she hadn't considered her posture to be bad. "Do you have a few minutes to talk?"

"Actually, I do. My private isn't for fifteen minutes. Come on into my office." Summer led Kelly toward the employees only area and then into her office.

The office was as sleek as the rest of the studio. White dominated the walls and furniture while the glossy dark wood floor warmed up the space. Before Summer walked toward her desk, she corrected Kelly's posture again.

"Pilates would strengthen your powerhouse. Otherwise, you'll end up hunched over by forty."

Kelly arched a brow. So, not only did she have to worry about middle-age spread, she had to worry about becoming a hunchback?

"I appreciate the heads up." She sat on a chair in front of the desk, making sure she didn't slump. "I'm hearing things about Tawny's business. There are lawsuits and accusations made against her."

Summer leaned forward, resting her forearms on the neat desk. Clearly, there was a theme in the studio. "What are you up to?"

"Nothing. I'm just curious. And worried."

"Worried about what?"

"Breena."

Inwardly, she chided herself. She shouldn't use her friend like that, but if it got Summer to talk, then she had no choice.

Besides, she was still worried about her friend. Even though Breena seemed happy with the program, Kelly would hate to know that her friend had shelled out big bucks to a scam artist.

"She paid for the PBF program. I'm worried she might have thrown her money away. You know, she's working part-time jobs and going to school. And she has a daughter."

"There's no need to worry. Tawny wasn't a fraud." Her eyelids lowered. "I can't believe I'm talking about her in the past tense."

"I'm sorry for your loss."

Summer nodded. "Thank you. With Tawny dead now, I don't think there will be anyone to support the program going forward."

Kelly inched to the edge of her seat. "You mean Breena could be out the money she spent?"

"I'm afraid so. There's a chance for a refund, but I wouldn't hold my breath for it."

Kelly's shoulders sagged but only momentarily, thanks to Summer's gesture to straighten up.

"Breena can come here for classes. I've always liked her, and I'd be happy to offer her a discount," Summer said.

Even with a discount, classes at the studio were pricey. But it was a nice gesture from Summer.

"I'll let her know. So, you don't think the claims those women made are valid?"

"Goodness no. Sure, Tawny was facing some backlash. But everyone wants immediate results without putting in the effort, without doing the work. I've had my share of clients like that."

"The allegations were that the personalized programs weren't personalized."

"I doubt that was the case. It's possible that several women can have the same goal and share the same physical conditions, so it makes sense that they would have the same program. In some areas of our lives, we're not unique snowflakes."

Kelly drew her head back. Did Summer just throw some shade at PBF's disgruntled clients? It was a whole other side of her aunt that Kelly hadn't seen before. She kind of liked it.

"Now for you, I would love for you to do a mix of reformer and mat classes. The mat classes will teach you how to control your muscles while the reformer will add resistance to improve strength and correct your body's imbalances. I have a client who had far too many imbalances in her body, so I scheduled her for reformer classes. She won't be on the mat for several more months."

Kelly wanted to hate Summer's program, but she couldn't. Maybe she should sign up for sessions, after all, she'd been offered a family discount for months. Wait, she was there to talk about Tawny. She needed to get back on track.

"Do you know who Adrian Chase is?"

Summer nodded as she leaned back. "He funds start-ups in the wellness area. Two years ago, he took Buddy Gallo and his protein shake, The Buddy Body Shake, national and now it's a multi-million-dollar business."

"Impressive. He sounds like he knows what he's doing."

"He's a venture capitalist, but he's more vulture than anything else. I'd cautioned Tawny about going into business with him, but she was determined to up-level her business." Summer leaned forward again, and even though they were alone in her office, she lowered her voice. "I believe Tawny wanted to impress her husband. After all, Jason is a successful businessman, and he'd been married previously to a very successful, powerful woman. Luckily, I've never had to worry about impressing Ralphie. He already knew how business smart I was when he married me. And I don't have to fret over whether or not to expand. We're both happy with me running this studio. In fact, the studio may be moving to accommodate more clients."

Kelly was happy to hear that Summer wasn't looking to expand into a chain of Pilates studios like she'd wanted to around Christmas time. She'd vied for a spot on a reality show that would have given her and her studio national attention. It looked as if Summer had shifted her goals for the time being.

"Now I've answered your questions. What I want to know is why you're really asking questions about Tawny's business. I hope you're not interfering. Aside from the risk of jeopardizing the case the police are building, chasing down a killer is an unseemly thing to do. You know the Blake family has a certain status in town."

Kelly resisted the urge to roll her eyes. Appearances were important to Summer, and her uncle. To some extent, she agreed, but Summer and Uncle Ralph took it to a whole other level. They were all about the country club, the formal dinner parties, and fancy cars while Kelly was happy in her little apartment and driving a hand-me-down car.

"I don't intend to do anything to compromise the police investigation. I'm just curious."

Summer gave Kelly a pointed look. "Well, stop being curious. Remember what it did to the cat."

Kelly swallowed. Summer made a good point. Her curiosity had gotten her too close to death a few times. Her own death.

"The police have arrested that horrid woman you worked for. Really, Kelly, she has a reputation for being a tyrant and a bully, and she finally snapped."

"Serena Dawson just doesn't snap." No, Serena had always been cool and collected even when she was torpedoing the career of a rival or designer. She never raised her voice and she never resorted to anything physical. She was cunning and smart. Murder was far too messy for her.

"You'd be surprised by what people are capable of. You wouldn't believe the things I saw when I was modeling. To be honest, I'm glad I'm out of the business."

"Thanks for the information about Adrian, and I promise to keep in mind your advice."

"Do that."

Kelly nodded and then stood. She exited the studio with a tinge of regret for making a promise she probably wouldn't keep and sucking her belly in. Maybe she should have signed up for a few sessions. The door closed behind her, shutting down those thoughts. She headed back to the boutique.

Halfway to the boutique, her phone rang with Marvin Childers' ringtone, and she smiled. He was an old friend of her granny, and she'd met him last Christmas. Since then, they'd kept in touch. She figured he was calling to invite her to dinner at his house again. He was a widower, so he liked the company from time to time.

"Hi, Marvin." Kelly held the phone to her ear. "What's up?"

"How's my girl doing?" When they first met, it was a little bumpy. His relationship with her granny had been a little murky and uncomfortable for Kelly to accept. Still, since then, she found that she liked him and enjoyed spending time with him.

It was too easy to dump her problems on him. He'd listen with a sympathetic ear and then offer advice. Being she was already up to her eyeballs in problems and advice, she needed no more of either.

"I'm thinking of signing up for Pilates classes with Summer."

"Interesting. I've tried it a few times. Never stuck. Not like yoga."

Kelly's eyes widened at the statement. She didn't know he was a yogi. The man certainly was layered and full of surprises.

"I'm hoping you don't have any plans for dinner tonight," Marvin said.

Talk about short notice. "Ahh…none actually. Mark is working late again. What time should I come over?"

"No, not my house. We're going to Gio's for dinner tonight."

"Fancy. Do you want to tell me why we're going to Gio's for dinner tonight?"

Marvin laughed. "No. Call me when you close the boutique, and then I'll head into town. See you later, sunshine." He ended the call.

Sunshine. She smiled again. Yes, it was a silly smile. At twenty-six, she shouldn't be getting all mushy over a cute nickname, but she couldn't help herself.

Her silly smile didn't last long. Before she tucked her phone back into her purse, a text message came through, and it was from Buck, the roofer. He wanted to know if she'd made a final decision about the roof.

It really wasn't a decision since she didn't have a choice. The building needed a new roof. End of story.

She texted him back, telling him to start the process.

Now all she had to do was get the money.

Easy-peasy. *Not.*

Well, definitely not if she didn't get her focus back to business and away from Tawny's murder. Maybe she should keep her promise to Summer after all.

There wasn't enough money in the boutique's bank account. There was no choice but to get a loan to cover the cost of the project. The thought of a monthly payment looming over her for the next decade or longer made her nervous. The business had no outstanding debt and she owned everything outright. A loan would change everything. She'd owe money.

Many businesses took out loans at various times; there was nothing to worry about. So why did every nerve in her body buzz, and not in a good way, at the thought of taking out a loan?

No matter what her nerves did, she needed the money. There wasn't any other option. Resolved to begin the loan process, she opened the boutique's front door and stepped inside.

Breena was helping a customer decide between two dresses. She opened the boutique while Kelly was at the Pilates studio and got right to work selling. While she was happy to have her friend working with her, she was also a little sad knowing one day, after graduating, Breena would leave the boutique. Luckily, she had about another year or so left before they crossed that bridge.

Kelly then spotted Liza standing at the sales counter. What was she doing back so soon? She was just there yesterday.

Instead of her usual safe outfit of a button-down shirt with a dark skirt and mid-heeled pumps, Liza wore a navy sheath dress that accentuated her curves and more stylish shoes.

"Good morning, Liza. What brings you by today?" Kelly crossed the sales floor, nodding to Breena as she passed by, and then stepped behind the counter. She placed her purse into a cubby beneath the counter.

Liza lifted a shopping bag up on the counter. "I have more clothes to consign. I don't know what's come over me. I'm digging through my closet and every drawer."

"Sounds like you're starting early with spring cleaning. By the way, your dress is lovely."

"Thank you. I got it yesterday, and I couldn't wait to wear it." Tears welled in her eyes. She fanned her eyes in an attempt to dry them. It didn't work. "I also bought a black dress for Tawny's funeral service."

Kelly plucked a tissue from its box, which was tucked under the counter, and handed it to Liza.

"I'm sorry. I know everyone is shocked by her death. It still feels unreal."

"No need to apologize. Losing a friend isn't easy, especially given the circumstances," Kelly said.

Liza nodded vigorously. "Only a few days ago we had coffee, when Tawny visited the church office."

Kelly pulled out the clothing, mostly button-down shirts and tank tops. She sorted through them to identify any imperfections or excessive wear.

"The other day…" Liza cleared her throat.

Kelly glanced up from the shirts. "What is it?"

Liza chewed on her lip and looked hesitant. "I may have been wrong about Serena Dawson killing Tawny."

"What do you mean?" Out of the corner of her eye, she saw Breena lead her customer to the changing rooms, so they could talk in private for a few minutes.

Liza patted her eyes with the tissue. "Tawny confided she and Jason were having problems." She blew her nose. "I couldn't believe it. They seemed to be the perfect couple. Oh, I'm sorry to dump this on you."

Kelly reached out and patted Liza's hand.

"Don't be. It's okay." She knew what it felt like to need to unburden herself. There were times, though, that she made poor choices when it came to the people she ultimately unburdened herself to. One time, she over-shared with a colleague whom she thought she could trust. In a New York minute, the co-worker used Kelly's confession against her when it was time for a promotion. Lesson learned. Aside from sympathizing with how Liza felt, she was interested in the Fallow's marriage. Was it connected to Tawny's murder?

"You're very kind." Liza covered Kelly's hand and squeezed before pulling back.

"Tawny said it was mostly her fault. The troubles with her business had her stressed, and she was snapping at Jason constantly. She said he didn't like it and was getting angrier. She finally admitted she was a little afraid of him."

That nugget of information shocked Kelly. Then again, she hadn't known the couple at all. Behind closed doors, anything was possible.

"On two separate occasions she shared that she was afraid of her husband and Serena with you? How close were the two of you, if you don't mind me asking?"

"I guess she trusted me. Wait, do you think Jason and Serena were in on it together?" Liza asked.

"Hey, Kelly. I need to get in here." Breena approached the counter with a dress and a pair of shoes in her hands. She shuffled behind Kelly to get to the cash register.

Liza dabbed at her eyes again. "I should get going. I don't want to be late for work. Can you email me the contract for these clothes, and I'll get it back to you?"

"Absolutely." Kelly gathered up the clothing and returned it to the shopping bag. She'd prep the garments later for sale. After Liza and the other customer left, Kelly asked Breena to come with her to the staff room.

They propped the swinging door open, so they'd hear the bell over the front door jingle if someone entered the boutique. Kelly poured two cups of coffee for them. Standing beside the counter, they sipped their hot beverages.

"When you told me about PBF the other day, you seemed happy with the program," Kelly said.

"I am. I've lost ten pounds, and I'm down a size. Now that Tawny is dead, I'm not sure what will happen. I guess I can still follow the program. But it's not going to be the same." Breena pouted.

"You don't feel like she ripped you off? The program seems to be personalized for you?"

"Oh, yeah. I've read things online about PBF recently, but I don't think Tawny scammed anyone. I really think those women could have been lying because they wanted their money back. There was a clear no-refund policy. I made sure I did everything Tawny said, and I'm getting results. No, PBF is the real deal. I hope someone else will pick up the program and continue with it." With her cup, Breena walked out of the staff room. On her way out, she removed the doorstop.

Kelly stood there, staring at the swinging door and sipping her coffee. She was relieved Breena felt like she hadn't been scammed. One less thing to worry about.

Now onto her next area of concern—the roof.

While finishing her coffee, she began the loan process. She emailed Buck, letting him know she was going to apply for a loan and optimistically asked when the work would begin. She also inquired about a down payment.

The thought of having to come up with any percentage of what the job would cost made Kelly's stomach somersault.

Online she found five tips to help secure a business loan. The first tip was to tell her story. The bank's loan officer would want to be sure she could pay back the loan. She needed to articulate what her business was, who her customers were, the growth in her industry, and where the money would be going. She'd also have to prove to him she had a track record of success. The upswing in sales since she took over would answer the question.

She also needed to prepare for higher expectations. It went back to the bank feeling confident she would prepay the loan.

Ah, the next tip was one she'd already rocked.

Even with her ups and downs over the years, she always maintained a good credit score.

Proof that she wasn't as flighty as her family believed.

The last tip was to be friendly with her lender. She nodded. She could be friendly.

Those tips were helpful. Even so, Kelly wanted to make sure she was prepared.

She got lost in her research, and with each passing click and jot on the notepad of what was in store for her, she became more and more concerned she wouldn't qualify.

She once had a t-shirt she loved wearing on Sundays when she met friends for brunch and spent the day traipsing around the city. It was soft, oversized, and had an inspiring quote written on it—Do It Scared. The t-shirt was long gone, but she carried the message with her. She channeled all of her fear into creating the best loan package the bank had ever seen.

With her head down and all of her energy focused, she got back to work.

Once she had all the paperwork and prep work done for the loan, she moved on to finishing her column for Budget Chic. Surely, having a side gig would show the loan officer she was enterprising and a hard worker.

Kelly added in her bio and saved the post. She'd find time later to give the article one more read before sending it to her editor.

While she was writing, an email came in, but she was being more disciplined and didn't read emails or scan social media until she finished her work. So far, so good.

Buck replied to her with a start date for the project. She added the date to her calendar. The next paragraph was the payment schedule, and he referenced the attached document, which was the contract.

She dropped her head and rubbed her temples, which were throbbing.

Breena came into the staff room with the cash bag, prompting Kelly to glance at the time on her computer. It was closing time. Where had the day gone?

"The front door is locked, and I tidied up." Breena set the cash bag into the small safe. "I sorted out Liza's clothing and entered everything into the inventory system. You'll send her the contract, right?"

Shoot.

Kelly had forgotten all about Liza and the contract. "I'll do it now. Thanks for taking care of the clothing."

"No problem. Looks like she's a big fan of consigning."

Kelly tapped on the keyboard and opened the file where the contract was kept. She then opened her email and sent the document to Liza.

"It seems so."

"She sure has been in here a lot lately." Breena grabbed her jacket off the coat rack.

"She has, hasn't she? Do you think it's a little odd?" Kelly closed out of her email.

Breena wrinkled her nose. "No, not really. She's what we call a repeat customer. We need more like her."

"I know, I know. But she started coming in..." Kelly couldn't help thinking Liza's sudden interest in the boutique had something to do with Tawny's murder.

"Kelly, you're reading too much into this. Liza is just excited about the fact she can earn money from her closet. Gosh, when did I become the voice of reason around here?" She laughed. "I have to get going. I'm picking up a pizza on the way home because tonight is movie night with Tori. I think we'll be watching her favorite princess movie for the hundredth time." Breena shrugged into her jacket.

"Sounds like fun. Give her a kiss for me." Kelly closed out of the bazillion websites she had opened. She needed to change for dinner with Marvin.

"Will do." Breena grabbed her purse and left through the back door.

Kelly closed her laptop, grabbed her purse, and headed upstairs. She intended to leave all her worries and suspicions behind and enjoy a nice dinner with Marvin because Breena was right. Liza was an enthusiastic customer, nothing more. She needed to chill and not suspect everyone of having an ulterior motive.

Chapter 10

Kelly arrived at Gio's for the second time that week, and found Marvin at a table looking dapper in a dark navy suit. He'd added a pop of color with a lavender tie. She was glad she had taken the time to change, or else she would have felt underdressed even in the casual restaurant. She'd slipped into a ruffled houndstooth printed wrap skirt and tucked in an off-the-shoulder black knit top. For her own pop of color, she'd added red ankle boots. While she was happy to see him, she was even more thrilled to see the bottle of wine he'd ordered. After the past few days she'd had, one or two glasses of wine would hit the spot.

He rose when she reached the table and gave her a kiss on the cheek.

"You look lovely, as usual." His warm smile made all her worries vanish for the moment.

"And you look so handsome in your suit. What's the special occasion?" Kelly sat and placed her clutch on the table.

Marvin returned to his seat and poured two glasses of wine. "Every visit with you is special. You remind me so much of your grandmother. You have her spark. Her joy for life."

Kelly offered a small smile. It wasn't until her granny died and she moved back to Lucky Cove, that she learned they had so much in common. It explained why she was the only person in the family who understood Kelly.

"You flatter me." Kelly reached for her glass of wine and took a sip. "Very nice choice."

Marvin nodded appreciatively. "You know how much I treasure our meals together. They're always so much more pleasant than the ones with Barlow."

The mention of Marvin's grandson was a buzzkill. She and the uptight vice-president of Childers Enterprises had gotten off to a rocky start when he believed he had ownership of the boutique and Kelly's apartment. While they settled the matter that he didn't, he still hadn't apologized for his behavior. It appeared the young Childers had little self-awareness.

"I am prettier than Barlow." She batted her false lashes and smiled before taking another sip of wine.

"You most certainly are." He sipped his wine and then set his glass down. He cleared his throat. "There is something I wanted to discuss with you."

Kelly's heart thumped. He sounded serious. Was he ill? He battled the flu in January. Could there have been complications that he'd kept to himself until now? Until it was too late to do anything?

Whoa. Slow down the worst-case scenario scene, Kell.

She took a gulp of wine and then set the glass down, bracing herself for bad news.

"It has come to my attention you need a new roof."

Kelly exhaled the breath she hadn't realized she'd been holding. "Roof? You want to talk about my roof?"

"Yes." Marvin nodded.

"Oh…okay." Phew. At least he wasn't sick or dying. "How do you know about the roof?"

"Buck's dad and I go way back. We still meet for breakfast once a week. Your name came up in conversation."

"It did?" Kelly wasn't sure how she felt about the two men discussing her. Then again, being a small business owner in town she was sure her name came up plenty of times. At least now, her name popped up in conversations for good reasons. Progress, it was a good thing.

"I know you don't have the money to pay for the new roof, so I want to take care of it for you."

Her tensed shoulders relaxed. Marvin wasn't delivering bad news. Instead, he wanted to help her. Her lower lip trembled. She was going to cry.

"That is such a sweet offer. Truly it is. But I can't take your money."

"Your grandmother would want me to help you. Please let me." He gave an expectant smile.

The mention of her grandmother tugged at Kelly's heart. She was confident her granny would have been pleased knowing her longtime friend was looking out for her granddaughter. Still, Kelly couldn't take that much money from Marvin, even though he was a wealthy illustrator. She needed to stand on her own two feet and be the business woman her granny believed she could be.

"I appreciate your offer, but I'm applying for a business loan."

"You'll pay too much in interest. With my offer, there's no interest. Not even a payback plan."

Wow. He wasn't talking about a loan but a gift. The money would be free and clear. It was more tempting than an end-of-season sale at a Stuart Weitzman outlet store. She pressed her lips together. She'd resist the lure of easy money. Staying firm with her decision not to take his money was difficult.

"I love you for caring about me, but I can't take your money." Why was adulting so hard?

Marvin looked a little disappointed. "Well, if the loan doesn't work out, you need to let me know. I'll even charge you interest if you want."

"Deal." She laughed. "You're paying for dinner, though, right?"

He let out a hearty laugh and opened his menu. "Of course. Order whatever you like."

"Thank you." She opened hers and browsed the list of specials. For the first time in days, she finally felt relaxed. Maybe it was Marvin's unconditional support, or perhaps it was the wine. Whatever it was, she didn't want the feeling to slip away. She needed to drink more water than wine with dinner, though. The last thing she needed was a wine hangover in the morning when she planned to meet with the loan officer.

They gave their orders to the waiter and enjoyed their salads before the main courses came out. While they ate dinner, they talked about their upcoming summer plans.

Marvin had arranged to rent a cottage farther out on the island, in Montauk, so he could paint. He always found inspiration from the ocean and was drawn to the rugged beaches out on the tip of the island. He invited Kelly to visit and suggested she bring her sister, Caroline.

When it was Kelly's turn to share her plans, it paled in comparison to spending the summer creating art in a quaint cottage by the sea. No, she'd be working to pay off her roof.

They each finished with a cup of chocolate mousse. Kelly had second thoughts about the order, but when hers arrived, she didn't hesitate to dive into the chocolatey bowl of heaven.

While Marvin paid the bill, Kelly read a text that came from Ariel. According to her friend's sources, aka the Lucky Cove gossip mill, Serena had rented a house in town earlier in the day. It must be nice to have money and to get a rental so fast. In the city, Kelly jumped through countless hoops to get her rental apartment. Then again, she didn't have unlimited funds, and everyone knew how money greased a lot of wheels. Ariel's dad, a real estate agent, arranged for the rental. So, the Lucky Cove gossip mill was actually Ariel's dad.

Kelly slipped her phone back into her clutch and walked out of the restaurant with Marvin. He gave her a kiss on her cheek and then headed toward his beat-up old car. He'd told her it may look like a junker, but it ran just fine so there was no reason to get a new one. Her granny was also frugal, and didn't bother to replace things just for the sake of replacing them. No wonder those two had been such good friends.

As Kelly began her trek back to the boutique. She texted Ariel for the address of where Serena was staying.

Moments later, Ariel texted back, and Kelly had the location of Serena's whereabouts. Other than Jason and her, Serena didn't know anyone else in town. Despite her strong, boss lady façade, she had to be scared. Kelly knew she would be. Maybe seeing a friendly face would help Serena feel as if she wasn't alone.

When she arrived at the boutique, instead of going inside, she slipped into her Jeep. It felt like a responsibility, though she knew she ought to just mind her own business. She made a firm decision to start minding her business tomorrow.

Kelly arrived at the two-story, cedar shake Colonial on a tidy lot within walking distance of Lucky Cove's small stretch of beach. The last-minute rental must have cost a pretty penny, even off-season.

As she made her way to the front door, thoughts of the marketing plan for spring that she should have been working on popped into her head. There was also prep work to do for the unofficial start of summer that was only a few months away. She could have been doing those things instead of paying a surprise visit to Serena.

The lights were on inside, so at least she wouldn't be waking Serena. She knocked on the door and waited.

When the door opened, Serena appeared. She sighed, signaling she was unhappy. Verbal cues were what Kelly relied on. She couldn't count on any facial clues thanks to all the tucks, lifts, and injectables Serena had done.

"Why are you here?" Serena's voice dripped with irritation, giving Kelly pause and causing her to rethink the welfare check.

"I heard they released you, and I wanted to check on you. See if you're okay."

Serena cast a cool, appraising gaze on Kelly. "You're here to see if I'm okay? I came to this...wannabe Hampton enclave to settle a legal matter with my ex-husband, and I'm arrested for murder. What do you think?"

"I think you're scared," Kelly said.

"Since you're here, you might as well come in." Serena turned and walked away, leaving the front door open. She padded along before disappearing into a room off the hallway.

"Geez, thanks." Kelly entered and closed the door behind her. She followed Serena into the living room.

Serena swiped a wine glass off the end table and then collapsed on the sofa. Which was so unlike her. She usually moved with grace, poise, and a massive dose of superiority. She didn't fall like a sack of potatoes onto a sofa. Then again, she was wearing athleisure wear. Something Kelly didn't think the always-fashionable Serena owned. Granted, the two-piece French terry was no doubt from Bishop's exclusive designer floor.

"Welcome to my temporary housing."

Kelly's gaze zoomed in on the opened pizza box on the coffee table. Serena didn't eat carbs or cheese or takeout.

Good God, the woman was coming apart at the seams right in front of Kelly.

"Thank God this place was available. After being let out of that horrid jail cell, I was fingerprinted like a common criminal. I needed a hot shower." She lifted her hand and inspected the pads of her fingers. "The shower in this house is about the size of the cell I was in."

Kelly opted not to indulge Serena in her whining about the size of the shower in the house. No doubt, it had to be bigger than her own at the apartment.

"Why are you staying in Lucky Cove? You've been released, can't you go back to the city? If you can't, why are you staying here and not at the inn you were at?"

Serena gulped the remaining wine in her glass and then refilled it from the bottle on the coffee table next to the pizza box.

"You're full of questions, aren't you? I'm staying put because it's a condition of my bail. And that inn had the nosy innkeeper. I'd get no peace there." She leaned back and tucked her bare feet under herself before taking a swig of the wine. "Besides, I want to be here for Jason. Even though we're divorced, I still care about him." She took another drink of wine.

Kelly arched her brows. If what she saw the other day between them was caring, she'd hate to see them when they were upset with each other.

"Do you think you should slow down on the wine?"

"No." Serena lifted her glass in a toasting gesture before taking another drink. "Help yourself."

"I'll pass, I'm driving home." Kelly cautiously moved toward Serena and sat on the sofa, keeping one cushion between them. "How does Jason feel about you staying to be here for him?" If he believed she killed his wife, would he look to her for help or a shoulder to cry on? Kelly thought that would be unlikely.

"It doesn't matter what he thinks. I'm here, and I'll help if needed." She topped off her glass again. Because her words were slurring, Kelly wanted to suggest again she cool it on the drinking, but knew it would fall on deaf ears. "Why don't you tell me what's going on between you and that boring detective? She doesn't seem to like you very much."

Now it was Kelly's turn to sigh. She explained how she'd inserted herself into a few of the detective's cases. She was helpful in solving those cases, but was frustrated because Wolman wouldn't acknowledge her assistance. Kelly also shared how she and Liv were arrested but, fortunately, they were released with no charges filed. Yeah, that was a night she'd not soon forget. Neither would Liv's mother, who had come to the police department to get her daughter. To this day, Mrs. Moretti still muttered something in Italian, which Liv refused to translate, whenever she saw Kelly.

A slow smile crept onto Serena's face, something Kelly had never witnessed before. "I didn't think you had it in you to be a thorn in someone's side. I'm actually impressed." Serena straightened and set her glass on the table with a clang. "I'm so impressed that I want you to help me."

Kelly tilted her head. Maybe Serena wasn't the drunk one, perhaps it was Kelly, because she could have sworn Serena asked her for help. That wasn't possible.

"You look confused. Did you not understand what I said, child?"

Okay, that sounded more like Serena.

"I understood you," Kelly answered tightly. "What I don't understand is how I could be of help to you."

"By finding out who killed Tawny and clearing my name. I need for you to stick your busybody nose into this case because I have little confidence in that small-town detective who wears sensible shoes." She glanced at Kelly's footwear. "Thank goodness you haven't succumbed to that fate."

Kelly smiled. She loved her red booties. *Whoa.* Wait, a minute. She couldn't get caught up in fashion flattery. No. No. She had to keep her head clear. After firing and humiliating her, Serena wanted Kelly's help.

Nope. Not. Going. To. Happen.

"I don't think it's a good idea. And I probably should go." Kelly began to stand.

Serena fell back into the cushion. Her chin lowered to her chest, and her shoulders sagged. The three-digit designer zipped hoodie looked baggy on her slender frame.

"It's true what people say about me. I am short-tempered, iron-willed, and brutally honest. I have had to be. You don't get where I am by being voted the most likable woman in the room." She licked her lips. "But that doesn't mean I don't have feelings."

"I'm sure you have feelings." But Kelly wouldn't bet on it.

"The truth is I'm worried about my daughters."

Kelly fell back down onto the sofa. Had she heard Serena correctly? "Your daughters?"

Serena nodded. "Twins."

How did Kelly not know that? How was it that nobody at Bishop's ever mentioned Serena had twin daughters? How had the press never published a photo of a pregnant Serena Dawson?

"Since when?" Oops. She clasped her hand over her mouth. That probably wasn't the right question to ask.

Serena laughed. "You have no filter, do you?"

Look who's talking.

"I keep my private life private. My girls live in Vermont with their father. I thought it would be best if they were raised out of the city, some place where they wouldn't be surrounded by everything that goes with my life. My ex can be there for them 24/7, something I could never do. I'm hardly the type of woman who could do a carpool or bake sales."

"You sound like a lot of women, but they make it work." *Way to go, Kell.* "I'm sorry, I don't mean to judge."

"Why not? Everyone else does." Serena waved her hand dismissively. "I know I do. Even though they don't live with me, we spend a lot of time together. I'm up there for long weekends and summers, and we take vacations together. There's not a day I don't talk to them. It shattered my heart, not talking to them today." She wiped away a falling tear.

Kelly studied Serena. Seated there, she didn't look like the person who terrorized Bishop's and all of Seventh Avenue. With her swollen, red eyes and frail-looking body, she looked incapable of yielding so much power that the legends of the design world buckled if she was unhappy with their new lines. No, she looked more like a scared mother of two children.

And it was that new perception of Serena that had Kelly relenting and breaking her firm decision to not get involved. So much for minding her own business.

"I'm not a detective, but if I can help, I will." Kelly watched Serena's reaction and the relieved smile on her face, and her shifting made Kelly brace for an unprecedented hug.

Instead, Serena stood and set her glass on the coffee table. "Wonderful to hear. I'm going upstairs to get some sleep. You can show yourself out." She turned and headed for the staircase in the hall.

"Of course, I can. Good night, Serena," Kelly called out as her former boss disappeared.

When Kelly got around to telling the story of how her visit ended, Serena's dismissal and lack of gratitude would surprise people because they didn't know the woman as well as Kelly had. She wasn't surprised by Serena. Only by herself. She was a sap for a sob story. But seriously, how could she let herself be dragged into Serena's drama?

Now, that was a question she'd be asking herself all night.

She stood and let herself out. Inside her Jeep, she sent off a quick text to Ariel asking her to research Serena's claim that she does indeed have two daughters.

She might have been a sap, but she wasn't a fool. If she was going to stick her neck out, she wanted to make sure she had good cause to do so.

Chapter 11

Kelly took a detour on her drive home after she got a call from her cousin, Frankie Blake. He invited her over to his condo for recipe testing. When she heard what he'd just baked, there was no way she could say no.

A night-owl off-season, Frankie swooped her inside and plated up a dish of piping hot apple cobbler topped with a generous scoop of vanilla ice cream. He'd just finished filming the recipe for his YouTube channel.

Kelly knew she shouldn't indulge after her delicious dinner with Marvin, complete with chocolate mousse. Still, the aroma of baked apples and cinnamon had her throwing caution, and possibly her size four jeans, to the wind.

"Holy bananas. This is so good," she said with a mouthful of the cobbler. Apparently, she was throwing her manners to the wind too. But, hey, Frankie was family.

The eldest of Ralph's two children, Frankie, chose not to follow in his father's footsteps—pursuing real estate domination on Long Island. Instead, his passion for food had taken him to Paris to study and then to cook for some of the most renowned restaurants there and in New York before landing back in Lucky Cove. Even though he'd landed jobs others would kill for, he wasn't happy. He wanted something of his own, along with a simpler lifestyle. Much to his father's dismay, he opened Frankie's Clam Shack. Not exactly the over-priced cuisine he'd cooked before, but he'd received rave reviews in newspapers across the island.

* * * *

"I'll be uploading the recipe video next week. Here's your tea." He set the mug on the peninsula's countertop, pushing a pile of papers to the side. He normally didn't have clutter. He was one of those rare individuals that sorted his mail over a recycling bin. His neat freak genes came from his mother. Kelly remembered how her aunt would spaz out at the sight of water marks on glasses. Heaven forbid there was ever a pile of papers like there was now on the countertop. Kelly could hear her aunt freaking out.

"What's with the mess?" She dunked her tea bag before setting it on the edge of the plate.

"Results from my DNA test." Frankie dropped a chamomile tea bag into his mug and then filled it to the brim with hot water.

"Huh. Ariel is doing one of those tests, too. Maybe I should do one."

"You should. I did one where I not only learn about where I came from, but also health information. It's very in depth."

Kelly shrugged. "I'll think about it. Back to your videos. How many do you have up so far?" She scooped up another bite of the cobbler. She needed to take some of this home for a snack tomorrow.

"Ten. I'll need a lot more. I'm hoping to get enough subscribers to start earning some ad revenue. Every little bit helps." Frankie carried his bowl around the peninsula. Barefoot, he wore his usual distressed jeans and thermal top. He settled on a stool next to Kelly.

During the winter season, he worked at local restaurants and as a private chef to pay the bills because his establishment was slow without summer tourists. The condo was a gift from his father, but he had to pay the HOA fees. The word gift was debatable.

When Frankie walked away from his chef career in New York City, his father asked him to work at the real estate company for a few months. He said it would be a trial, to see if Frankie liked developing properties. He'd thrown in the condo to sweeten the deal. In need of a place to live, Frankie took the offer and worked for his father just long enough to satisfy the requirements to get the condo. He may not have had the heart for real estate, but he knew how to work a deal.

"You'll get there. Before you know it, you'll have thousands of subscribers all making your recipes. This is to-die-for." Kelly scooped up another bite.

"Thanks for the vote of confidence. There's plenty, so you can take some home with you."

Kelly smiled. She loved her cousin. Well, most of the time. He had a way of letting his imagination run off with him. Like the time he had gone along with a séance in her boutique. If Kelly was ever asked for advice about running a boutique, top on her list would be never have a séance in your shop. It really wasn't good for business.

Frankie sipped his tea. "See, I knew you'd be happy. Kinda like I know something is bothering you. What's going on?"

She sighed. He could always read her like a book. They'd been raised more like siblings than cousins, and he knew how her mind worked. Sometimes it was a good thing, other times not so much.

"It's Serena. And it's a long story."

"Like usual?" He grinned and nudged her with his shoulder.

"Haha. I was just at her rental."

"What? Why? Oh, come on, Kell. You know she's bad news."

"I know. I know. I went there to check on her. To see if she was okay. You should have seen her. She had eaten pizza and drunk too much wine. I think she'd even cried."

"Sounds like she had a moment of being human."

"I know. It freaked me out. Then she asked me to help her clear her name." Kelly took a long drink of her tea and braced herself for Frankie's reaction.

"Which you agreed to do." See, Frankie knew her too well.

"How could I refuse? She's worried about her two daughters. I'm sure her arrest has already made the news. I've just been too busy to check online."

"It has. I saw it on TV earlier. Look, she's not your responsibility. Remember how she treated you when you worked at Bishop's?" Frankie's fork clanked in the bowl as he scraped up the rest of his cobbler.

Kelly let out a breath. "I do. It's still burned into my brain. So why do I feel obligated to help her?"

"Because you're a sucker for a sob story." Frankie popped up from the stool and dashed around the peninsula. He scooped out another helping of the cobbler from the glass baking dish. He gestured to Kelly's bowl, but she declined. She envied her cousin's lean, muscled frame. He could eat the whole cobbler and not gain one ounce, while she probably gained three pounds between dinner with Marvin and dessert with Frankie.

How was that fair?

"Am not." Kelly pouted.

"You need to be careful."

"I know. Trust me, I don't intend to get arrested again."

"I'm not talking about that. I'm talking about you and Mark." Frankie covered the baking dish and then refilled his mug.

"I don't understand."

"Sticking your nose in the investigation might cause a problem between you two since you'll be going up against his sister." Frankie looked concerned.

Kelly's heart sank. She hadn't thought about the effect her inquiring about Tawny's murder would have on her relationship with Mark. Could her cousin be right? Would Mark object to her asking some questions, helping Serena out? No, of course, he wouldn't. He'd understand what she was doing wasn't in any way a result of her not respecting his sister and her job. She would only help. Helping wasn't a bad thing, so it shouldn't be a problem. No problem at all.

* * * *

The next morning, sunlight streamed into Kelly's apartment, promising a beautiful day. She guzzled down a bottle of water first thing to counteract all the food she'd eaten the night before. Today she'd watch every bite that went into her mouth. Dressed in a black A-line dress that hid her puffiness, she swept her hair up into a sleek twist. She slipped on a pair of nude pumps and filled her water bottle before heading downstairs.

In her small entryway, she stopped in her tracks when she found a leak. The past few days had been warm. Warmth meant all the snow on the roof was melting right into her home. Maybe she should have taken Marvin up on his offer last night. She'd have a check by the afternoon and Buck on the roof ASAP.

No, she had to go and be a responsible adult.

She returned to her apartment to fetch a bucket from the kitchen. After placing it beneath the leak, she got a text from Ariel. She was an early riser who started work at the crack of dawn.

She confirmed Serena's story about having two children living up in Vermont.

Serena had been married to business consultant Arnold Parkerson. Arnold preferred keeping a low profile and avoided all spotlight. They had twin daughters, Chloe and Rachel. The girls were two years old when Serena divorced her husband. Arnold got full custody of the children and returned to his hometown.

It looked like Serena had told the truth.

Now she felt better about helping her. The truth was, the faster Serena was gone, the better it was for Kelly.

Back out in the hallway, she set the bucket under the new leak and then inspected the other buckets. They were only half filled so she'd check them after lunch.

She headed down the stairs, dreading more leaks. She opened the stairwell door and then made the turn into the staff room. She pushed opened the swinging door, and when she entered the room, her mouth gaped open.

It wasn't the discovery of new drips that shocked her. It was the fact someone had ransacked the room.

"What the heck?"

Kelly backed out and hurried to the photo studio. The tripod was knocked over, all of the cabinet drawers, where she kept her photography accessories, were opened. Their contents were scattered on the floor. Her digital camera was still on the table, which seemed odd, seeing as it was an expensive investment for her. Why wouldn't a burglar take it?

She returned to the staff room and did a closer inspection. The desk drawers were pulled out. The closet where she stored office supplies was opened, and its items were scattered on the floor. She looked at the kitchenette. All of the cupboard doors and drawers were open, and their contents were tossed all over the floor.

The place was a mess. Someone was looking for something. But what?

She pivoted and dashed out of the room. Her next stop was the accessory department. She came to a halt at the sight of the mess. All the displays were knocked over. Handbags and shoes were scattered all over the floor.

She shook her head. She must have been sleeping unusually soundly because she hadn't heard anything. Her quick look around didn't alert her to anything being taken. The six Coach bags, two Kate Spades, and one Dooney and Bourke were still there. Surely, they would have been taken since they were expensive.

Kelly pulled her phone out of her pocket, and she dialed 9-1-1. It was becoming a habit. One she wanted to break.

She was telling the dispatcher what she'd found when Pepper entered the room and gasped.

"What happened? The staff room is a mess." Pepper walked to Kelly. "The back door was open. Are you okay?"

Kelly ended the call. "I am. I came downstairs, and this is what I found. It looks like the staff room and photo studio were also searched."

"Searched? Oh, my goodness. What on earth for?"

Drip.

"Good grief. Could this day get any worse?" The moment she asked the question, she regretted it. Tempting fate was never a good idea.

"Over there." Pepper pointed. "In the corner. The leaks are coming in all areas. Those horrid ice dams. I'll get a bucket. And I'll call Clive. He'll arrange for a locksmith to come over and fix the door." She turned and hurried out of the room.

"And more buckets, please. There's a new leak upstairs," Kelly said as she took another look around before heading to the staff room. "Wait! Maybe we should stay out of the staff room until the police arrive."

When she reached the room, Pepper was already on the landline talking to her husband. She gave him a recap of what happened and then a list of things to do. Locksmith, home center, and Doug's to pick up donuts. The last action item on the to-do list perked up Kelly a bit. She could go for a donut.

She saw the *Lucky Cove Weekly* on the table. The front-page story was Tawny's murder. It wasn't a shocker considering it was the biggest news story in town. The byline wasn't a surprise, either. Ella wrote the story.

Kelly lifted the paper up and scanned the article. Two quotes caught her eye. One from Liza and one from Breena. There was also a scathing description of Serena. If Kelly hadn't known the woman better, she would have felt bad for her.

"Clive will drop off more buckets, and he'll get Burton to fix the door. You have an appointment this morning at the bank. Go on. Breena will be here soon, and we'll clean up."

Kelly looked up from the newspaper. "Are you sure?"

"I am. We *need* the loan." Pepper walked to the kitchen counter and prepared a pot of coffee. "Interesting article, huh?"

"I hope Serena doesn't see it." Kelly set the newspaper down, and that's when a loud frantic knock at the front door startled them both.

Pepper glanced at her watch. "We're late opening. The front of the boutique wasn't trashed. So maybe we close off the accessory department until we clean it up?"

"I don't think we'll be opening at all today. We have to wait for the police to arrive before we can clean up. And then we have to take a full inventory. It doesn't look like anything has been stolen but we need to make sure." Kelly's shoulders sagged. "Great. As if dealing with trying to get a bank loan isn't enough, I might have to deal with an insurance claim."

"Take a deep breath. And find out who's at the door and make them stop. Go." She shooed Kelly out of the room.

Kelly did as she was told and scooted out of the room. She was both annoyed and elated she had a customer banging down the door to get in, even though the boutique was in no shape for customers. Whoever it was, she'd have to send the person away. As she passed through the main sales area, everything looked good, so maybe she could close off the accessories department and open the rest of the boutique. She hated losing sales.

Kelly's annoyance ratcheted up when the person on the other side of the door came into view. Not a potential customer.

Serena.

Kelly guessed she saw the newspaper. She unlocked the door and opened it but didn't get out of the way fast enough. Serena barreled in at full speed and waving the newspaper, confirming Kelly's suspicions.

"Can you believe this? Who is this…this…" She unfolded the paper and looked at the front page. "Ella Marshall? I'll sue this rag and make sure this hack doesn't get another word printed ever again. Not even on some lame blog."

"Serena, calm down. Considering the past few days and last night, you might be over-reacting," Kelly said.

"What are you talking about?" Serena propped a hand on her hip. Kelly admired how good she looked, considering she nearly polished off a bottle of wine last night. Her makeup was flawlessly applied, her eyes were bright, with no sign of bloodshot or puffiness.

"This article makes me sound like I'm responsible for Tawny's death. I'm not! I'm innocent!" Serena swatted the newspaper. "You know, it was probably Jason who killed her. I bet he finally realized what a fraud she was, and the only way of getting out of the marriage without costing him a fortune was to kill her."

"What are you saying? Tawny wasn't a fraud."

"Ha! Dear child, she most certainly was. Before she married Jason, she was a spinning instructor, and overnight she became a fitness guru? Seriously?" She propped a hand on her hip. The belt at the waist of her cashmere coat was expertly tied and slightly off-center for a chic look. A plum silk blouse peeked out from the coat's neckline.

"What's going on here?" Pepper had come up behind Kelly.

"Who's this?" Serena asked.

"I'm Pepper Donovan. You must be Serena Dawson." Pepper's voice was tight with displeasure. Kelly recognized the tone all too well.

Serena didn't look the least bit interested in Pepper. Her attention snapped back to Kelly.

"What are you going to do about this?" she asked, shoving the newspaper into Kelly's hands. "How are you going to prove Jason killed her?"

"You?" Pepper's lips pursed, and she leveled the "Pepper glare" on Kelly.

Suddenly, it was getting hot in there for Kelly. She was bookended by two unhappy women. But not for long. Pepper yanked her by her arm and dragged her over to a rack of dresses.

"What is going on? Don't you think you have enough to deal with? You have to go to the bank to get the loan. You have to deal with the break-in and run this business."

Kelly raised her palm. "Enough," she blurted out and regretted it.

Pepper drew back, clearly offended.

"I'm sorry." She inhaled a cleansing breath. "It's been a rough morning so far."

"After what she did to you, she doesn't deserve your loyalty." Pepper grabbed Kelly's arms and looked her directly in the eyes. "Ever since Ariel's accident, you go out on a limb to help people. Sometimes it's to your own detriment. You have a big mess here at the boutique, the roof, the leaks, the loan. You shouldn't be chasing down a killer for a woman who treated you like dirt."

Kelly dropped her head. She knew Pepper was right, but she'd given her word to Serena. After a decade of being someone people couldn't rely on, she would keep her word even if it was to a self-absorbed, judgmental diva who crushed her career with two little words—you're fired.

She looked over her shoulder at Serena, who was casting disdainful looks at the merchandise, and she reconsidered her plan. No, she'd promised.

"Trust me." Kelly freed herself from Pepper's grasp and walked back to Serena. She thrust the paper back into Serena's hands, shocking the woman. "Go back to the house. I'll see what I can find out, but first, I need to tend to some business."

There was a little movement in Serena's eyebrows, showing Kelly that she needed another injection of Botox and that she was surprised by Kelly's directness.

"Fine. I expect regular updates." Serena spun around and left the boutique.

Kelly looked back at Pepper. The glare was still in place. Darn.

"I'm going to head out to the bank." Kelly hitched her thumb over her shoulder and then turned. She scurried out of the room before Pepper could say anything.

Before leaving the boutique, Kelly slipped on a red Balmain-inspired blazer she found in a shop in the city. The real deal was about two thousand dollars, well beyond her budget. This jacket's exquisite tailoring, tapered waist, and the quality wool-blend fabric was pretty darn close to the original.

Approaching the loan officer's desk, she channeled nothing but positivity.

Red was the color of power, determination. She squared her shoulders, lifted her chin, and embraced her confidence, which was at an all-time high. Jed Callahan stood when Kelly reached the desk, extended his hand, and gave her a firm shake. He then gestured to one of the two chairs in front of his desk before returning to his seat.

He had tanned skin with deep lines around his eyes and a head of white hair. Jed looked very professional in his navy pinstriped suit. Its smooth shoulder lines showed it was a well-tailored suit. While Kelly didn't know much about men's fashion, having male friends who worked in fashion helped her recognize the difference between off-the-rack and tailored.

"Good to see you, Miss Quinn. Hopefully, I'll be able to assist you today."

Kelly hoped so too.

She settled on the edge of the chair and leaned forward to provide him with the paperwork she compiled.

After his perusal of the papers, he smiled. "I'm impressed by your thoroughness." He returned his attention to the documents.

A compliment so early on. Kelly relaxed into the chair. She'd be leaving with the loan.

Jed hemmed.

Kelly's eyes narrowed. What was he hemming about? She tried to see what document he was reading.

He flipped the page. Then frowned.

Kelly leaned forward. What was he reading?

He flipped the page. A slight shake of his head. If she'd blinked, she would have missed it, but he'd definitely shook his head.

Why? Why the head shake? She'd filled in all the boxes. Revenue was up last month over the same time a year ago,

All of that was a good thing. Wasn't it?

Jed looked up at Kelly, gathered all the documents together, and then clasped his hands.

"Well?" she asked, on pins and needles.

"I'm sorry, but I cannot authorize the loan you're seeking."

Kelly went to say something, but she was speechless. How could he deny her so fast? So easily? The money she was asking for was to improve her building so she could keep the business open. With the uptick in sales, it was a sign her little resale boutique could repay the loan. Why couldn't Jed see it?

"I don't understand. I have good credit." Her voice had returned, and she leaned forward and jabbed at the top form.

"I see. While it's impressive, it's not enough to carry such a large loan. Besides the building, your business's assets are pretty much nonexistent. Retail is a risky business."

Kelly agreed. The risk was a part of the allure for her. From the first time she set foot on the sales floor at Bishop's and felt the adrenaline of selling, she was hooked. Her shoulders slumped as Jed's words seeped farther inside of her. The denial crushed her.

She'd done everything the bank requested.

She'd done everything to turn the boutique around with little money and experience.

She'd done everything right.

"Perhaps the best thing to do is to sell the building. You'd walk away with a hefty check and no headaches because, with such an old house, there are bound to be more problems down the road." He smiled, but there was no warmth, only his unusually white teeth baring at her. Did he sleep in whitening strips?

Sell? She lowered her eyelids and shook her head. He sounded like her uncle Ralph.

She opened her eyes, blinked, and then her gaze traveled past Jed to the window, behind the mahogany desk, and that's when she noticed a framed photograph of three men, golfers, on the credenza.

Jed was in the center with her uncle next to him, an arm around Jed's shoulder.

Annoyance bubbled in her belly. What was with her uncle? He was so desperate, to the point it was pathetic, for her to sell the building. Why? He stood to gain nothing since she owned the house free and clear.

And that's when it hit her.

This wasn't about money like she'd assumed. No, her uncle was still bitter he'd been cut out of his mother's will. Being made executor was another blow. If he couldn't have the house and business, no one could.

She wanted to be furious with him, but all she felt was pity and sadness for such a petty and greedy person.

Kelly checked herself before speaking. The last thing she wanted to do was become an emotional, hot mess after working so hard to be taken seriously as a businesswoman. She inhaled a deep, cleansing breath, set her shoulders, and crossed her legs.

"I see your point, Jed. Loaning me the money wouldn't be a smart business decision for your bank. I have given thought to selling."

A small victorious smile tugged at Jed's lips. The poor sucker thought the little ploy he'd cooked up with her uncle was working.

"However, I've decided not to sell. I love the boutique, and I'm determined to carry on with my grandmother's business. She left me her legacy. Now, there has to be another way for me to get the money to replace my roof."

And Jed's smile slipped away.

"Do you need to check with someone before continuing our conversation? Perhaps your manager? I'd welcome the opportunity to speak with him or her. I can wait." Wow. Her dupe Balmain blazer was working wonders. She could only imagine how she'd feel if she ever slipped on a real one.

"You golf?" she asked, nodding to the photo on the credenza.

He looked over his shoulder and then back to Kelly. A shadow of guilt clouded his eyes. She could tell he knew she knew what he'd conspired to do with her loan application.

"There are other options." Jed unclasped his hands and patted the paperwork.

"Wonderful. I'm listening."

"Since the building is paid off, you can use it as collateral."

It took all her self-control not to ask Jed, "Was that so hard?" Instead, she maintained a blank expression even though that option wasn't appealing. Heaven forbid something happened. She'd not only lose the business but her home too. Then again, if she got the loan and couldn't pay it off, she'd lose her home also.

"Anything else?" she asked.

"You could open a line of credit." Jed pinched the bridge of his nose as a pained look covered his face. It was clear to Kelly he was reluctant to share the option. Even so, he did his job by explaining the line of credit to her. He continued and laid out how to use it to pay for the needed roof repair. When she left, she had two viable options plus Marvin's offer of a no-strings loan.

Outside the bank, Kelly tilted her chip upward to the late-winter sun. She squinted and smiled. Her granny had always said to look at the bright side of things because the dark side was too depressing.

Ain't that the truth.

The meeting with Jed hadn't gone as she expected, but she couldn't let it discourage her. She had a business to run, employees relying on her, and a cat who demanded food and catnip.

While Jed hadn't confirmed her suspicion, she'd bet her small Louis Vuitton collection that her uncle had something to do with his reluctance to work with her in securing a loan. Over a game of golf, she could easily imagine Ralph strongly suggesting—that's how he liked to phrase his arm twisting—it would be in the bank's best interest not to lend money to her.

"Kelly Quinn!"

Kelly froze at the sound of her name and the familiar male voice. Just great.

Chapter 12

"You've got to be kidding," Kelly muttered before she looked in the direction of the voice that had called out her name. There was a sliver of a chance she was hearing things.

Nope. She wasn't hearing things. It was indeed Barlow Childers. Heir apparent and Marvin's grandson. A blast from the past she'd soon like to forget.

What did he want?

"Good morning, Barlow." As with Jed, the loan officer, she checked her voice before speaking. The young business man was the last person she wanted to run into after a disappointing visit to the bank. Truth be told, Barlow was somebody she never wanted to run into. Their previous interaction, when he barged into the boutique declaring it was his rightful inheritance, had left a lot to be desired. Eventually, the whole matter had been straightened out. Still, his bull-in-china-shop behavior left a bad taste in Kelly's mouth.

"Glad we ran into each other. I was going to call you today." He shoved his hands into the pockets of his leather bomber jacket. Unzipped, it revealed a lightweight gray crewneck. He didn't seem the type to be adventurous with color. No, he was more of a safe bet kind of guy. A quick glance at his creased khakis, and his traditional loafers confirmed her assessment. He wasn't a fashion risk-taker. Her guess was that he shopped at L.L. Bean.

"Oh? About what?" A pit formed in Kelly's stomach. This wasn't shaping up to be a good conversation or a good day.

"My grandfather." He stepped forward, closing the space between them. Kelly caught a whiff of his aftershave or cologne and she, momentarily, forgot they were adversaries. "And his money." That snapped Kelly out of her silly teenage age girl stupor.

"What…what are you talking about?"

Barlow chuckled. It wasn't a lighthearted laugh. It was more like a so, *we're-going-to-play-this-game*, kind of laugh. A breeze kicked up, ruffling his dark brown hair as his intense dark eyes fixated on Kelly. They were pools of intriguing darkness she could easily get lost in if it wasn't for the fact that they were his.

"I trust you've taken care of your financial situation so you won't be needing any of his money." He gestured to the bank.

Marvin must have told his grandson about his generous offer to loan Kelly money. Being the greedy little heir, Barlow would want to stop such a transaction. Heaven forbid his grandfather do what he wanted with his own money.

"You don't have to worry about your inheritance. I have no intention of taking Marvin up on his offer to lend me money."

Barlow nodded. "Good to hear it. My grandfather sometimes acts out of emotion rather than logic. Guess it's because he's an artist."

"Something you'll never have to worry about. Good for you." Kelly walked past Barlow. They had nothing to discuss.

"Are you implying I have no emotions?"

"No, of course not. I think you have emotions. You love money." Kelly plastered on her sweetest smile and batted her false lashes.

"Correction, Miss Quinn. I respect money. I respect how hard it is to earn it, and I respect how my grandfather struggled to build his estate. Which is why I won't allow anyone to swindle him out of his money."

Kelly's smile fell, and her eyes widened.

"Swindle? You think I'm trying to do that to Marvin? I turned him down. I'm here at a bank getting a loan."

Barlow leaned in closer. "Keep in mind, my grandfather isn't a backup plan if you fail to get a loan. I'll be keeping a close eye on him and you, Miss Quinn." He pulled back and then continued down the street without so much as a look back.

Kelly balled her hands into fists and huffed. The man had some nerve. He acted as if Marvin was a senile old man who needed protection from her, the young shop girl down on her luck.

Well, she wasn't down on her luck. She was a smart woman with a college degree and ambition. She didn't need a handout, no matter that it came from a place of affection, from Marvin or anyone else.

A honking horn caught her attention, and she looked to the curb. A police vehicle pulled up, and Gabe was inside behind the wheel. When she reached the lowered passenger window, he removed his sunglasses.

"Ahh…finally, a friendly face." Kelly did her best to keep from sounding sorry for herself. Still, there was a little inflection of pity in her voice despite her internal pep talk a few moments ago.

How many times was a gal supposed to rebound from being kicked down before she threw her arms up in surrender to the universe?

"I take it the meeting didn't go as you'd hoped." Gabe leaned toward Kelly.

"No, it didn't. I have a lot to think about and very few options." After the words came out of her mouth, she realized all wasn't lost. At least she had options.

"Everything will work out, you'll see."

Her heart swelled. He always knew the right thing to say, unlike Barlow. And she appreciated Gabe. "You don't know how to roof a building, do you?"

Gabe grinned. "Sorry, not a skill I possess."

"Maybe I can learn by watching a few YouTube videos."

"I don't think that's a smart idea."

"No, it's a desperate idea. What I could really use right now is some good news. Got any?"

"Sorry. The only news I have is there was a break-in at Jason Fallow's house overnight."

"What? It sounds like someone was busy last night. Don't leave me hanging, tell me more."

Gabe shrugged. "Not much to tell. Jason was woken up by the sound of the intruder, and when he got downstairs, the person was gone, but whoever it was broke the patio door."

"Huh." Kelly's mind churned. Was the intruder an opportunist looking to score some pawnable items from the home of a grieving widower, or had the killer come back to kill again? Or, was it the same person who'd broken into her boutique? If so, why?

"Oh, boy."

"What? All I said was 'huh.'"

"It's never that simple with you."

"Haha. His wife was just murdered, and now someone broke into his house. Also, my boutique was broken into overnight. Do you think it's a coincidence? Because I don't." That reminded her, she hadn't checked her phone to see if there was an update from Pepper. So much for being a responsible business owner. Maybe Jed was right to turn her loan request down.

"Not my call. Detective Wolman is looking into it. I've got to get back to work. You okay?"

"Sure. Don't worry about my financial woes or the leaky roof. As you said, it'll all work out." She pulled back and waved as Gabe eased his vehicle back onto the road. She pulled her phone out of her purse and checked her messages while she walked back to the boutique. There was a message from Pepper. An officer had arrived, and Kelly needed to get back ASAP. She picked up her pace and made it back to the boutique in record time. Well, she never timed the distance between the bank and the boutique, but it felt like she beat a personal record all the same.

Before she entered, she noticed the police car parked out front and then looked up at the biggest pain in her bottom line. The roof. The timing of its decay was unfortunate, to say the least. Even if it waited months or a year to fail, there wasn't any guarantee she'd be in better financial shape. Retail wasn't for the faint of heart. She reminded herself she was Martha Blake's granddaughter. She would survive this hiccup.

A five-figure roof repair was more than just a hiccup. Kelly shook her head. Everything had to work out. It just had to. She reached for the door handle and saw that the *Closed* sign was still displayed. When she discovered someone had ransacked the downstairs, she was scared, mostly. Someone had been in her space while she was sleeping. The thought was unnerving. Now, that fear morphed into anger because she was losing money. The process of reporting the crime, having evidence collected, and checking inventory took time. In the business world, time was money. She blew out a breath. Everything would work out. She entered the boutique with what she hoped was a better mindset than only a moment ago.

Inside, Pepper was telling the officer she completed an inventory of the merchandise and found nothing missing. See, finally some good news.

The officer had a few more questions for Pepper and then for Kelly. When they were done, he went into the rooms that had been searched to process those areas for evidence.

"Do you think they'll find any evidence? Like fingerprints?" Pepper stepped out from behind the sales counter and joined Breena beside a display stand of hats and umbrellas.

Kelly shrugged. "Whoever broke in probably wore gloves."

Breena nodded. "We heard that Jason's house was broken into last night. What's going on in town? First, the murder and now break-ins? Lucky Cove used to be such a safe place."

"I think it still is. Mostly." Pepper tidied the umbrellas.

"I just saw Gabe, and he told me about what happened at the Fallow house. By the time Jason got downstairs, the intruder was gone." Kelly set her purse on the counter. "To answer your question about—"

The front door opened, prompting Kelly to look over her shoulder.

"Mark, what are you doing here?" Kelly asked.

"I heard about what happened here last night. Why didn't you call me? You could have been hurt if the intruder..." He hurried to her and pulled her into an embrace.

"Aww," Pepper and Breena said in unison as they leaned into each other and pasted silly smiles on their faces.

Kelly ignored them and their tween behavior. "I'm sorry. It was just so crazy this morning. I just got back from the bank, and I could use a cup of coffee. How about you? Come into the staff room with me, if it's clear."

"Yeah, don't worry, we got everything covered." Breena's silly smile widened, and her eyes went all dreamy.

Kelly took Mark by the hand and led him to the back of the boutique. The police officer emerged from the staff room and indicated he was finished in there. He was on his way into the accessories department.

Kelly slipped out of her jacket while Mark looked around the mess.

"Wow. Was anything taken?" he asked as he refused a cup of coffee.

"No. It looks like the person was looking for something. What? I don't know." She poured a cup of coffee.

"How did things go at the bank?" Mark sat at the table. He must have been in court or heading there because he had on a suit. Usually, he dressed more Friday casual when he only had office hours. She glanced at his footwear, a pair of polished Oxfords. A stark difference from Barlow's laid-back loafers. "Kell, the bank?"

"Oh, sorry." She snapped out of her thoughts. Why Barlow popped into her mind then was a mystery to her. She sat across from Mark and sipped her coffee. "Not good, but I have a couple options for getting the money for the roof repair."

"Good. Good. Being a business owner isn't ever easy. There's a lot of potential for this business. You just need to make sure you apply yourself a hundred and fifty percent." He leaned forward and covered Kelly's free hand with his.

"I'm doing that. The marketplace for consignment is exploding, and I have every intention of taking full advantage in that upswing."

"Do you really?" His eyebrow arched as he pulled his hand from Kelly's.

Kelly stiffened.

She didn't appreciate the question or the slight shift in the tone of Mark's voice. She wondered if he thought she'd miss it. Not a chance when she was applying a hundred and fifty percent to him at the moment. She wanted to know what was going on with him.

"What's that supposed to mean?"

Mark pressed his lips together. "I'm sorry. What I said was stupid. You're doing an amazing job with the boutique. So, just think how great business would be if you were here more focused on the business."

Too bad he removed his hand from Kelly's because she wasn't able to yank hers back. It would have felt so good.

"I don't recall asking you for business advice."

"You didn't. I'm only offering an opinion. An opinion I probably should have kept to myself. I didn't mean to overstep."

Kelly sipped her coffee while mentally counting to ten, hoping to rein in the fiery response on the tip of her tongue. Saying it out loud would do neither one of them any good. Besides, he'd just apologized.

"I guess I'm worried about your safety. I want to make sure you're safe. Look, your shop was broken into after you found Tawny's body. I don't think it's a coincidence."

"I appreciate your concern. I really do. There's just a lot going on right now. The roof, the money situation, Serena."

"What about Serena?"

"She asked me to help her clear her name."

"She had the nerve to ask you for help? After what you told me about her and how she treated you, you can't seriously be thinking about helping her?"

"It's true she was awful to me. She was awful to many people. But she has two daughters she's been shielding from the public eye, and if she goes to prison, it will ruin their lives."

"Well, Serena should have thought about that before she murdered Tawny."

Kelly's mouth fell open. Had she heard Mark correctly?

"I'm shocked. How could you say such a thing? You're a lawyer. What about that whole innocent until proven guilty?"

"You're right. She is entitled to the presumption of innocence. Again, I'm worried about you."

Kelly reached out and covered Mark's hands with hers. She believed his gaffs were because he was concerned about her safety. It was charming. She realized how lucky she was to have Mark in her life.

"I'm going to be okay. You don't have to worry. But, since we're talking about this, I think it's a good time to ask this question." She'd worked up the courage to broach the subject Frankie pointed out might be an issue for the couple.

Mark grinned. “This sounds serious.”

“It’s not bad. Just something we need to talk about. Aside from you being worried about me, will helping Serena cause a problem between us?” Once she asked, she held her breath, waiting for Mark’s answer. It was stupid. Of course, it wouldn’t be a problem between them.

His gaze dropped for a moment. When it met Kelly’s again, it had become more severe.

“It may. The last thing I need is to have to bail you out of jail if you’re arrested for interfering with a police investigation.”

Kelly pulled back her hands. She couldn’t believe what he’d just said. Where was his unconditional support? It’s what couples did.

“Look, Kelly, I’ve worked hard to build up my law practice, and I can’t have anything jeopardize that.”

“Or, anyone.”

“And Marcy is my sister. It’s complicated. And it’s dangerous for you to track down a killer. Let the police do their job.”

And I should do mine.

“I appreciate your honesty,” she said, despite the lump in her throat and the breaking of her heart.

“All relationships need honesty. I’m glad we can talk about anything.” He glanced at his watch. “I should get going. I’ll call you later about dinner.”

“Sure.”

Mark stood and gave her a kiss before dashing out the back door.

She huffed as she swiped up her mug and took it to the sink. She was on a roll with disappointment today. First, Jed the banker and now Mark the unsupportive boyfriend.

His response had been like a sucker punch to her stomach, and it knocked the breath out of her.

All relationships need honesty.

He said it, but was he being candid with her? Was he anxious about her safety as he claimed, or was he more concerned with how things looked to his peers, his colleagues, and his family?

The door swung open, and she wiped away her tears. Darn. She hated crying over a guy.

“Hey, the officer is all finished,” Breena said. “And, Mrs. Addison called, and she has a closet full of clothes that no longer fit, so she’s bringing in some dresses and pants later today. I guess it’s true what they say about the divorce diet.”

"Pretty darn close." Having the seal of approval from her big sister was right up there with an organ donation for Kelly.

Caroline rolled her eyes while smiling. "I have to get back to work, and I suspect you do too. You'll probably need to get your building appraised for the line of credit. If you do, let me know. I know an appraiser who doesn't live in Lucky Cove, so he doesn't have a connection with Uncle Ralph."

"I hadn't thought about an appraisal. Thanks. I'll let you know." Kelly grabbed her jacket and purse.

"Do you want to do dinner next week? The four of us?" Caroline was talking about a double date. Her and her fiancé, Kelly, and Mark. She opened the files and spread them back out on the table.

"Sure. Let me check with Mark." Kelly did her best to sound upbeat, but right now, Mark wasn't someone she wanted to talk about, let alone go out to dinner with. They had to have a serious talk about his comments earlier before they'd be going out on a double date. Or, any date.

Kelly said her goodbye and left the law firm to head back to Lucky Cove. Before shifting her Jeep into gear, she texted Buck to let him know she was applying for a line of credit. She was looking forward to the job starting soon.

On the drive back home, she did her best to relax and allow the stress of the past few days to dissipate. To help, she turned on the radio and cranked up the volume when a Cyndi Lauper tune played. She bopped along to the 80s icon as she traveled along a narrow stretch of road.

The passing landscape was filled with the hope of spring—tulips on the verge of blooming, trees waiting to fill in with leaves, and the water gradually warming.

Longer days of sunlight and warm breezes were only weeks away, and she could barely contain her excitement for the change of season. She would trade her boots in for flip-flops, her wool caps for straw hats, and turtlenecks for tank tops.

Kelly's daydreaming of warmer days to come was cut short when up ahead the sign for Jason's street caught her eye.

Impulsively, she flicked on her blinker and made the turn. As the house came into view, she told herself the reason for the impromptu visit was to pay her condolences. It was mostly true.

The day she'd found Tawny dead had been chaotic, and in the days that followed, she hadn't had the opportunity to speak with him.

She arrived at his front door and used the ornate knocker to announce her arrival. There wasn't any fancy video doorbell, which she made a note of looking into for her home. On second thought, the boutique probably needed a full on surveillance system—inside and outside. Good thing she was about to have a sizeable line of credit.

The door opened a crack before Jason appeared. “Oh, it’s you, Kelly.”

“I hope I’m not interrupting.”

“No, no. There have been reporters trying to get a statement.” He opened the door wider, giving Kelly a glimpse into the beautifully furnished entry hall and carpeted staircase. Decorated in warm tones, the space set a welcoming and classic tone for the house.

“I was driving past, and I thought I’d stop by. If it’s a bad time…” Of course, it was a bad time. His wife had just been murdered and his house broken into.

“No. Please, come in. There’s a fresh pot of coffee. Would you like a cup?” He ushered her inside and closed the door once Kelly was inside the small vestibule.

“I’d love one.” Kelly followed Jason through the house to the kitchen. The room was bright and equipped with top of the line appliances, including a to-die-for espresso machine. Though she didn’t drink them too often, it would be nice to whip up an espresso and sip leisurely while reading her beloved Vogue magazine.

Jason nodded and then gestured to the pedestal table, large enough for eight, before walking toward the coffee pot. Kelly crossed the kitchen to the table and sat.

“I guess you heard about the break-in.” Jason filled two white porcelain mugs with coffee and set out cream and sugar before joining Kelly. Even though his wife had been murdered and his house broken into last night, he looked well rested and pulled together in his plaid button-down shirt and chinos.

“Yes. Are you aware that someone also broke into my boutique overnight?” She sipped the coffee. It had a robust kick to it, precisely what she needed.

“No. What’s going on? First Tawny and now break-ins?” He rubbed his forehead for a long moment before he stirred a spoonful of sugar into his coffee.

Kelly shrugged. “I wish I knew.”

“Could it have been Serena?”

“Serena? Why would she break into your house and my boutique?” Kelly added milk to her coffee and stirred. It appeared both exes suspected the other.

Jason leaned back with his mug in hand. He took a drink and then sighed. His well-rested face had clouded over with an emotion Kelly couldn’t read.

"I truly don't know. I thought I knew her. But a woman like Serena is complicated. She'd project a confident aura, and all the while she was simmering with insecurity and jealousy inside," he said.

"Are you saying she was jealous of Tawny?"

"Serena is jealous of everyone."

"Well, I'll be—"

"It's not a pretty characteristic. It's downright ugly." His next drink of coffee was a long one.

Kelly sensed he'd regretted what he just said. They had been married, and he probably still felt a little sense of loyalty toward Serena. Similar to what Kelly was feeling and the reason she agreed to help her ex-boss.

"Jealous enough to kill?" Kelly heard how blunt the question was and wondered if Jason would answer it or show her the door.

Jason set his mug on the table with a thump, prompting Kelly to reach for her purse. She stepped out of line and would be asked to leave.

"I have no idea what my ex-wife is capable of."

It looked like she wouldn't be tossed out. Jason wasn't afraid of uncomfortable questions.

"Is there anyone else you can think of who wanted to harm Tawny?"

"I thought you owned a thrift shop?"

"A consignment boutique," she corrected him.

He gave a half-shrug. What she called her business didn't matter to him. To her, it was branding and sales.

"And that reminds me. I have the clothing and Fendi purse Tawny consigned. What would you like for me to do?"

Jason scrubbed his hand over his face. "I don't know. Maybe I'll donate whatever it brings to charity in my wife's name."

"I didn't know Tawny, but I think she would like that. I have to get the purse appraised before I can put it up for sale."

"Do whatever you need to do. I have more important things to think about."

"I understand." Kelly offered a weak smile before taking another drink of her coffee.

A silence fell between them. Jason focused all of his attention on his mug. She could imagine the thoughts racing through his mind. Was her being there too intrusive? Maybe she should leave and let him get back to his private grieving.

"I probably should go and let you get back to what you were doing. But I do have one question if you don't mind." When Jason didn't object, she continued. "How was the relationship between Tawny and her business partner?"

“Are you sure you’re not a cop or reporter?” Jason stood to get a coffee refill.

“I’m sure. I apologize for being nosey. Finding Tawny’s body wasn’t easy.”

Jason leaned back against the counter. “I understand. Adrian always rubbed me the wrong way. He always seemed like a used car salesman to me. Slick, smooth-talking, pushy. He rushed through the whole process of setting up Tawny’s business.”

“Why do you think he rushed the process?”

“I think he did it because, with Tawny’s focus spread out and her being under constant deadlines, she wouldn’t look too closely at the details.”

“You think he was cheating her? Did you talk to Tawny about it?”

“Until I was blue in the face. PBF was her baby, and she made it clear to me to stay in my lane of advertising.”

Ouch. Hearing his wife tell him that must have stung him. Enough to kill?

“I guess I can see her point of view. You have a successful ad agency, and she was looking to create her business on her own.”

Jason pinched the bridge of his nose. “Tawny was a remarkable woman. Hardworking, determined. It’s what I loved about her.”

“Did anything else happen?”

Jason stepped away from the counter and went back to the table. “She’d been acting oddly the past few weeks, and I eventually confronted her. She believed Adrian was embezzling funds from the business and generated phony financial paperwork to get loans he used to promote the programs he sold. I’m pretty sure Tawny’s wasn’t the only program he was being taken to court over. He needed to keep the money coming in to cover his legal fees and pay his bills.”

“Did Tawny have any evidence to back up her suspicion?”

“As far as I know, she didn’t have any proof. I don’t know if she confronted him about her suspicions. Why don’t I know that?” He looked regretful before he dropped his head into his hands.

Kelly reached out her hand and touched his arm. She knew a thing or two about blame and how easy it was to take it on and let it consume you.

“You can’t blame yourself for what happened to Tawny. The person responsible is the murderer. Not you.”

Jason lifted his head. His pale blue eyes were filled with pain. “I’m not sure how I’ll forgive myself. She raised a red flag, and I did nothing about it. I should have.”

“Let’s change that now. Have you told the police about this?”

“No, I haven’t told the police yet. I know I should have but my head… it’s been muddled with everything that has happened. I guess I’m starting to think clearly now. Think about who could have killed my wife." He dropped his hands onto the table and balled them into fists.

"You need to call Detective Wolman and tell her. She needs all the information in order to do her job. Aside from investigating Serena, she now can look into Adrian."

There was a knock at the door, signaling to Kelly it was time to leave. She stood and lifted her purse from the back of the chair.

"I will. I appreciate your visit. It's been beneficial to me." Jason also stood and guided Kelly out of the kitchen and to the front door. He sidestepped around Kelly to open the door.

Liza swooped in, holding an insulated bag.

"I apologize for dropping by unannounced, but I've brought food. You probably haven't been eating properly." Liza's gaze drifted from Jason to Kelly. "Oh, hi. I didn't think I'd run into you here."

"Kelly dropped by because she heard about the break-in, and her boutique was broken into overnight as well." Jason accepted the bag from Liza.

"Oh, how terrible. You don't suppose it was the same person? Why on earth would someone break into both places?" Liza dropped a hand on Jason's arm. "I'm taking care of the funeral arrangements myself, so you don't have to worry about a thing. Since I'm here, can I get those documents we talked about earlier?"

"Right. Right. They're in a folder on the desk in the study. Kelly was just leaving," Jason said.

"No need to rush. The study is that way, on the right?" Liza pointed ahead and then looked back at Jason for confirmation. He nodded. "I'll set this in the fridge first." she murmured a goodbye to Kelly and walked away.

"Thank you for the visit and for taking care of Tawny's purse. Perhaps you could come back and go through her closet." His voice was shaky, and he looked hopeful Kelly would agree.

"Of course. When the time is right, call me."

"I want to do it as soon as possible. Having her things around is just too hard for me. I'll call you to set up a time."

"Okay, whatever you want." Before stepping out onto the welcome mat, she stopped. "I'm sorry, I have one more question. The day I came to pick up the clothes from Tawny, I saw her later in the day outside my boutique. She was arguing with a woman. Have any of the clients who are suing PBF threatened Tawny?"

Jason's eyes fluttered closed as he shook his head. "I'm not aware of any personal threats. But you say you saw a woman arguing with Tawny? Was she a client?"

"I don't know. I'm sorry."

"This is all Adrian's fault. I'd warned her about him. All he's interested in is money. He's the one who created PBF for Tawny, and he was supposed to manage it. Any problems with customers are all because of him. The guy refused to take any responsibility for his blunders. He was ruining Tawny's reputation. If anyone should be dead, it should be him."

A loud gasp drew Kelly and Jason's attention behind them. Liza stood there with a folder in her hand.

"You can't mean that, Jason." Liza hurried to his side. She rested a hand on his arm again.

"If we find out one of those PBF members killed my wife, I certainly mean it. Now, if you don't mind, I really need some time alone. Thank you for taking care of the funeral arrangements and for the food. You've been a great support." Jason smoothly shuffled Liza and Kelly out the front door.

"I can't believe what he said. Can you?" Liza zipped her jacket as she walked away from the front door.

"He's obviously distressed over what has happened. We shouldn't read into what he said." Kelly was familiar with grief. It could be so consuming it trampled rational thinking.

Liza dug into her purse for her car key. "I hope that's all it is. The last thing Lucky Cove needs is another murder."

They walked to the driveway in silence. Liza's Jetta was parked behind Kelly's Jeep.

Kelly stopped at her driver's side door. "Since you seem to know Jason better than I do, do you think he's capable of killing someone?" It wasn't a secret the police usually look at the spouse when investigating a murder.

"People are capable of a lot of things. Have a nice day, Kelly." Liza hurried away to her vehicle, and within moments, she was backing out of the driveway.

People are capable of a lot of things.

Wasn't that the truth?

As soon as Liza's vehicle disappeared from sight, a familiar-looking BMW pulled into the driveway and parked

What on earth was Mark doing there?

"Kelly, I didn't expect to see you here." He closed his vehicle's door and approached her. A laptop bag was slung over his shoulder, and he had his Ray-Ban sunglasses on.

"I came to pay my condolences to Jason. I haven't had the proper opportunity before to do so. Why are you here?"

"I'm his personal attorney. And I was Tawny's also." Mark slipped off his sunglasses and carefully slid them into a pocket in his bag.

"You are? You handled their estates? Their wills? Tawny's will?" She couldn't help but wonder how much Jason would inherit. Then again, prior to their marriage, Tawny was a spinning instructor. And her business seemed to be coming apart at the seams. No, it was more likely Tawny would have benefited from Jason's death rather than the other way around.

"I do. Before you ask, I can't tell you anything."

"Right. Client privilege. Anyway, I wasn't going to ask." It was a little fib, but she didn't want to give him any more ammunition regarding her curiosity about Tawny's murder.

"Glad to hear. How's he doing?" Mark's gaze diverted to the house.

"As well as you could expect. He's angry. He's grieving. He wants to clear out all of Tawny's clothing."

"So soon?" Mark did a double take.

"Everyone handles grief differently. I'll be sensitive to what I take for consignment. I'm sure there are some sentimental items he'll want to keep even if he doesn't realize it yet."

"Very thoughtful. I'm sure he'll appreciate it. Look. About our conversation earlier..." Mark's lips pressed together. Kelly wasn't sure if he was about to apologize or expand on his lecture because of where he just found her.

Their relationship was not up for discussion while they were standing outside of Jason's house. She reached out and grabbed his hand. What would it hurt to give him the benefit of the doubt?

"You're here to do work, and I have to get going."

"We'll talk later?"

"Sure." She slid into the Jeep, but didn't close the door right away. "Quick question, did you handle Tawny's business matters?"

"No. Only her personal legal matters. Why?" His voice went flat on the last question. Kelly sensed he was second-guessing her claim of being there only to pay her condolences.

"No reason. Talk soon." She closed the door and started the ignition. Mark had parked his BMW off to the side behind her so she'd be able to back out without him having to move his vehicle. He was always considerate. Well, when he wasn't criticizing her business management style.

After she backed out of the driveway and was on the road, she called to check on Pepper and Breena. Both reported everything was fine. Hearing there were no new leaks or crises, she considered taking a trip to Adrian

Chase's office. The round trip would take over an hour, but she'd be back in time to close up the boutique.

What harm could it do to pay a visit to the man who, on the surface, was a successful venture capitalist? Other than finding herself alone with a potential killer. She drove toward the highway. She assured herself they wouldn't be alone. She pulled over to search for his address. Once she found it, she used her phone's map app to get directions to the corporate park. There were bound to be plenty of people around. So, she had nothing to worry about. Nothing at all.

Chapter 14

After taking the exit off the highway, Kelly followed the directions from her app to the corporate park. A sign for the corporate park came into view, and she slowed to take the upcoming right turn into the parking lot. Searching for a spot, she realized she hadn't come up with was a way to approach Adrian.

Walking up to him and asking flat out if he killed Tawny didn't seem like the best way to break the ice with the guy. No, she needed something else.

The parking lot was practically full, so it took a couple minutes to find a space. By the time she parked and got out of her Jeep, she'd come up with an idea, one she was sure Adrian would have no interest in, but it would get her in the door—or, so she hoped.

The sleek, two-story building was impressive, and inside she found a directory. She scanned the list and located Adrian's office. Suite 216. When the elevator door whooshed opened, she stepped in and pressed the button for the second floor.

The ride up gave her a moment to second-guess being there. What was she doing? The visit could go sideways quickly. Was helping Serena worth it? As the door slid open, Pepper's reminder that she owed no loyalty to Serena repeated in her head. While she wanted to be annoyed with Pepper, she had a point. There was no payoff for her by helping Serena. No job, no promotion, no raise. Nothing. So why was she stepping out onto the floor where Adrian's office was?

Because she promised. She gave her word. Lordy. She vowed never to let anyone else down after Ariel's accident.

Look at where her vow had gotten her. At Adrian's office door.

She opened the door and stepped inside. It wasn't as impressive as she expected given he'd reportedly made millions launching lucrative fitness products and programs. The reception desk wasn't staffed, and the inner office door was closed. Darn. She had expected people to be around. At least a receptionist.

The interior office door opened, and a tall, bald man with a thick beard and broad shoulders appeared.

"Can I help you?" His voice was gruff, and he scowled. He wasn't very welcoming.

"If you're Adrian Chase, I hope you can help me. I'm Kelly Quinn. I'm a relative of Summer Blake." She hoped dropping the name of a fitness professional Adrian had an interest in would open him up to a conversation. She extended her hand, and he moved forward to shake it.

Adrian's scowl quickly disappeared and was replaced by a toothy smile. His beady eyes lit up with interest. "How is Summer doing? I heard a rumor she's expanding her studio. She has a lot of potential. Come on in. Would you like a coffee or something?" He gestured for Kelly to come into the office.

"No, thank you. I apologize for showing up without an appointment."

Inside the inner sanctum, Kelly's gaze swept over the average-sized office with a view of the parking lot and a mall off in the distance.

A collage of framed photographs featuring Adrian with C-list celebrities hung on one wall above a seating area. The two leather chairs and sofa looked brand new. As did the highly polished desk. The space was streamlined and professional but had a staged look to it.

She couldn't help but wonder how much work actually got done there.

"Not a problem. Please, have a seat." Adrian walked around the desk while Kelly settled on a chair in front of the desk. His smile was still in place. He reminded Kelly of a street vendor selling knockoffs. "Summer has a great studio. And unlimited potential. I've been trying to make a deal with Summer for a long time, so I'm glad she's sent you to..."

"I'm sorry. It looks like I wasn't clear. Summer hasn't sent me here." Kelly hoped her uncle's wife would never go into business with the guy sitting across from her. She wondered how Tawny had partnered with him. Tawny was a smart woman. And the vibes he was sending were slimy and untrustworthy. She had a sudden urge to take a hot shower as soon as she got home.

"Oh, I see. Then why are you here, Miss Quinn?" Adrian's sly smile vanished as he clasped his thick fingers together and waited for an answer.

"I own a consignment clothing boutique, and the resale market is hot. Actually, hot is an understatement. It's on fire. What I'd like to do is expand, but I really don't want another brick and mortar location. Instead, I've been thinking about creating an online business. Women would sign up for a subscription box of clothing curated especially for them from resale shops all over the country. Before taking over the boutique, I was a fashion buyer."

She believed there were several things challenging her idea to make it profitable. The first was logistics. She would need a warehouse of some sort to receive consigned clothing, prep the merchandise for sale, and then ship the boxes. Next, she'd need a much bigger staff than she had now and that meant a larger payroll. The list went on and on. But since she wasn't there to make a deal, it didn't matter how many holes her idea had.

"You want to send people used clothing on a subscription model? That's a thing?"

"Yes." The more she thought about the idea, the more intriguing it became even though she had no clue how to make it work. She guessed that's how Tawny felt about her online fitness business and what led her to Adrian.

* * * *

"Huh." He drummed his fingers on his desk as he appeared to consider the idea. Shoot. That wasn't the outcome Kelly wanted. She already had too much on her plate, and he wasn't definitely someone she wanted to work with. For one thing, he may have murdered his previous partner.

"Sorry, but fashion isn't my area. I'm all about fitness." He pointed toward the framed photographs of his business associates on the credenza. There was a photo of him and Tawny. It looked like they were on a television set. She guessed they were doing promotion for PBF.

Kelly nodded. "You have quite a reputation in the fitness field. You've launched many successful fitness businesses. From what I hear, you were behind the launch of Tawny's PBF program. The photo of the two of you, where was it taken?"

"A TV studio. We planned on doing an infomercial."

"Wow. How expensive is one of those to produce?"

"Well, you can't make money without spending it." He followed up his financial advice with a smarmy chuckle. She wondered whose money he was using to pad his bank account. "Look, I'm sorry, hon, that I can't help you with your business idea. Good luck with it."

Hon? Did he really call me hon?

Kelly tamped down her annoyance. Schooling him in twenty-first century etiquette would get her tossed out in a nano-second. Instead, she forced a smile.

"Thank you. I guess I'll have to continue looking for an adviser. Or, a business partner like you were with Tawny. She was lucky to have someone with your experience working with her."

"If I do say so myself, I do bring a lot to the table. Now, if Summer would like to go into a partnership, I can take her one-studio Pilates biz nationwide and have her streaming into hundreds of thousands of homes like that." He snapped his fingers.

"I'm sure you could. One thing you definitely brought to the table for Tawny was the ability to put out fires. Like those lawsuits against PBF." When Kelly worked at Bishop's, it was her job as the assistant buyer to make sure small issues didn't morph into big disasters for her buyer.

Adrian stiffened and he raised a palm. "What's going on? Why are you really here? Do you even know Summer or Tawny? Wait. It doesn't matter. If you're here for a refund, you'll have to go through the website we created for the process. Yet another thing we did out of our own pocket to show we are legitimate. Though by the looks of you, it appears the program worked."

Kelly tilted her head. "Thank you…I think. And, no, I'm not here for a refund. I haven't purchased PBF."

He widened his hands in a questioning gesture. "Then, why are you here? Oh, don't tell me you're a reporter? If so, I don't have any comment."

"I'm not a reporter. I knew Tawny and would like to find out who killed her. Her husband said he didn't know of any enemies except maybe for the customers who felt cheated by her. And just before she died, she had suspicions of some irregular accounting. Since you were her business partner…"

Adrian jabbed a finger at Kelly. "Hold on there. Hold on there right now. I've already talked to the police. Answered all their questions, which forced me to miss a lunch meeting to sign on an up-and-coming fitness star. Now, with all this publicity around Tawny's death…it's not good for *my* business."

His voice was loud, and his nostrils flared while his dark eyes bulged. Alarm should have sounded in Kelly, but instead, she was still curious about why he was so defensive. What was he hiding?

"Aside from the refunds that have been requested, you and Tawny were facing lawsuits. Those can be bad for business too."

"They're nonsense lawsuits and will be tossed out."

"Won't that take time? Cost you money? Are you going to settle them? Then what happens next? Do you dissolve the company and move onto the next great fitness star?"

Adrian chuckled, but it wasn't jovial. "Most gals would have high-tailed it out of here by now. But you? You got guts, hon. It's admirable. Even so, I'm not at liberty to share my plans with you, but I am looking at all available options."

Kelly nodded. "Tawny's murder has given you options."

Adrian slammed his hand on his desk, startling Kelly and making her jump.

"Listen, lady, I don't know what you're thinking coming here, but let me give you a piece of advice. Mind. Your. Business."

Kelly's cell phone buzzed, notifying her of an incoming text message. Her nerves were jumbled by Adrian's outburst, so pulling out her phone from her purse wasn't close to being smooth. It fell to her lap, and grasping it with her shaky hands was a challenge.

"Apparently, you're a busy lady. You can show yourself out." Adrian shifted and pulled a handkerchief out of his back pants pocket. He blotted his creased forehead as Kelly stood and darted out of the office. She didn't stop moving until she was inside the elevator heading down to the main floor.

During the ride down to the lower level, she checked her phone and saw the message was from Serena.

Come over. We need to talk.

Kelly finished her text before the elevator door opened to a group of professionally dressed women.

Can't. I need to get back to the boutique.

She made her way through the crowd and headed for the exit.

Kelly sent her text and stepped out of the building. She welcomed the fresh air. Inside, Adrian's office was stale and suffocating, especially at the end of her visit. His rage seemed to have sucked most of the air out of the room.

"Miss Quinn." Detective Wolman approached with a grim look on her face.

Kelly quickly rethought her relief of being outside. Running into Wolman was going to be as unpleasant as her visit with Adrian.

"What are you doing here?" Wolman asked after she stepped up onto the sidewalk. The concrete path wrapped around the front of the building, bordering evergreen shrubs and tired looking mulch.

"I came to talk to Adrian Chase." Being honest and direct was the best policy with the detective. Or the fastest way to get arrested. Kelly wasn't sure which. Too late now since she blurted out her reason for being at the corporate park.

Wolman stared at Kelly and chewed on her lower lip. It appeared to Kelly the detective was struggling to maintain a professional demeanor.

"I didn't see the harm in talking to him."

"No, of course, you didn't. You didn't stop to think your interference could cause a killer to walk free."

"By talking to him?"

"Yes, by talking to him. You've probably agitated him, which means he'll be less willing to talk me."

"He said he already talked to the police."

Wolman took a step forward. "You think we talk to persons involved in a murder investigation only once?"

"No…I'm sorry…I never intended for—"

"You didn't because you don't know what you're doing. This is my last warning, Kelly. Stay out of my case or I will arrest you, and this time you won't be out in an hour without being charged with a crime. Do you understand what I'm saying?"

Kelly nodded. "I do."

Wolman stepped around Kelly and headed for the main entrance.

Kelly didn't look back; she propelled herself forward, hoping she hadn't messed up the investigation.

By the time she reached her Jeep, her phone had buzzed. Serena had texted back.

We have a deal. Don't be long.

Just like old times. Kelly sighed as she dropped her phone into her purse and backed out of the parking space. She was back on the highway and heading to Serena's house. She'd find out what Serena wanted, and maybe break their deal. There was no doubt in her mind Wolman would follow through with her threat to arrest and charge her. She didn't need a mug shot plastered all over social media. No one ever looked good in them. Nor did she need Pepper having to bail her out. Definitely not a situation she wanted to happen. Facing Pepper after being arrested was scarier to Kelly than facing a murderer. A lot scarier.

* * * *

Kelly jabbed at the doorbell. She was there for a command performance for her fashion majesty. One thing the two of them would get straight was that

Kelly wasn't at Serena's beck and call. Nor would she stand out in the cold. The temperatures were dipping again. A radio news show meteorologist tossed around the "s" word—snow. Snow, rain, any type of precipitation was the last thing her roof needed. She jabbed at the doorbell again. Her patience was wearing as thin as a pair of Spanx leggings.

The door opened, and a bored-looking Serena greeted her. She made a show of glancing at her vintage Rolex.

"There was traffic on the highway. May I come in, or do you want to have this discussion out here on your front step?"

"Aren't you a little petulant thing today? I'm not sure why you sound so perturbed. I'm the one accused of murder." Serena turned and walked away, leaving the door open.

As if Kelly needed the reminder. Had Serena not been arrested for the murder, she would be back in the city, terrorizing a new crop of assistant buyers. Kelly entered the house and closed the door behind her.

"What's so important that I had to drop everything?" Yes, it felt like old times. Serena snapping her fingers and Kelly jumping.

Entering the living room, Kelly reminded herself it would be for only a few days. At least, she hoped so. What if no other viable suspect surfaced? What if they uncovered no other evidence to cast a shadow of doubt on Serena's guilt? What if Serena remained in Lucky Cove throughout the whole messy trial? She needed to corral her racing thoughts of doom and gloom before her head exploded.

"Kelly, are you listening to me?" Serena had settled on the navy sectional with a glass of wine in her hand.

Dressed in sequin pants, a silky halter-top, and bejeweled mules, Serena looked like she was ready for a cocktail party, not for a night of being housebound in a town lacking a fabulous zip code.

"What? Sorry. A lot is going on."

"Tell me about it." Serena lifted the glass to her barely nude lips and sipped. Her natural look was far from effortless. With the aid of fillers, patience and a lipstick that cost three digits, she'd created a subtle yet bold statement.

Kelly worked her lower lip. She hadn't even applied a swipe of lip gloss since leaving for the bank earlier.

"You know, Serena, everything isn't about you. Sure, I'm not accused of murdering someone." *At least not this time*. "But I still have problems." *One of them is you.*

Serena lowered the glass from her mouth. "Being arrested for murder and facing God knows how many years in prison away from my daughters isn't a *problem*. It's a nightmare. It's terrifying. It's all I can think about. It's taking every ounce of strength I have not to break down."

When Serena put it that way, maybe Kelly was being too tough. Her shoulders slumped. Her visit needed a reboot. She walked to the sectional and sat, not too close to Serena but not too far away. There was always a delicate balance when it came to personal space with the Dragonista. Kelly gave herself a mental shake. She needed to stop referring to her former boss by that derogatory nickname.

"I'm here now. What can I do for you?" Kelly eyed the bottle of wine. She could use a glass or two. But Serena didn't look like she was about to play hostess anytime soon. Which was fine because it was too early in the day for her to indulge.

Serena sighed. "It seems my assistant has fallen and broken her ankle, so she's unable to come out to this God-forsaken place."

The wheels started turning fast in Kelly's head. She'd agreed to help clear Serena's name. Nowhere in the agreement was there a clause for her to be Serena's Gal Friday.

"While I'm here, I have to work, and I need an assistant." Serena sipped her wine. "You've worked for me before. Well, not directly for me. But close enough."

Kelly opened her mouth to protest but was cut off by the ringing of the doorbell. Serena looked at her expectantly, but she had no intention of answering the door. This wasn't her home, and she wasn't Serena's employee. Finally, after another chime of the bell and a stare down, Serena huffed and stood.

She marched out of the room, leaving Kelly feeling a little victorious. She never had the nerve stand her ground with the powerful Serena Dawson. Not until that moment.

Maybe coming back to Lucky Cove and taking over her granny's business had given her self-confidence the boost it needed. Feeling proud of her personal growth, she leaned back into the cushions and surveyed the room.

Pretty nice digs.

Gleaming hardwood floors, interesting artwork, and spectacular furniture that Kelly couldn't imagine ever being able to afford.

A buzzing noise drew her attention to the spot where Serena had just stood from. The culprit was a cell phone. Not just any cell phone. Serena's was encased in a ridiculously expensive phone case. The price tag was over seven hundred dollars. Kelly knew because she drooled over it whenever she spotted it on Instagram. Still, she shook her head. Why would anyone pay so much money for a phone case?

Then again, Serena was probably gifted it from the designer. One of the perks of Serena's title.

She glanced up to check on Serena, who was still out of sight at the front door, before she reached for the phone and turned it over. The text notification said AC.

She grabbed the phone and pressed the home button, and the main screen came up. She was amazed Serena didn't have a passcode. If she did, it probably would have been six-six-six. Ugh. She gave herself another mental shake. She needed to be nice.

She tapped on the messaging app first to read the string of text messages.

Call me ASAP. Had a call. Getting too risky.

Who was AC referring to? She continued to read the messages from AC.

Reporter snooping around. Need to fix.

Kelly read Serena's reply.

Don't panic. Let me see what I can do. Name?

AC replied an expletive and then added:

Ella. I'll take care of her.

Kelly's heart thumped. Was AC Adrian Chase? Could Serena and Adrian be involved? She did a mental scan of the collage of photos on the wall in Adrian's office. She hadn't seen Serena in any of them, but they could still know each other. She needed to stop focusing on how the two of them knew each other and focus on Ella. She could be in danger. What was Ella doing poking around Adrian? Had she gotten a lead about the possibility of him engaging in financial fraud? Had Tawny gone to her with her suspicions?

Focus, Kell. Deep breath.

Kelly's ears perked up at the sound of the front door closing. She tossed the phone back on the sofa cushion and sprang up. She had a bunch of questions for Serena, but first, she needed to check on Ella.

"Now, where were we?" Serena entered the room and went for her wine.

"Sorry I have to go. But we do have to talk. Soon." With her purse in hand, Kelly swept by Serena and ignored the woman's outrage at her quick departure.

Running out of the house, Kelly pulled her phone from her purse and found Ella in her list of contacts. As she yanked open the Jeep's door, her call went to voice mail. Frustrated and worried, she used the AI function on her phone to call the newspaper. The receptionist told her Ella wasn't in the office. Kelly opted not to leave a message.

Chapter 15

Behind the steering wheel, Kelly pulled out of the driveway and headed back to town. Nightfall was setting, and she tried to figure out where her day had gone. Oh, yeah, she'd been busy sticking her nose into Wolman's case. Now wasn't the time to give herself a good talking to. She had to get to Ella's place. ASAP.

She didn't have a phone book handy, but the next best thing was Liv. The Moretti family knew everybody in town, and she was confident her friend would know where Ella lived. While she waited for Liv to pick up the call, she considered calling Gabe, but she had no solid proof Ella was in danger. She only had vague text messages she wasn't supposed to have seen.

"Hey, what's up?" Liv's chipper voice should have made Kelly smile. Instead, she frowned. She hated to be the one to burst her friend's happy little bubble.

"Nothing good. Do you know where Ella lives? I need to see her. Now."

"What's going on?" Liv's voice lost its perkiness. Now, a severe tone came through the phone line.

"She could be in danger."

"What? Kelly, what's going on?"

"No time to explain. Do you know where she lives?" Kelly rolled through an intersection despite the *Stop* sign. A woman's life could be at risk. One little traffic infraction wasn't a big deal in the grand scheme of things.

"Sure. In the cottage behind the house I live in."

"Seriously?" Talk about a lucky coincidence.

"For about a year now. I'm on my way home. I'll meet you there. Shouldn't you call the police?"

"And tell them what? I have a bad feeling. Hopefully, I'm over-reacting." Kelly disconnected the call and pressed down on the gas pedal a little harder. What was one more traffic infraction?

Kelly arrived at Liv's residence. The adorable yellow Victorian house had a wrap-around porch with planters waiting for summer blooms. The first floor housed a pottery shop while upstairs there were two apartments.

The businesses at this end of Main Street didn't have the luxury of communal parking lots behind the shops. Navigating her Jeep into a space between a van and a pickup truck, she spotted Liv's mini coupe a few spaces away. Her breathing hitched before she saw Liv appear from the building. She let out her breath. Thankfully, Liv hadn't taken it upon herself to go back to the cottage. With the Jeep parked, she got out and met Liv on the walkway.

"Now, are you going to tell me what's going on?" Liv propped a hand on her hip and gave Kelly a firm look. It was clear she wanted an explanation.

"I'm not sure."

Liv shook her head and then led Kelly around the back of the Victorian. "I know you know more. Spill."

"I think Adrian Chase and Serena are in cahoots. I think his business dealings are shady, and Ella must be onto it also."

"Cahoots, huh?" Liv tossed a look over her shoulder.

"It's a real word," Kelly tramped behind, trying not to obsess on the worst-case scenario.

Between the house and the enchanting cottage was a small patch of grass. A lit gravel path led to the cottage's front door.

Liv pointed to the blue compact parked beside the cottage. "Looks like she's home. I wish I could afford to rent this cottage. It's charming inside. I got a peek before Ella moved in."

They reached the white vinyl-sided cottage, and the front door was open. Liv stopped and turned around to Kelly.

"Maybe we should call the police now," Liv said.

"Let's look first. Maybe the door didn't latch all the way." Kelly walked toward the cottage and eased the door open, calling out Ella's name. When there was no answer, she peered in. A kitchenette was to the right, and the living area was to the left. She entered and called out Ella's name again.

"We have to call the police." Liv followed Kelly inside the cottage.

Kelly passed a wooden desk, cluttered with takeout menus, flyers, church bulletins, and other papers. The thick carpet absorbed the sound of her footsteps. She reached another partially opened door, and after inhaling a deep breath, she pushed the door open and then let out the breath.

"What is it?" Liv hurried to Kelly's side. "Is she…dead?"

"Who? Who's dead?"

The loud, demanding voice had both Kelly and Liv jumping. They spun around and found Ella standing in the doorway.

"You're alive," Liv cried out.

"Of course, I am. What are you two doing in my house?" She shut the door. "I'm waiting for an answer."

"I thought you were in trouble," Kelly said.

"She did. She thought you were dead. Well, you heard that." Liv rested her hand on Kelly's shoulder and squeezed. She always had Kelly's back and now facing a very unhappy looking Ella, she wasn't going to waver.

"Or you thought you could break in and search my house. What are you looking for?" Ella marched over to the desk and scanned it before she pulled her cell phone out of her jeans back pocket.

"We did no such thing! Your door was open. And the only thing we were searching for was for you." Kelly stepped forward. "Who are you calling?"

"Hello, I'm calling to report two intruders in my house." Ella cast a cool look at Kelly and Liv.

"She's calling the cops!" Liv hurried to Kelly's side. "Do something. I can't get arrested again."

"I'm sorry, Liv." Kelly's stomach knotted. The last thing she wanted was for Liv to get into trouble because of her.

"Don't be sorry. Just fix this." Liv shoved Kelly forward. Kelly tripped over her feet and almost knocked right into Ella. That wouldn't have been a good thing.

"Please, don't do this. We were worried about you. We…I think you're in danger." Kelly gave her best sad face and prayed to any power-to-be to help her and Liv get out of this mess.

Ella studied Kelly for a long second and then rolled her eyes. "Never mind. There's been a misunderstanding." She disconnected the call and set the phone back down.

"Thank you." Kelly glanced over her shoulder.

Liv laid a hand over her heart and mouthed, "Thank you."

The knot that had bundled up in her belly vanished, and Kelly turned back to Ella with her arms wide open for a grateful hug.

Ella raised her palms, staving off an intrusion into her personal space.

Kelly immediately stopped. She realized she overstepped once already and didn't want to do it a second time. She lowered her hands and took a step back.

"Why don't you tell me what's going on?" Ella shrugged out of her blazer and draped it on the chair at the desk.

"I saw a text message with your name in it, and the person who wrote it said they'd take care of you." Kelly now considered the fact she may have indeed jumped to conclusions. AC could have been the initials for anyone. A name from the past popped into her head. Andrea Cooper, the director of cosmetics at Bishop's. Shoot. She'd forgotten all about Andrea or AC as everyone called her. Ella could have reached out to her for a comment on Serena's arrest. Double shoot. She probably did just make a really big mistake.

"From whom? To whom?" Ella demanded.

"Tell her." Liv came up beside Kelly and nudged her.

"Actually, I'm thinking...Have you been in contact with an Andrea Cooper?"

"Why do you ask?" Ella asked.

A loud banging at the door startled all three of them.

"Lucky Cove Police!"

Kelly's head dropped. It was Gabe at the door. Of all the officers in Lucky Cove. Wait, there weren't that many officers in the town. Maybe that's why it seemed like he was always on duty, catching Kelly where she wasn't supposed to be.

"Gabe?" Liv paled. "What's he doing here? We're going to get arrested. My Nona will be heartbroken. It would kill her."

"We're not going to get arrested. Besides, your Nona dotes on you. She'll forgive you. Eventually." However, Kelly was certain there would be no more homemade lasagna in Kelly's future if Liv got into any trouble because of her.

"He was probably dispatched because of my call." Ella walked to the door and yanked it open. "Good evening, officer."

"Officer Donovan. You called 9-1-1. Is everything okay?" Gabe looked past Ella and his baby blues landed on her visitors, or intruders, depending on how you viewed the whole situation. "Kelly? Liv?"

Kelly smiled and gave a little wave. How was she going to explain this to him?

Liv leaned over to Kelly. "The bright side is at least it's not Detective Wolman at the door."

"I apologize for the call to emergency services. It was an accident, and I promise it won't happen again," Ella said.

"What led to accidentally calling 9-1-1?" Gabe entered the cottage.

"We can explain, right, Kelly?" Liv asked.

Kelly's gaze bounced from Liv to Ella, to Gabe, and back to Ella. Oh, boy. It looked like she didn't have a choice but to tell Gabe the entire truth of how she and Liv ended up inside Ella's cottage.

"I'd forgotten they were coming over," Ella jumped into the conversation. "I stepped out, leaving the front door unlocked. I don't know where my mind is today. Anyway, they let themselves in, and I jumped to the wrong conclusion when I saw my door open. Again, I'm truly sorry for my mistake." Ella offered a small smile, but Kelly doubted Gabe was buying the story.

"Liv, is that what happened?" Gabe asked.

Kelly had to give him points for directing his question to Liv and not to her. Her friend was an honest person who didn't intentionally break into someone's house. Whereas Kelly, well, it was a gray area.

Liv cleared her throat. "She's correct. She wasn't inside when we arrived, and we let ourselves in."

Nice way to skirt the truth.

Kelly almost gave her friend a high-five but stopped herself. "Look, Gabe, we're all sorry that the police got involved in this misunderstanding." Now, that wasn't a lie, because she'd probably misinterpreted the text message on Serena's phone.

"Well, I'm glad everyone is okay. Please be sure to lock your door next time, Ella."

"I will. I promise." Ella walked to the door and grabbed hold of the knob. Before leaving, Gabe gave Kelly a look that told her they'd be having a talk soon.

"That was close." Liv headed for the door after Gabe was gone.

"Hold on. I covered for you two trespassers." Ella stepped in front of the doorway and propped her hands on her hips.

Kelly wasn't surprised the reporter wanted something in return for lying to Gabe. "What do you want?"

"I want to know what led you to my home. Why did you think I was in danger?" Ella lowered her hands to her side.

"The good news is I'm probably wrong about you being in danger. I think I jumped to a conclusion." Kelly averted her gaze downward. She hated sounding so impulsive and flighty. Shades of her younger self were emerging, and she didn't like it.

"Shocking." Ella's tone was mocking, and Kelly deserved it.

"Look, I promise to tell you everything once I figure it all out." Kelly hoped the promise of an exclusive would suffice the reporter.

"Oh, come on. I need more. Does this have anything to do with Tawny's murder? Serena Dawson? Was it her text message you read?" Ella walked toward Kelly, her steps deliberate, and her gaze intense. "It was her text!"

"I promise you'll be the only reporter I speak to." Kelly held out her hand to Ella.

"We have a deal." Ella shook Kelly's hand.

"Great. Let's get out of here, Kell." Liv didn't wait for a reply; she was out the door in a flash.

Kelly followed, wondering if she'd done the right thing. Had she really misunderstood the text? If not, Ella could be in danger.

* * * *

The next morning, Kelly tied her sneakers' laces while Howard batted a catnip toy around in the living room. He'd burn off his breakfast calories while tiring himself out just in time for a mid-morning nap. She tried not to be envious of the fur ball, but she couldn't help it. He hadn't a care in the world. Meanwhile, her belly was tangled up with worry over a myriad of things.

When she returned home after her breaking and entering situation, she made a call to Julie, her closest friend from her time at Bishop's. Julie still worked at there and graciously shared her employee discount from time-to-time. She asked Julie to find out if Ella had reached out to Andrea Cooper. Her friend was full of questions, but Kelly didn't have the energy to explain her request. She promised to do so very soon. Then they spent the next half hour talking about their relationships, the upcoming trends, and possibly a girls' weekend in the fall. Being in retail, they were always planning months in advance.

Her phone buzzed with a reminder to get a move on. She told Marvin, last night when he'd called, she'd meet him for coffee at Doug's Variety Store. After Christmas, she closed the boutique on Sundays until spring. Between the low sales on the shortest business day of the week and operating with a lean staff, it didn't make sense to be open. Even Pepper welcomed the change. Now, though, she had the whole day to dwell on how close she'd come to getting into serious trouble with the police.

Her stomach somersaulted again. It had been doing that whenever the scene at Ella's cottage flashed in her mind.

With her sneakers laced up, she slipped into a jacket over her yoga pants and graphic tee. She then grabbed her key holder, where she stashed her credit card, and headed out of the apartment after saying goodbye to Howard.

So far, the lazy Sunday morning greeted her with no new leaks. Even though the repair would cost a small fortune, she looked forward to waking up not on pins and needles expecting to find the roof collapsed because of water damage. Downstairs, she left through the back door and hurried to Doug's.

Stepping inside Doug's, she scanned the store and found Marvin had not only secured a table for them, but he'd ordered them coffee and muffins. Bless him.

She made her way toward him. When she reached the table, he stood and kissed her on the cheek. He wore a navy fisherman sweater over gray pants. He looked alert and well rested. It was a stark contrast to when she first met him. He'd been living in isolation and feeling unwell. Now he was out and about daily, organizing an art show with the Lucky Cove Arts Council and making a weekly card game at the senior center. He often said that it was because of Kelly that he felt the zest of life again. She wasn't too sure about that, but whatever role she'd played in him finding the joy of living again made her heart warm. He'd been a good friend to her grandmother, and she wanted to be a good friend to him.

"Good morning, Kelly. I got us coffee and something to eat. Doug said you love apple crumb muffins." Marvin beamed. He enjoyed doting on Kelly.

"I do. To be honest, I don't think I've met a muffin I haven't loved." This morning, though, she had little appetite. There were too many worries jumbled in her head, and unanswered questions about Tawny's murder matched them. Not showing interest in the muffin would disappoint Marvin, so she tore back the liner paper from the pastry and took a bite.

"You sound like your grandmother." Marvin took a drink of his coffee. He always ordered a decaf black.

Kelly smiled. "She loved her baked goods."

"How are you doing?" Marvin bit into his chocolate chip muffin.

Kelly set the pastry down. "Honestly. It's all a mess. Somehow, I got caught up in Tawny's murder. I thought Serena and Tawny's business partner conspired together to kill her. But I think I'm wrong. I don't see how they'd even know each other. They don't exactly travel in the same worlds. Unless Serena is involved with Jason and they schemed with the business partner to kill Tawny. You know, it's possible. Then…I'm…I'm worried Mark and I are breaking up because of the murder." She stopped talking when she realized how certifiable she sounded.

Marvin pushed aside his plate and reached for Kelly's hand. "Slow down, dear. With all that you've just said, is there anything you can do right this very minute?"

Kelly shook her head. There wasn't.

"Exactly. So, let's enjoy our coffee and muffins. While we do, we can talk through each thing you mentioned. Okay?"

Kelly nodded. He had a way of talking her off the ledge. While she hadn't much of an appetite when she'd left her apartment, her stomach grumbled now, and the muffin didn't seem like it would be enough.

"Could I get an egg sandwich?"

Marvin smiled. "Of course, dear. You stay put. I'll order it for you." He stood and walked to the counter to place the order.

Kelly reached for her coffee and leaned back. She sipped her hot beverage and let it warm her insides. The morning was frosty and made her wonder if spring would ever arrive. Marvin returned with her sandwich, and while she ate, she talked through all of the things that were weighed on her mind.By the time Marvin left to go home to let his dog, Sparky, out, Kelly felt a hundred times better. Thanks to Marvin, she had a plan. She would tell Serena she was on her own now. Whatever guilt or misguided loyalty she felt was gone. She had the boutique to manage, and she needed to be laser-focused if she wanted to achieve her financial goals. Next, she and Mark would have a talk. As much as she dreaded the conversation, it had to happen. And soon.

She stayed to finish her second cup of coffee and ponder the advice Marvin had given her over breakfast. All sound guidance and she should follow it. But then, her track record with following good advice was pretty iffy.

She glanced at her empty plate. She'd wolfed down the egg and cheese sandwich along with the muffin. There was a ten-mile run in her near future to burn off those calories.

Kelly lifted her gaze and noticed the store was filling up with the after-church crowd. Sundays were a busy day at Doug's all year long. The line at the counter was growing, and she realized she'd have to give up her table soon.

"Come on, it's an old story. Remember Mandy Gallagher?" a petite redhead said as she passed Kelly's table with a coffee and a wrapped sandwich. Her voice was thick with a Jersey accent and nasal to boot.

"Sure, I do. She was in love with her best friend's husband," said the woman, following the redhead. She carried a coffee and muffin while a Kate Spade satchel dangled off her wrist.

The women settled at the table behind Kelly and her ears perked up.

Eavesdropping was wrong and impolite, but she was curious about the person the women were talking about. Who was Mandy, and what had she done?

"She wormed her way into their lives. All those articles recounted how she got them to trust her, and then she set out to seduce him, lure him away from his wife," Satchel Lady said.

Kelly made a face. Mandy Gallagher sounded like a horrible person. Now she needed to know more. She lifted her cup and sipped, impatiently waiting for one of the women to finish the story.

"When he wouldn't stray, she killed the wife," the redhead said.

"I bet Serena Dawson is still in love with her ex-husband, and she killed Tawny to get her out of the way," Satchel Lady said.

Kelly peeked over her shoulder, tempted to say something in Serena's defense, but remembered her vow only moments earlier. Whatever she was about to say vanished before it could reach her lips. She wouldn't defend her former boss any longer.

The two women continued their conversation, and Kelly tuned them out. Their topic was too close for comfort for her. It seemed the Mandy person they were talking about had been overwhelmed with jealousy, anger, or a combination of both emotions, and lashed out. And quite possibly, Serena could have fallen victim to the same fate.

"Good morning, Kelly. Do you mind if I join you?" Liza stood beside the seat Marvin had vacated a few minutes ago, holding a cup and a wrapped sandwich.

"Oh, hi, Liza. Please do." Kelly gestured to the empty seat across from her.

"I always forget how busy Doug's gets after service." Liza removed the lid from her cup and took a drink. She then unwrapped her bacon and egg sandwich, and its aroma got Kelly's mouthwatering again. No, she wouldn't indulge in another bite.

"Me too." Kelly always forgot because she didn't go to church service on Sundays. Until December, she worked on the seventh day, so her morning began late, resulting in her missing Mass. And more recently, she relished leisurely greeting the day. If the weather was good, she'd head out for a run, popping into Doug's for a post workout coffee to go.

"This morning, the service was even more beautiful. The reverend spoke about Tawny and how much her light will be missed by all of us, but now it's shining up in heaven." Liza took a bite of her sandwich.

"Wow. What a striking image." Kelly leaned forward. "Liza, could I ask you a question?"

"Sure. What is it?"

"You said Tawny confided in you that she was scared of Jason. He'd lost his temper with her."

Liza's gaze darted downward for a moment, and she then pushed aside her breakfast.

"I shouldn't have said that. I guess all marriages have their difficulties. Bad moments, you know. While I'm sure Tawny felt unsafe at the moment, I don't for a second believe Jason killed her. You saw how grief struck he was yesterday. No, it was his ex. She did it. I'm certain of it." Liza's eyes were serious, and her tone was confident.

Yep, she tried and convicted Serena, much like the press had.

"It's for a jury to decide on Serena's guilt or innocence." Darn. There she went defending the woman again.

Liza's head tilted slightly to the side. "You're a good person, Kelly Quinn. You're standing by Serena, and I'm sure she's very appreciative to have you on her side."

Not exactly.

Kelly chose not to share with Liza her own suspicions and doubts about Serena. Why add fuel to the fire?

"Did Tawny ever mention being threatened by anyone in Lucky Cove? Like an unhappy PBF customer?" Kelly couldn't shake the image of Tawny being chased out of the gift shop the day before her murder. While it probably was only an argument, there was a chance that the woman confronted Tawny one last time.

Liza rolled her eyes, and then a shield of embarrassment covered her face. "I'm sorry. That was unkind of me."

"What do you mean?"

"PBF was an idea Tawny came up with to expand her fitness coaching business. Once she partnered with what's his name...Damien...Andrew..."

"Adrian."

"Right. Adrian. She mentioned it several times when she volunteered at church. Once he got involved, she was sucked into working sixty hours a week. She barely had time for anything but her work. Never mind, Jason. Now, look at what happened to her. All that drive and ambition. For what?"

Kelly's cell phone buzzed, and she shifted to retrieve it from her jacket pocket. The text was from Julie. She spoke to Andrea Cooper's assistant who confirmed there had been a message left by Ella requesting an interview. Kelly groaned. It was official. She jumped to the wrong conclusion yesterday and it had almost landed her and Liv in a big freaking pot of hot water—all the more reason she should walk away from the investigation.

"Anything wrong?" Liza pulled her sandwich back in front of her.

"No, nothing. But I should get going." While she had the day off from working in the boutique, she still had administrative work to do. Today was a perfect day to tackle those things. It would keep her mind off Serena and how close she'd come to sitting in a jail cell overnight.

"Have a good Sunday." Liza took a sip of her coffee. "Oh, Tawny's service will be on Thursday. Her parents have to fly in from overseas. They're on a relief mission with their church."

Kelly's heart constricted. She couldn't imagine how devastating the news of their daughter's death was.

Outside, the morning turned bone-penetrating cold, and a cover of gray clouds drifted overhead. She picked up her pace back to the boutique.

Her pace slowed and she came to a stop. Neither Jason nor Liza knew who the name of the person who accosted Tawny on Main Street the day before she died, but there was one person who might know. And Kelly was standing in front of that person's store.

Chapter 16

A bare flower box ran the length of Courtney's Gift Shop front window, but in a few weeks, it would spill over with colorful annuals. It was another reminder to Kelly that she needed to up the game at her storefront. A beautiful window merchandise display wasn't enough. She needed to draw passersby close enough to stop and look at the window.

Peering into the gift shop, she didn't see anyone except for Courtney. Good. They'd be able to have a private conversation.

Kelly opened the door and walked inside. She told herself she was satisfying her own curiosity. This had nothing to do with clearing Serena. Only a few steps in and her senses were on overload. The shop smelled like vanilla and cinnamon with a light note of salt air from the abundance of candles for sale.

"Hey, there, neighbor." Courtney looked up from the display counter of decorative birdhouses. Surrounding her were stacks of unpacked boxes and discarded tissue paper.

"Those are beautiful." Kelly weaved through the shop, passing shelves of pretty items and plush throws draped over chairs and wooden display ladders.

"They are, aren't they? It's taking all of my self-control not to keep them all for myself. Kind of like the chocolates." She glanced to the sales counter where she sold gourmet chocolates from a local chocolatier.

"You have more willpower than I do." Kelly lifted a birdhouse and admired it.

"They're all handmade. Perfect gifts for Mother's Day." Courtney pulled out another birdhouse from a box and found a spot for it on the shelf.

Mother's Day was right around the corner, and then it would be a quick blink-and-you'll-miss-it slide into summer. Kelly had the urge to buy one for her mom and mail it to her as a surprise, but her mom wasn't big on birds, their homes, or gardening. Actually, Kelly couldn't recall if her mom had any hobbies. All she remembered was how much her mom loved working, much like her brother, Ralph.

"Has Opal spoken to you yet? The flower sale is coming up for Mother's Day, and they're looking for donations for the 50/50 raffle." Courtney balled up a handful of tissue paper. She was a few years older than Kelly and several inches shorter. Her brown hair was kissed with golden highlights and cascaded below her shoulder. Enamel ladybug earrings added a pop of color to her round face.

"No. Thanks for the warning." Kelly enjoyed being a part of the community and supporting the many charitable causes in town, but being hit up for donations was a financial burden for the boutique. Even still, she always came up with something to contribute. She didn't want to be known as the Scrooge among her peers.

Maybe she'd offer a gift certificate because once she had the customer in the boutique, it was easy to upsell a few more items.

Courtney squatted and adjusted a few birdhouses on a lower shelf.

Kelly noticed her dark jeans—mom jeans, to be exact. How had they ever made a comeback? The white and black polka dot sweater tucked into the waist of the jeans was cute and a good choice for the unpredictable weather between seasons.

"What brings you by? Do you need another candle? We just got in a delivery of lemon lavender scented. They are heavenly." Courtney straightened and stepped back from the display to give it a once over.

Kelly never *needed* another candle. They were an indulgence, and she justified them because the soothing scents helped calm her. These days, she needed a lot of calming.

"Tempting but maybe next week. I'm hoping you can help me with one of your customers. The other day, Tawny Fallow was in here."

Courtney frowned. "So sad about what happened to her. I heard her husband's ex-wife was arrested for the murder. Unbelievable."

"It most certainly is. Anyway, the day Tawny was here, she argued with another customer who followed her out of the store. I saw them arguing on the street. Do you know who the woman was?"

"Talk about a scene. I was so thankful that Tawny left on her own because I had other customers in here."

Kelly could relate. Last October, her big three-day sale was turned upside down when a psychic had a vision of a dead man in the middle of the boutique. The spectacle mesmerized all of her other customers, and they'd stopped shopping, preferring to gawk at the show that unfolded in front of them. Courtney was indeed lucky Tawny and the other woman had taken their disagreement outside. If only Kelly could have been so lucky last fall. No, instead, the police and an ambulance had arrived. Lucky her.

Courtney folded her arms and tapped her check with her forefinger. "Let me think. Della. No. Delia…Wyland. Yes. She loves Camellia Blossom candles and those artisan soaps I sell. Anyway, as soon as she saw Tawny enter, she went ballistic. She started yelling at Tawny, who looked like a deer in the headlights. She never saw Delia's wrath coming. Wait. You don't think Delia killed Tawny?"

Kelly shrugged. "I have no idea. I was simply curious who the woman was. When she was yelling at Tawny, did she say why she was upset?"

"Something about scamming money out of people and preying on vulnerabilities. Tawny looked so shocked. She tried to calm Delia down, but Delia was having no part in it. I swear she was out for blood."

Out for blood? Kelly's mind quickly concocted the scene at Tawny's cottage. Delia arrived, still enraged, to continue their argument. Tawny tried to get Delia to leave. One of them laid a hand on the other, and then a struggle ensued, leading to Delia pushing Tawny and her body falling through the coffee table.

"Kelly, are you okay?" Courtney asked.

Kelly snapped out of her fictional murder scene. Where had that come from? Probably one too many *Law and Order* episodes, and one too many dead bodies discovered since coming back to Lucky Cove.

"I'm…I'm good. Does Delia live in town?"

Courtney stacked the empty boxes into each other and lifted them. "Yes. She lives near Pepper."

The bell over the door jingled, letting them know a customer entered, so it was time for Kelly to leave. She'd gotten the information she came for.

"Kelly."

She turned around at the sound of Mark's voice. He was the last person she thought she'd run into at Courtney's store. "Hey, what are you doing here?"

"I need to pick up a gift for my mom. I'm heading over to her house for lunch." He gave Kelly a kiss on the cheek. "I left you a voice mail earlier, didn't you get it?"

Shoot. She'd been so involved with working out her problems with Marvin and then eavesdropping on the two women at Doug's, she hadn't noticed the message. How could she have missed it?

"I'm sorry. I had breakfast with Marvin this morning. But, if you give me a few minutes, I can change and be ready to go with you." Even though things had been rocky between them, she still wanted to work things out. Being a couple was never easy, but it was impossible if both partners didn't make an effort.

"Did you want a jar candle for your mom? Or, we have beautiful decorative globes. She collects them," Courtney said.

"I think a candle. Something summery." Mark flashed an appreciative smile while Courtney went to find a candle for him. He shoved his hands into the pockets of his khakis, and his smile slipped away. "Look about lunch. I'm going solo."

Kelly blinked. "What? Why?"

"Well, my dad's buddy and his wife are going to be there. I think it's best if I go alone. Hey, you're busy today. You have stuff to do."

"You don't want to introduce me to your dad's friends? Are you serious?" Kelly's insides twisted as she saw flashes of red.

Mark pulled his hand out of his pocket and guided Kelly out of Courtney's earshot. "Kell, don't make a big deal out of this. It's not a social occasion. It's business. My dad's friend is a partner in a prominent law firm. I have to make a good impression."

Kelly yanked free of his hold. Her mouth opened and closed several times before she could trust herself to speak. Had he heard what he'd said to her? Had he realized how insulting it was?

"So, you're saying having me there won't make a good impression?"

"You tell me. When Gerald asks what you're doing, you'll say what? You're chasing down a killer, interfering with a police investigation, and neglecting your business. What part of that sounds like a good first impression?"

"Did you want to pay with a credit card?" Courtney asked from the sales counter.

Mark averted his gaze to her. "Yes. Be right there." He turned his attention back to Kelly. "Don't be like this. I'm doing this for us."

"Excuse me? For us? You mean for yourself. I…I can't have this conversation. Not now. Not here."

Mark drew back, and his eyes darkened. "When do you want to have this conversation?"

"Never. How dare you say I'm neglecting my business." She jabbed a finger into his chest. "I work twenty-four seven to keep the boutique open. It's my number one priority."

Courtney approached the couple with her purse slung over her shoulder. "Mark, Angie will ring you up. I have to run out for a minute. Kelly be careful with Delia. If her outburst with Tawny is any indicator, you need to watch yourself if you talk to her." She dashed out of the shop.

Kelly cringed. Why did Courtney have to mention Delia in front of Mark?

"What are you up to, Kell?"

"Nothing you need to be concerned about. Enjoy your luncheon." She stormed past him and exited the store in a huff. Her walk back to the boutique was quick because she was moving so fast to put a lot of distance between herself and Mark. He had some nerve.

"*Going solo*. Yeah, well, get used to it, buddy," she muttered to herself as she approached the boutique. Her ringing phone interrupted her private rant. Despite the urge to ignore the incoming call, she pulled the phone from her purse. "Hello," she said after she raised the phone to her ear.

"Kelly, it's Jason. Sorry to call on a Sunday." His voice sounded shaky and profoundly sad.

"Hi, Jason. No worries. Is there something I can help you with?" She welcomed any distraction from thinking about Mark.

"I'd like you to come over and take Tawny's clothing for consignment. I was talking to Liza after service, and the proceeds can go to the food pantry."

Kelly stopped herself from saying, *so soon*. She reminded herself everyone grieved differently, and for Jason, he needed his wife's clothes out of his home.

"I can do that for you. And I'm sure the food pantry will be grateful for your donation. When did you want me to come over?" Kelly arrived at the back door of the boutique.

"Tomorrow. Morning would be best."

"Tomorrow?" Kelly's mind raced through the items on her to-do list for the following day. Both Breena and Pepper would be in, so she could get away early for the clear out. That shouldn't be a problem. What could be a problem was that she didn't know how much clothing she'd have to remove from the house.

"I realize it's short notice." He paused. "I can't keep this stuff here any longer."

"I understand. It's not a problem. See you first thing tomorrow." She ended the call and then entered the staff room, closing the door behind her. Since she didn't know how much stuff she'd have to go through, she planned to bring all the clothing back to the boutique and then inspect each item for the estimate. This way, she'd be in the boutique available to work. She doubted Jason would be too concerned with the number. Raising money wasn't a priority for him.

She dropped her purse on the desk and pulled out the chair. There wasn't a luncheon, but there was someone she wanted to speak with, and she needed an address.

After a flip-through of the phone book, Kelly found Delia Wyland's address. To think, she'd almost tossed the brick of a book into recycling weeks ago. She grabbed a jacket and left to pay a visit to Delia.

Courtney was right. Delia did live near Pepper, but not too close. Kelly was grateful because there was a lesser chance she'd be spotted at the Wyland house.

Kelly arrived at the bungalow and knocked on the red door. Moments later, the door opened, and Delia appeared. She wore a bright tunic over black leggings and slippers. She also had a look that was a mix of curiosity and annoyance on her face.

"I'm not buying anything or changing my religion." Delia went to close the door.

"Good, because that's not why I'm here. I'm Kelly Quinn. I own the Lucky Cove Resale Boutique."

"You're going door to door to get clothes?"

"No. I'm here to talk to you about the day you were at Courtney's Gift shop, and Tawny Fallow showed up. I saw both of you come out of the store." Kelly wanted to be careful about what she said. Stating that she saw Delia chase Tawny while screaming at the top of her lungs didn't seem to be the best way to get the woman to talk. She'd probably have the door slammed in her face.

"Not my finest hour, I admit." Delia's gaze cast down.

"We all have bad moments. You sounded furious with Tawny."

Delia narrowed her eyes and lifted her chin. "I was. She ripped me off."

"You enrolled in her PBF program?"

"I did."

"It sounds like you didn't have success with it."

"Honey, look at me. You can see I didn't have any success with it." She glanced down at herself. Kelly guessed Delia chose a tunic to hide the extra pounds on her small frame. She'd seen it too often. Women trying their best to hide their bodies rather than love what they had now. Pounds came and went. It was a part of life. Dressing like a potato sack wasn't the answer, and it wasn't the way to feel self-confident. "Why are you asking about PBF?"

"My friend signed up recently..."

"Good Lord, not another one. How many women had Tawny scammed? I don't have a lot of time. I'm working, but I can spare a few minutes. Come on in."

"You work from home?" Kelly entered the home.

"I'm a virtual assistant." Delia closed the door.

"Sounds interesting."

"It can be. It's also one reason I've packed on the pounds. Well, along with perimenopause. I'm home all day by myself. There's no commuting, and there's no other walking than from my bedroom to my desk over there." She pointed toward the living room.

Kelly looked into the tidy room. Tucked into a corner were a desk and laptop among the tasteful furnishings.

"You signed up with PBF to lose the weight."

"Sure did. I believed Tawny's pitch. I had done a few of her free workouts and then signed up for the fitness program. I thought, since she lived in town, she was honest. Who would cheat a neighbor? Turns out, I was wrong."

"Why do you say that? Doesn't everyone have different results with fitness?"

"Of course, we do. I'm not an idiot," Delia snapped, "I followed her plan faithfully for eight weeks, and I expected to see a change. Either on the scale or in how my clothes fit. I didn't expect to lose all the weight I've gained in such a short period of time. But something should have changed. Well, nothing did. I even went to the doctor to check my hormones. She found nothing that would prevent me from losing weight."

"Did you contact Tawny?"

"Certainly, I did. All I got from day one was generic replies to my messages. Keep up the good work. Way to work it, girl. Sweating is the way to reshape your body. You'll see a change. Keep working. Blah, blah, blah."

"Those were through her app?"

"Yes. A complete waste of time. I finally emailed her several times and got no replies. Then I started seeing online other women were experiencing the same thing, and it turns out, we had the same fitness plan. It was supposed to be customized to us. Tell me, why was I doing the same workout and eating the same foods as a twenty-something? I'm fifty years old." Delia threw her arms up in the air, startling Kelly with the quick motion.

Kelly didn't have an answer for Delia. Instead, she stepped back. "When you saw her at the gift shop, you confronted her about all of this?"

"Darn straight, I did. It was the first time I'd seen her in town. Trust me, I'd been tempted to go to her house, but doing something like that would be crossing the line. Then I finally saw her, and I couldn't stop myself. I'm sorry your friend also fell for the scam."

"Oh, I don't think she did. Well, I mean, it seems to work for her."

"Then, why are you here?"

"When you chased after Tawny…"

"I didn't exactly chase after her. We left the shop together."

Nice spin. "You threatened her before you walked away. I heard you."

Delia stiffened. "You think I had something to do with Tawny's murder? Sure, I'm angry and out several hundred dollars, but I wouldn't kill someone over that. How dare you come into my home under false pretenses. You should go." Delia opened the door.

Kelly was barely over the threshold before the door slammed shut. It seemed someone needed to work on her anger management. Maybe some yoga.

She dashed to her Jeep, flipping up the hood of her jacket to keep the light rain that started while she was inside, off her hair. In the vehicle, she debated whether to call Wolman. Kelly should tell her about the visit to make sure Delia was on the detective's radar as a potential person of interest. But after what went down between her and Mark in the gift shop, she really didn't want to talk to anyone connected to him at the moment. In fact, what she wanted to was erase the guy from her brain so she'd have no memory of him or his stupid "going solo" comment. *Jerk.*

Out of the corner of her eye, she caught movement in a window by the front door. Delia was staring at her with a phone in her hand. It was time to go before Delia called the police and reported Kelly for something like trespassing.

Chapter 17

The rainy dampness penetrated Kelly's body right down to her core. It was shaping up to be a miserable day. So, when the unexpected delivery came into view as she walked toward the boutique's back entrance, it was a welcomed sight. She was giddy with delight. How could she not be? The start of the roof's makeover was imminent. There was no turning back now.

Buck had gotten a dumpster delivered. On a Sunday of all days.

Standing with hands clasped and a silly smile on her face, for sure, she stared at the large metal container. Never had there been a more beautiful sight. There were days when she was sure she'd be broke and homeless with a cat. There were other days when she had seen the light of hope. She was eternally grateful for those moments. They got her through tough periods.

The sound of a car pulling into the parking lot drew her gaze away from the roof. She frowned at the sight of her uncle's Mercedes.

"Great. Now what?" she mumbled, as she stepped away from the dumpster and readjusted the hood of her jacket. There was still a light drizzle, and she was hoping to get another day out of her blowout.

Ralph unfurled himself from the front seat of the car. He gave an appraising look at the dumpster and then up at the roof. "See you're moving forward with the new roof."

"I am." Kelly plastered a smile on her face and added oomph to her voice. She wasn't going to let him bring her down. Nope. She would be as resistant to his negativity as her new roof would be to all inclement weather.

He shoved his hands into his pants pockets, sweeping back the sides of his raincoat to reveal his navy suit.

"It's going to be a mess for sure. You know, the roof could only be the beginning of the problems with this old building. Plumbing, electrical.

Your line of credit may not be enough to cover all the expenses you could run into."

Kelly's smile slipped away as exasperation twisted inside of her. Just once, she'd like a visit from her uncle that didn't revolve around him reminding her of her inexperience in running a business. It seemed the visits were an effort on his part to undermine her confidence. She hated to admit it, but if that was his goal, he'd accomplished it many times.

"Thanks for the heads up. You know, you don't need to be concerned with my finances. I have everything under control." *No thanks to you.*

"You think so?"

"Look, let's stop doing this. Everything has been settled with the estate. I don't see any reason for you continuing to come here if you're going to be negative and intent on sabotaging my efforts to turn this boutique around."

"I don't know what you're talking about." He grinned like a Cheshire cat.

She barked a laugh at the blatant lie. "Really? The next time you and your buddy Jed plot to keep me from borrowing money, you should suggest he remove the photo of you two playing golf. Your plan didn't work."

"Your imagination is in overdrive. No wonder you're running around town playing detective. Maybe if you spent more time taking care of your business, you wouldn't need to rely on getting money from a bank for the roof repair."

Kelly huffed. She'd had enough. She wasn't going to be lectured anymore. It was time for her uncle to own his role in this whole matter.

"Maybe if you'd showed the slightest interest or respect to your mother, the business wouldn't have fallen into disrepair."

"Watch your mouth, young lady."

The irritation she'd felt earlier turned into a raging anger in her belly. He was going to tell her how to speak? Not anymore. She'd had enough of his interference, lack of respect, and general disdain.

"Or what? Look, I have no idea what I did to earn such contempt from you. Whatever it was, I apologize. I'm sorry. I am truly sorry. It's just I can't go on like this anymore. If you're not going to support me, then we should stay out of each other's lives." As she spoke those words, they sliced into her heart. Breaking off from her uncle meant she risked being kept out of Juniper's life. She loved the baby and had tried to keep things civil between her and Ralph to maintain a relationship with her cousin.

"You'll never be sorry enough for me." His expression hardened, and it matched his tone.

She drew back. What was he talking about? What could she have possibly done to him? She began searching her memory, but what did it really matter now? He made it clear he didn't want to have a relationship with her by his actions and deeds since his mother's death.

"Whatever." Kelly gave a dismissive wave and turned. She stomped back to the boutique. Inside the staff room, she shrugged out of her jacket. With all her might, she threw it on the desk. She was desperate for some form of satisfaction, but tossing the jacket fell short of her goal.

"That man is so irritating!"

A door slammed behind her.

"Right back at you!"

Her uncle had followed her inside.

"We have nothing left to talk about." She crossed her arms over her chest and stared at him. He advanced forward, but she remained rooted in place. She wasn't going to acquiesce to him. She wasn't going to back down.

"You're wrong. Listen to me and listen good. You're going to sell this place, take the money and move back to the city."

"Why would I do that?"

"Because it's what's best for our family."

"Ha! If you wanted to do what was best for our *family*, you'd support me in making this business successful. This is your mother's legacy for goodness sakes. Doesn't it mean anything to you?"

"Family legacy. How rich coming from you. Tell me, how long will it be before you run off again?"

"I didn't run away. I went to college and stayed in the city to work. Never mind. It doesn't matter now. What matters is that I'm here to stay. Why do you think I'm having the roof redone? Why do you think I've invested in a new inventory system?"

"You wasted your money."

"Why? Why do you hate me so much? Tell me, for goodness sakes! Get it out in the open!"

Ralph's jaw tightened, and his posture stiffened. "Every time I look at you, I see Ariel in the hospital bed."

Kelly jerked her head back. What in the world was her uncle talking about? He barely knew Ariel when she was growing up. Heck, he hardly knew Kelly when she was growing up. Though she did remember, he had gone to the hospital to see her friend after the accident.

"Uncle Ralph, I'm very confused. You know I wasn't driving the car when the accident happened, right?"

"But you were there with her! And you left her!" He jabbed his finger into the air. "Because of you, Ariel was paralyzed!"

“What? You hate me because of the accident. You’re my family. How can you hate me so much because of that?”

“You can’t just hurt my little girl and then waltz away without taking responsibility! Because of you, my daughter is paralyzed!” Ralph staggered to a chair and dropped down, his hand covering his mouth as if he couldn’t believe what he’d said.

Kelly’s eyes widened; she couldn’t believe what she’d heard. It didn’t make sense. A sudden coldness hit her core, and she felt weak-kneed. She clutched onto the back of a chair opposite Ralph to steady herself.

“What? Your…your daughter? I don’t understand.”

Ralph ran a hand over his balding head and looked away from his niece.

“Ariel doesn’t know. No one knows. Only her mother.”

Kelly sank down onto the chair and stared at her uncle. What he’d said couldn’t be correct. Kelly knew Ariel’s dad. Geoffrey was a real estate agent and always made time for his daughter. From school events to taking Ariel and Caroline camping, he was always present.

He was Ariel’s dad.

“I…I…Wow, I can’t wrap my head around this.” Kelly rested her arms on the table. “Does Frankie know?”

He shook his head. “No one knows. And it’s going to stay that way. Do you understand me?” He lifted his gaze and glowered at her.

“Ariel’s parents have been married for years. Are you telling me her mom cheated?”

“I told you to watch your mouth! She’s a wonderful woman.” Ralph leaned back and shook his head. He looked like someone had let the air out of him. She couldn’t help but wonder if there were any more deep, dark secrets in her uncle’s past. “Things weren’t going well in their marriage, and they separated.”

Oh, goodness, she didn’t want to hear details. No details. She only wanted to hear how he was going to fix this. And by fix, she meant find a way to time travel back to before he followed her into the boutique and bared his soul to her. His cheating soul.

“Lily and I went on a few dates quietly. Then she had the chance to work things out with Geoffrey. They did. Not long after they reconciled, she found out she was pregnant.”

“Wow.” Kelly dragged her fingers through her hair while she continued to digest what her uncle had just shared. “Watching her grow up and never being able to let her know you are her father must have been torture.”

He grunted.

"At least now I know why you despise me so much." She rested her head in her hands. Everything finally made sense.

Right after the accident happened; Ralph had become cold, more distant than before. While her parents and sister verbalized their disappointment in her decision the night of the party, he'd barely said a word to her.

"She was always full of life. Active in everything," Ralph said. "Then, one night, one bad decision, and she was disabled."

Kelly lifted her head and looked at her uncle.

"You have to know I never meant for her to get hurt."

"You left her." His tone was accusatory and harsh.

"I did. But she decided to get into the car with Melanie."

"You're blaming Ariel?"

While Melanie had finally gotten out on parole after seven years, Kelly felt like she was still stuck in the prison of public judgment. It was time she got her pardon.

"I'm saying while I played a part in the events of the night, I wasn't the one who got into a car with someone who had been drinking. And I wasn't the one who drove drunk and crashed the car. There's a lot of blame to go around. It just seems I got more than my fair share."

Ralph drummed his fingers on the desk. "I can't help it. When I see you, I see Ariel in the hospital. Broken. When I got the news of the accident, I went there and saw her fragile body lying there and her mother crying. It ripped my heart apart."

Emotion caught in Kelly's throat. She remembered the night. She remembered seeing Ariel hooked up to machines and fighting for her life. She remembered Mrs. Barnes wailing in the waiting room and her husband trying his best to comfort her. The night would be forever etched in her memory, along with the guilt of her choices.

"I'm so sorry." She wiped away tears from her face with the back of her hand.

"Right. You're sorry."

"We're family. We have to work through this."

"Well, what we need to understand is that this conversation goes nowhere else. Ever."

Kelly raised her palms and nodded. "I won't tell anyone your secret."

"I suppose you want something in return for your silence."

"Wow. You don't know a thing about me, do you?" Kelly stood and walked to the door that led to the hall. "There is one thing you can do for me. Stop making my life miserable. You can also show yourself out."

She pushed the swinging door open and walked out of the room. Upstairs in her apartment, Howard greeted her. His body slinked along her legs, and he meowed softly. His welcome made her smile. She squatted down and stroked his back. Her fingers burrowed in his fur as she settled on the floor.

He took her action as an invitation and climbed onto her lap. His whiskers brushed her chin, and the dam burst. Tears streamed down her cheeks, and she sniffled.

The memory of the summer party slammed into her. Flashes of the fire pit, bottles of beer being passed out, and her walking away from the crowd with Davey.

No, no, no. She couldn't blame herself anymore.

Not only did she have to stop punishing herself, but she also had to stop letting people blame her. Like her uncle had.

Oh, goodness. She inhaled a sharp breath.

How was she going to face Ariel? How was she going to be able to keep her uncle's secret?

Ariel had the right to know who her biological father was, didn't she? What about Frankie and Juniper? Didn't they have a right to know they had a sister?

How had she gotten into this situation?

She just had to tell her uncle off. Now, look where it had gotten her. Right in the middle of a life-changing secret.

Kelly rested her head against the wall.

Why did she have to open the can of worms? Why hadn't she just accepted her uncle's crummy behavior? Why did she have to question it? There was something to be said for leaving things alone.

Lesson learned.

Howard meowed, drawing her attention downward. She scratched his head.

"Why is life so complicated? It reminds me of Granny's soap operas," she said to her feline companion. Yes, her life had all the makings of a top-rated drama. "Maybe I should have taken that offer to appear on reality TV last winter."

Howard meowed again. This time it was clipped and followed by a flick of his tail before he jumped off her lap and sauntered off to the living room.

"Wow. That didn't last long." She scrambled to her feet, and before she reached the bathroom to wash her face, her cell phone buzzed.

She checked the caller ID.

Ariel.

Good grief. Kelly couldn't talk to her friend now. She tossed the phone onto her bed and let the call go to voice mail as she entered the bathroom.

She slammed the door shut. Maybe running away from Lucky Cove again wasn't such a bad idea.

Chapter 18

After taking a bubble bath, consuming a pint of mint chocolate chip, and catching up on *Project Runway*, Kelly finally fell asleep. Waking the next morning was slow going, but she gave herself some grace. Yesterday had packed a wallop.

She indulged in a little extra pampering while she got ready for the day. And when she leaned into the mirror over the bathroom sink to apply false lashes, her mood instantly brightened. It was amazing what a good pair of lashes could do for a gal.

Despite her sluggish start to the day, she arrived at Jason's house on time. Pulling into the driveway, she was passed by a speeding car heading out to the road. The vehicle looked like Serena's Mercedes, but the car was moving too fast for Kelly to get a good look at the driver. The only thing she was sure of was that the driver was a woman.

If the driver was Serena, what was she doing there? And why was she leaving so fast? What exactly was her relationship status with Jason these days? Even though Kelly had decided to step away from Serena's situation, it didn't mean she wasn't still intrigued. Hence, her visit to Delia yesterday.

After parking her Jeep, Kelly got out and walked toward the house. When Kelly reached the welcome mat, she knocked on the door. While she waited, she glanced around the front of the house. Evergreen shrubs dotted the mulched gardens, where the tips of bulbs started to emerge from their dormant winter. The morning air was refreshing in an almost-spring-kind-of-way after yesterday's rain. Because of the shift in weather, she'd been able to pull out her favorite longline cardigan, and she'd paired it with leggings and a tunic. As she headed out of the apartment, she grabbed a scarf and wrapped it around her neck for a little added warmth.

Kelly checked her watch. It was now after nine. Where was Jason?

During their telephone conversation yesterday, they discussed her coming over "first thing" in the morning. Still, before she made dinner, she texted him to firm up a time. They agreed upon nine o'clock, which was perfect because she'd be in and out before the boutique opened. To make sure she was as efficient with her time as possible, she left the cargo door of her Jeep open so she could start loading it up right away.

She knocked again. And again, there was no answer.

She stepped back from the front door and yawned. Was Jason out, or had he overslept?

Her cell phone buzzed. It was Liv calling.

She was grateful that the call wasn't from Ariel. The jury was still out on how she'd deal with her friend. And the *secret*.

Kelly answered the call and wasted no time blurting out what happened with Mark to her best friend. She'd wanted to call last night and talk it through with Liv, but she hadn't had the energy. She still didn't. But it was impossible not to share one of the worst conversations she'd had in a long time.

Well, it had dropped in ranking once her uncle dropped the mother-of-all bombshells on her.

"Solo? He really said that to you? What a jerk." Liv sounded as peeved as Kelly was when Mark had uttered the word.

"Oh, he most certainly did." Kelly wandered back to her Jeep and leaned against the side.

"But you two are dating. He should have taken you with him."

"I know!"

"Have you spoken to him yet?"

"No. He hasn't called. He'll probably never call again."

"How do you feel about that?"

Kelly stared ahead, not focusing on anything, as she thought about her answer.

"Sad. I thought we made a good couple." She dropped her gaze to the ground and kicked at a twig. She paired a favorite pair of platform sneakers with her casual outfit for her appointment.

"Well, it sounds like he isn't ready to be a part of a couple. Maybe it's for the best you find out now rather than later."

Kelly sighed. Her friend was right. It was better to get out early than to waste time in a dead-end relationship.

Maybe it was for the best. The last thing she wanted to be was an embarrassment. If they stayed together, that thought would always be in the back of her mind.

"How about I meet you at Doug's before I go to the bakery?" Liv asked. "My treat."

"I'd love to. I was supposed to meet Jason at nine to take Tawny's clothing for consignment, but it looks like he's not home." Kelly pushed off from the side of the vehicle. Just then, a mini-van pulled into the driveway. She didn't recognize the car.

"Great. I'm almost out the door."

"Wait…there's someone here. I'll call you back." Kelly disconnected the call and approached the vehicle as a woman got out. "Hi."

The petite woman gave Kelly a quick once-over before she reached into the back of the mini-van for a canvas tote. "Good morning. Is there something I can help you with?" She hurried toward the front door, not giving Kelly time to answer. Her ash brown curls bounced with each step.

Kelly hurried to catch up. "I have an appointment with Jason. I'm Kelly Quinn."

The woman tossed a look over her shoulder as she unlocked the front door.

"He's usually here in the morning when I come, but who knows now? He has so much going on."

"Who are you?"

"Missy. I'm the housekeeper. I come twice a week." Missy entered the foyer and set the tote on the floor.

"Nice to meet you." Kelly followed Missy inside and looked around for any sign of Jason. "It seems odd."

"What does?" Missy dug into her tote and took out a clipboard. She jotted down some notes.

"He was insistent I come first thing this morning. He wanted to clear out Tawny's clothing."

"So soon? Wow. Guess he's wasting no time in moving on." And with that, Missy headed for the kitchen. Kelly wondered if the housekeeper cleaned as fast as she moved.

"What? What do you mean?" Kelly chased after the housekeeper.

Missy stopped short of entering the kitchen, at a utility closet, and pulled out a vacuum.

"Miss Quinn, I have work to do." Missy pushed the vacuum by Kelly and headed back to the front of the house.

"Please. Could you check upstairs? Maybe Jason overslept. I'm here, so I'd like to take the clothes back to the boutique so I can open for the day. I'd really appreciate your help."

"Fine. I'll go check. You stay right here." Missy set her clipboard down on the small chest of drawers by the coat closet and went up the stairs. She disappeared out of Kelly's sight.

Kelly glanced at her watch again. She'd be cutting it close to opening time. Even though Pepper was scheduled to work the morning shift, she didn't want to be away too long. While she didn't like how Mark or her uncle had spoken to her, they weren't entirely wrong about the distractions she allowed to into her life. Sure, being there at Jason's house was for business—new inventory. But her visit to Delia yesterday? No way she could chalk that up to being work-related. Well, she could if the category was none-of-her-business.

Her cell phone buzzed. It was Liv again. She answered the call.

"Sorry. I don't think I can make it," Kelly said as she walked to the first riser on the staircase and looked up, though there was nothing to see except a massive flower arrangement on a small table.

"Bummer. I'm already at Doug's," Liv said.

Kelly was about to ask Liv to drop off a large Top o' the Morning coffee at the boutique when a piercing scream from the second floor stopped her.

"What the…" Kelly bolted up the stairs and made a sharp turn toward where she heard the scream come from. She ran along the carpeted hallway to the bedroom.

"What's going on?" Liv asked.

Kelly barely heard Liv's question when she arrived at the doorway of the master bedroom. Missy was standing in the bathroom's doorway with her hands over her mouth. She rushed to the housekeeper's side and looked over her shoulder to find out what caused her to scream.

Kelly's stomach clenched. It was Jason.

His body was sprawled out on the tile floor, and a pill bottle was next to his hand. Small white pills were scattered around the bottle. Kelly shoved Missy out of the way and went to Jason. She checked his carotid pulse.

"Did you find Jason?" Liv asked.

Shoot. She'd forgotten Liv was still on the line. "Ah…yeah…we found him. I have to call you back." Kelly disconnected the call.

"He's dead, isn't he?" Missy had lowered her hands and now wrung them together.

"Yes. We have to call the police, but first, we have to go downstairs." Kelly stood and ushered Missy out of the bathroom. On their way out of the room, she noticed a sheet of paper on the bed. She took a slight detour over to the unmade queen-sized bed to get a look at the paper.

Missy started wailing, and Kelly couldn't linger, so she snapped a photo before rushing to the housekeeper's side.

"I've never seen a dead body before. This is awful." Missy buried her face in her hands, forcing Kelly to guide her along the hallway to the staircase.

Before Kelly descended the stairs, she glanced back at the bedroom. She wondered if Serena had gotten into the house and discovered Jason's body. If so, that would explain why she high-tailed it out of the driveway only minutes ago. Being present at the scene of two deaths in the same household would be suspicious and probably lead to her being taken into custody again. Either way, it wouldn't look good for her.

If there was any doubt in Kelly's mind she'd become a regular caller to 9-1-1 to report a dead body, it was confirmed by the dispatcher's subtle sigh. Barely audible, but Kelly still heard it. Yes, it was her again.

Police officers arrived minutes after her call. By some miracle, Gabe wasn't one of the responding officers.

The officers didn't know who she was and were surprised Kelly gave her statement succinctly and calmly. She was tempted to say, not my first rodeo. From the serious expressions on their faces, she figured the quip wouldn't go over well. Then she discovered why they were so solemn when she overheard them talking.

Jason was their first dead body.

Kelly remembered her first. Now, look at her. Cool, calm, and collected. She also had the presence of mind to take a photograph of the note on the bed, which she desperately wanted to read. To see if it was indeed a suicide note.

It looked like a suicide. Alone in his home and a bottle of pills. His body had been warm to the touch when she checked his pulse, indicating he hadn't been dead for too long.

Had he been thinking about killing himself when he talked to her last night? Or, had he woken up that morning and realized he couldn't go another day without Tawny? Or, had the guilt of murdering his wife overwhelmed him? Okay, she had no proof he'd killed Tawny, but the husband was always a suspect.

"Miss Quinn." The baritone voice drew Kelly's attention to the living room's entry. "I apologize for the interruption."

Not only was Gabe missing from the crime scene but also Wolman. Instead, Detective Nate Barber arrived and took her statement. She asked where Wolman was, but Barber didn't give her a direct answer. Instead, he asked why she was there, what she touched, how long she'd been in the house before discovering Jason's body. She answered the questions but did keep one bit of information to herself. It was that tidbit that caused beads of sweat to form on her temples.

"I apologize for keeping you waiting." He stepped out of the room for a few minutes, telling Kelly to sit tight until he returned. What else did she have to do?

"Detective Barber, may I go now?" She scooped her purse up from the sofa and stood. She gazed into the detective's kind eyes. They weren't as harsh as Wolman's were when she interviewed Kelly.

"Yes. Please be aware there may be some follow-up questions."

Not my first rodeo. Yeah, still inappropriate.

Barber reached into his blazer's breast pocket and pulled out a business card for Kelly.

"Thank you." She slipped the card into her purse.

"One more thing, Miss Quinn." Barber had at least six inches of height on her, and his bulk appeared to be solid. He could easily intimidate any suspect with not much more than a look. "I spoke with Detective Wolman."

Kelly could only imagine what Wolman had said about her.

"She says you have a way of…how should I say this? Let's go with you have issues with knowing your boundaries." A small smile tugged at his lips. He seemed amused by Kelly's reputation around the police department.

"I can't help it if I notice something or if someone tells me something. When it happens, I tell the police whatever I learn." Not exactly true since she failed to tell the detective about seeing Serena's car when she'd arrived. The million-dollar question was why hadn't she told him? It should have been the first thing she said to him when he asked what time she arrived. Instead, she left the detail out. Now it seemed too late to mention it. "You don't have to worry about my boundaries." *Only my knack for leaving things out.*

"Oh, I'm not the one who should be worried. Consider yourself warned." Barber stepped aside to allow Kelly to pass by.

"Noted." She hustled out of the room. On her way to the front door, she glanced into the dining room. Missy sat at the table with her head in her hands. A pang of sympathy rippled through Kelly. She knew precisely what Missy would go through over the next few weeks. Nightmares and what-if scenarios would consume her. Over time, the shock would lessen, and her life would return to normal.

Kelly continued to the door and left the house.

Behind the wheel of her Jeep, she took in a deep breath.

She couldn't believe Jason was dead. Had he really killed himself? Why? Was it grief? Was it guilt? Or was it murder?

Was that why Serena had torn out of the driveway?

There was only one way to find out. Kelly turned the ignition on and drove out of the driveway. She'd find out why Serena had been there and then convince her to go to the police. The question was, would Serena go as a witness or would she be turning herself in?

Chapter 19

Kelly arrived at Serena's house prepared for anything. Being in Serena's orbit meant life was unpredictable, and the past few days proved that to be true. However, she wasn't prepared to see Lucky Cove police vehicles parked in front of the house.

Oh, boy. This isn't good.

Kelly parked her Jeep off to the side so as not to block the official vehicles. As she got out of the car, the front door of the house opened.

Serena emerged from the house and behind her was a uniformed officer. Following them was a tall, lanky woman on crutches. Kelly guessed she was Serena's assistant.

"She's been here all morning." The injured woman's voice was loud and pleading. She looked to be around Kelly's age with shoulder-length brown hair and plump red lips. They reminded Kelly of a neon sign that you could see from a mile away.

Kelly hurried to the walkway, and it was then she noticed the handcuffs. Serena's hands were secured behind her back, and her hoodie was over her shoulders. Her hair was swept off her face by a headband, and she wore workout leggings and a tank. She was arrested while doing yoga? It was the only workout she ever did.

Why did she have to stop for gas on the way over to Serena's rental house? Filling her gas tank hadn't taken too long. It was the unanticipated conversation with Nan Phillips. Actually, it was more like an ambush. Nan was always looking for donations for her never-ending list of charity events. Today, she wanted a donation for the historical society's ice cream social. In a rush to get going, Kelly agreed, but then had to listen to the planned menu. Had she paid with a credit card rather than cash, she would have escaped before Nan got a hold of her.

"What's going on?" Kelly asked. The police must have found out Serena had been at Jason's house. But why arrest her?

"Please, ma'am," the officer said, as he held out his arm to keep her away from Serena.

"This is a mistake! I'll have your badge." Serena swung her head around and glared at the officer. "How dare you treat me like this."

"Ma'am, please lower your voice," the officer said.

Kelly cringed.

Serena hated being called ma'am.

"I will sue!" Serena wasn't heeding the officer's advice.

"I'll call your lawyer, Serena." The assistant followed along the best she could on crutches.

Kelly got a closer look and saw the woman's eyes were hooded and dark circled. She remembered the perpetual wary look on all of Serena's assistants all too well.

"Of course, you will! Always stating the obvious, Danica." She might have been handcuffed, but it didn't stop Serena from being her usual snarky self.

"Be careful." The officer assisted Serena into the back seat of his vehicle.

"Officer, you must believe me. She was here with me." Serena's assistant had a slight accent Kelly couldn't place. The position of being Serena's right hand was highly sought after and attracted candidates from around the world.

The officer slipped in behind the steering wheel of his vehicle and drove away.

"What happened? Why was she arrested?" Kelly came up beside Danica, who appeared visibly shaken by the whole ordeal.

"Good question! I got here about an hour ago from the city. Do you believe she threatened to fire me if I didn't come all the way out here? She knows I broke my ankle, and I'm on crutches. I had to get a car service. Geez. Now, what am I going to do?"

"Call her lawyer and then call the car service to go back to the city."

Danica rolled her eyes. "She doesn't pay me enough to deal with this stuff."

"I'm sure she doesn't. When you arrived, she was here? Inside the house?"

"Yes, yes." Danica nodded. "She was about to do yoga, and I went to set up my laptop. It's not easy carrying an overnight bag and a laptop bag. Do you think she helped me?" She shifted her weight on her crutches and grimaced. "Who are you anyway? Why are you here?"

"She's Kelly Quinn. She owns a consignment shop in town." Detective Barber stepped out of the house, and grinned.

"Boutique. It's a resale boutique." Why Kelly felt the need to correct the detective was beyond her. She guessed it was just automatic these days to distinguish her business from the consignment shops.

"Pardon me. Boutique. I'm curious, like Miss Quinn, why you're here." Barber walked down the granite front steps.

"I came to see Serena." Kelly fidgeted with her hair. If she played it cool, then she could skirt around the fact she'd withheld a piece of information from the detective.

"I'm glad you stopped by." The detective joined Kelly and Danica. "It saves me the trouble of tracking you down. Miss Welch, would you mind going back inside? I have a few more questions for you."

"Of course. I'm happy to be of service." Her sarcasm wasn't hard to miss. Danica turned and lumbered back to the house. She took a few missteps but regrouped quickly. Climbing the front steps challenged her beginner crutch skills, but she made it inside. Kelly saw she used one crutch to close the door with a hard slam. Impressive.

"Now, Miss Quinn, we need to talk." Barber unfolded his arms and rested his hands on his hips, pushing back the sides of his blazer.

"About?"

"I don't like games. Even if I did, I don't have time for them."

"Neither do I. Did you tell Serena that Jason is dead? How did she react?"

Barber cleared his throat. "Miss Quinn, I'm the one who asks the questions. It's not the other way around."

"Of course. My apologies. I've had a hard time getting a handle on the relationship between Serena and Jason. When I first saw them together, they were at each other's throats. Then later that night, they met for dinner. And I heard they held hands. Anyway, then she's telling me she's staying in town to be supportive of him and then the next thing I know, she's accusing him of murdering his wife. See? I can't figure their relationship out."

"Maybe it's because you're not supposed to. You're not the police detective. You're a shop owner."

Kelly huffed. "I know…shoot!" she glanced at her watch. "I need to get back to my boutique. Is there any way we can talk there?"

"No."

"Well, then. Where will we talk?"

"I'm thinking about my place."

"You're …what?"

"The police department. Follow me." He breezed past her with an air of confidence and arrogance, and it appalled her. Well, not completely.

"Do you think you can bark orders, and I'll obey?" She propped a hand on her hip and cocked her head sideways, waiting for an answer.

He shrugged. "It's usually how it works when I'm investigating a case. But if you prefer, I can cuff you and haul you in for interfering with police business. Either way works for me." He pulled out his key fob and opened the car door.

"Fine. I'll meet you there." Kelly rushed past him to get to her Jeep. She never wanted to be handcuffed again. It was the most humiliating, degrading experience of her life. Considering she had knowingly kept a piece of information from the detective, she couldn't blame him if he did arrest her. Once he found out what she'd withheld, he might change his mind.

Kelly unwrapped her scarf, shrugged out of her cardigan, and tossed them along with her purse on her desk. She spent over an hour at the Lucky Cove Police Department giving her truthful recount from the moment she'd arrived at Jason's house to her arrival at Serena's place. Barber really hadn't been interested in her conversation with Nan Phillips. She didn't blame him. She wasn't that interested.

The door to the staff room swung open, and Pepper entered carrying her reusable water bottle.

"You're back. Glad I didn't have to come down and bail you out." Pepper smiled as she headed to the sink to refill her bottle.

"Haha. I was only there to give a statement." Kelly pulled out the chair from the desk and sat. She massaged her temples. A wicked headache was spreading across her forehead.

"I thought you gave one at the house after finding Jason's body." Pepper turned off the faucet and took a swig of her water.

"I did." She didn't want to share with Pepper there had been a slight omission in her first statement. "Detective Barber wanted to make sure it was complete and accurate."

"He did, did he?"

Oh, boy.

There it was—the Pepper glare along with a tone that made it clear she wasn't buying a word Kelly was saying. The twofer made Kelly squirm.

Before she could respond, offer a defense, or just get the heck out of the room, the back door opened, and Summer barged in.

"There you are!" Summer pointed a manicured finger at Kelly as she advanced toward her.

"I should get back to the sales floor." Pepper scooted out of the room, leaving

Kelly on her own.

"Good afternoon, Summer." Kelly smiled, hoping to defuse the situation.

"How could you?" Summer lowered her hand and rested it on her hip.

If it weren't for the irritating twist to her rose-colored lips and death stare, which rivaled the Pepper glare, she would have looked lovely. Dressed in a bright orange dress with a flounce hem and nude-colored Valentino Rockstud ballet flats that left Kelly swooning, she looked ready for spring.

"What are you talking about?"

Summer sighed. "You know what you did! Tell me why do you keep interfering in my life? Last year it was the reality show, and now it's Adrian Chase? How could you use me as an excuse to talk to that horrible human being?"

"I did no such thing." Kelly got to her feet.

"You didn't tell him we're related? I sent you to see him?"

"No. Well…I told him we are related. But, I swear, I didn't tell him you sent me. He assumed it. What's the big deal? You said you have no intention of doing business with him." Kelly walked to the counter and poured a cup of coffee. She added an extra dose of cream. Her stomach was growling. She missed breakfast, and it looked like she would miss lunch if Summer kept yelling at her.

"While I don't plan on ever doing business with him, I can't afford to alienate him either. The fitness community is small."

"I'm sorry. Please believe I didn't intend to damage your reputation in any way. I understand how important your studio is to you. It's how I feel about this boutique." She had considered none of the fallout when she headed to Adrian's office. Well, she believed she might have been putting herself in danger, but she hadn't thought about Summer.

"He called me, and he was furious." Summer joined Kelly at the counter and poured a cup of coffee. She drank hers black. Kelly thought only psychopaths drank black coffee. "What did you say to him?"

"I asked about his relationship with Tawny, about the lawsuits and about her concerns about the company's finances." Kelly sipped her coffee.

"What concerns? Who told you that?"

"Jason."

"Oh, poor Jason. I heard a little while ago. Suicide? It's heartbreaking." Summer sipped her coffee as she moved to the table. She sat and crossed her legs. Kelly felt a twinge of envy. Summer's legs were long, lean, and already tanned. Kelly's were still pasty winter white.

"It appears it was." Kelly's eyes widened. The note! She'd forgotten all about it. She hurried to the desk, jostling her coffee, and opened her purse. "He left a note, I think." She took her phone to the table and sat.

"You read it?" Summer sounded surprised. Reading her facial expressions was tough since, like Serena, she was a repeat customer for injectables.

"No." Kelly tapped her phone.

"Thank goodness. It would be unseemly to read such a document. Remember, our family has a reputation to withhold in town."

Kelly paused for a moment. Oh, the Blake family had more than just a reputation to withhold. They had a deep, dark secret just waiting to be uncovered at any moment. It was only a matter of time, because secrets were like weeds, they always pushed their way through until they got out into the light. She gave herself a mental shake and then held up the phone to Summer.

"I took a photo."

Summer sighed. Her disappointment was evident.

"Now, I'm going to read it." Kelly turned the phone back to her, and she read the handwritten note.

I'm sorry for what I did. The mistakes I made. The trusts I betrayed. Living with this guilt is unbearable. I can't do it. It's my dying wish that Tawny will forgive me.

"What?" Summer leaned forward, her disappointment gone. "What does it say?"

"He's sorry for what he did, and he hopes Tawny will forgive him."

"Sorry for what? Killing her?"

Kelly shrugged. "It seems like it, right? His suicide and this note. Maybe Serena was right. Maybe he finally realized Tawny was only after his money. I heard they argued."

Summer gave a dismissive wave. "A lot of couples argue. Let me tell you about Jason. He wasn't very wealthy. He wasn't even a member of the country club. No, Tawny knew she had to work for her own money."

"It was after she married him she started her business. Before then, she had several jobs. It looks like she benefited a lot from marrying him."

"Sure, she did. But she'd been planning on launching her own fitness business before she married. In fact, she began talking with Adrian months before her wedding. She was going places even if she hadn't married Jason." Summer glanced at her five-figure gold watch. "I need to get to the studio for a class."

"Again, I'm sorry if I caused any problems for you with Adrian. You know the guy is a sexist pig, right? He called me "hon."

Summer laughed. “I’m not surprised. But seriously, be careful. He’s not a person I would want to cross.”

Kelly nodded. She’d gotten the message loud and clear when he’d exploded in anger at her. She sipped her coffee as Summer stood and left. When the door closed, she looked at the photo of Jason’s note.

It appeared to be precisely what it was—a suicide note.

She leaned back. The headache she felt bloom minutes ago exploded and she needed aspirin ASAP. She got up and walked over to the counter. From an upper cabinet, she took out the aspirin bottle. She shook out two pills into her hand, and that’s when she remembered.

Next to Jason’s opened hand was a prescription pill bottle and scattered around the bottle were pills. A lot of pills. If he’d overdosed, why were there so many pills left?

Chapter 20

Pepper came back into the staff room under the guise of checking on Kelly, but she really wanted to know what happened with Summer. After Kelly gave a condensed version of the conversation, she insisted a lecture wasn't required. Pepper went to object, but Kelly nipped the all-too-familiar speech in the bud. Pepper wasn't pleased so Kelly made a quick getaway to her apartment. Up there, she could work without any interruptions.

The boutique was woefully out of touch with the times when she took over and one of the first things, she did was create a website. Last fall, she didn't have much time to devote to the website, so it was pretty bare bones and she wanted to change that. Diving into the project would be a welcomed change, something positive to concentrate on.

She entered her apartment and set her purse on the cabinet by the door. The small piece of furniture was an unexpected find the day she bought the lamppost for the window display. Its cottage charm seemed to mesh with the vibe she was trying to achieve—shabby chic on a budget. It also provided added storage space that the apartment was short on. A little sanding and a new paint job brought the cabinet back to life. She took a moment to admire her handiwork.

Never in a million years would she have thought she'd be refinishing furniture and enjoying it.

Certainly, never while eating, breathing, and living in Serena's world.

She looked for Howard. He was a no-show at her arrival home, leaving her to guess he was curled up on the bed. The lazy bum had the right idea.

She took off her sneakers and stashed them in the hall closet. Next order of business was another cup of coffee. In the kitchen, she dropped a pod into her single drip coffee maker.

After she stirred generous drop of milk into her coffee, Kelly grabbed a cookie and then walked out of the kitchen and to the dining room table where her laptop was setup. She settled down and opened her Word document program.

One of the things that had been at the top of her to-do list for the website was to create a regular newsletter. And not just any newsletter. She wanted to create one that her customers would find value in, and when it landed in their inboxes, it would be the first email they opened. She knew it was a lofty goal for a newsletter, but it was good to have goals.

She opened her file of content ideas for the newsletter and read through the list. Special events, pop-up sales, fashion tips, the perks of decluttering (it can bring in cash) and the benefits of buying resale. She had a good start. So now, all she had to do was start sending out newsletters on a regular basis. She'd also have to come up with catchy subject lines to catch her subscriber's attention. Once she had their attention, she was certain she could sell to them.

In the mood for something fun and lighthearted, Kelly chose to write about color blocking. A former hot trend, now it was an outlier just waiting for its rebirth. Color blocking was fun, whimsical, and fresh. A trend Serena detested. One day, a secretary had worn a tunic blocked in three colors—army green, black, and cream. She styled it with velour leggings and a peep-toe bootie. Perfection. So Kelly had thought. It turned out Serena hadn't agreed. She'd marched to the secretary's desk, tossed a gray sweater at her, and demanded she change.

Kelly raised her fingertips from the keyboard. She needed to stop thinking about Serena and her own ill-fated career at Bishop's. Could that have been the reason why she agreed to help Serena? To ultimately show her former boss she made a mistake in firing her?

She shook her head. She had to stop thinking about the past. The what-ifs, the could haves and the should haves. What was of the utmost importance was the here and now. Here, she had a flourishing business, and the now was she had a newsletter to write.

She re-positioned her fingers over her keyboard and got back to work. She was on a deadline. Her plan was to send the newsletter within a week.

With that kick in her leggings, Kelly put her head down and wrote. When she looked up an hour later, she had a finished draft, her coffee, and the cookie was gone. She contemplated what to do about the coffee mug. Refill or no refill? Now, there was an easy decision. Finally. She swiped it up and, as she was about to stand, her cell phone dinged. A text from Ariel.

Kelly cringed. She'd been avoiding her friend since her uncle's confession. At the time that she agreed to keep his secret, she hadn't considered how she'd feel when she faced Ariel.

She sighed and picked up her phone to read the message.

Ariel was finishing her shift at the library but was staying to work on an article for a magazine she pitched to last fall. She asked if Kelly wanted to join her for some writing time and then they could get an early dinner.

A writing session and dinner. Could Kelly keep herself from blurting out the fact they're not only friends but cousins?

She replied.

Sounds good. See you then.

Sounds good? Sounds more like a recipe for disaster.

Ariel replied with a thumb's up emoji.

Kelly set her phone down and sighed again. Somehow, she'd keep the secret to herself. She had to. All thoughts about Ariel's biological father were pushed aside. She couldn't allow herself to be sucked into her uncle's twenty-eight-year-old indiscretion.

She quickly got a refill and another cookie. Back at her laptop, she started drafting the welcome portion of the newsletter. That section took more brainpower, as she wanted to convey a fun, cool, and modern tone that would draw the reader in. There were a few false starts until she found her voice but when she did, her fingers flew over the keyboard. When she had a first draft of the opening paragraph, she took an eye break by scrolling Instagram for a few minutes. When she finally caught up, she went back to her browser to check the weather and the news of the day.

The weather forecast was for a stretch of unseasonably warmer days, and the news hadn't reported on Jason's death yet. She was certain that would change once Serena's arrest leaked.

She propped an elbow on the table and rested her chin in the palm of her hand.

The question of all those pills after Jason's supposed suicide attempt lingered in her mind and finally pushed front and center. If Jason did indeed kill himself, why did the police arrest Serena?

She grabbed her phone and texted Gabe. Hopefully she could get a little info out of him.

Hey, have you heard anything about Jason's death?

While she waited for his reply, she checked her emails again and there was an email from MineNowYours.com. Her finger hovered over the mouse pad to click on the correspondence and then it hit her—the Fendi purse! With everything going on and her mind jumping from one thing to another, she'd forgotten about the precious Peekaboo. How could that have happened?

Out of sight, out of mind. That's how.

The purse was in her coat closet.

There was a ding from her phone. A text from Gabe.

Open investigation. Can't tell you anything.

She rolled her eyes. They both knew he'd tell her something about the case.

Why was Serena arrested if Jason killed himself?

With her phone in hand, she got up and went to the closet. She pulled the purse down from the top shelf and took it back to the table. Gingerly, she removed the purse from the dust bag. It was so beautiful. Classic. Timeless. And so far out of her financial reach. Darn. She caressed the smooth leather and wondered if Tawny's estate would accept monthly installments. First, she had to find out who comprised Tawny's estate or Jason's estate. Maybe no one needed to know she still had the purse?

Her phone dinged again, and she glanced at it.

All I can tell you is that there was evidence to indicate it wasn't a suicide. Gotta go.

Kelly stared at the message. They suspected Serena killed Jason. What was her motive? To get the jointly owned property? They'd been battling over it and with Jason and Tawny dead, it was hers now. But then there was the suicide note. Something was off.

She opened the photo of the note and studied it. The handwriting wasn't Serena's. She could have had a partner. Kelly dismissed the idea. Serena wasn't a team player. She zoomed in on the photo. She remembered the paper. It wasn't a plain sheet of white paper. No, it was creamier in color, and it looked thicker. She'd seen it somewhere before but couldn't remember where.

Kelly sat down and set her phone aside. The police would be able to sort everything out. At some point, they would discover the handwriting on the note wasn't Serena's. They had experts for that, didn't they? Her new top priority was to figure out what to do with the purse.

She opened the bag and examined the interior label. The more she checked, the more confident she was that it was authentic. It probably should be turned over to the police for safekeeping considering its value.

While inspecting the interior, she unzipped the pocket, reached her fingers in, and discovered a key. She missed it on her first check when Tawny presented it to her. Then again, she'd been so surprised it wasn't a wonder she'd missed the key. Anyway, it was common to find something hidden. She often left things in her purses because she changed them so often.

She set the key aside and looked for any other items left in the purse. There was nothing. Her attention shifted back to the key. It looked like the key she had for her granny's storage unit. The tag attached to the key read #116.

Was it a key for a storage unit? She got up and went for her purse. After visiting her granny's unit for the first time last fall, she'd added the key into her six-ring holder to keep it handy and not lose it. When she opened the accessory and compared the two keys, they looked identical.

It looked like Tawny had a unit. The key and the purse had to go to the police. She returned to the table and placed the key next to her laptop. It took only a couple minutes to transfer her wallet and key holder to the laptop bag. Next, she slipped her computer into the bag. She was ready to head out, but she stopped mid-way and turned back to swipe up the mysterious key. On her way out of the apartment, she grabbed her jacket. How bad would a detour on the way to the library be?

Chapter 21

Kelly pulled into the driveway of the storage unit facility and followed the maze of exterior units to the bank where unit 116 was located. She parked a few feet away and grabbed her bag as she exited the Jeep. At the unit's sliding door, she looked around to make sure there was no one around to see her break into and enter the unit. Well, there was that security camera angled right at her. She turned her head back toward the unit. So much for being stealth.

She pulled out the key she found in Tawny's purse and slipped it into the lock. Holding her breath, she gave the key a twist.

It worked. She unlocked the unit.

She exhaled. Now she had to figure out if she was doing the right thing? No, of course she wasn't. She was about to enter someone else's unit without permission. Totally not the right thing to do, and it was illegal. Yet, she tightened her grip on the handle and slid the door up. With the tips of her fingers, she gave a final push and the door locked into place above her.

If she was caught, she'd apologize. If she found a lead, a clue, or evidence, she'd bring it to Detective Wolman and then apologize. Either way, she'd be apologizing.

The contents of the small unit came into view, and any hope of finding something to help solve Tawny's murder vanished. Kelly was underwhelmed by the almost empty space. It looked very different from her granny's unit when she'd first visited.

Instead of boxes stacked on top of boxes and bins stuffed to the brink of not being closed, Tawny had a couple of chairs, an exercise bike, an aerobic step, some other workout accessories, and a card table set up.

On the table was an envelope. Kelly entered and went for the envelope. It was sealed. She shook it and something small jiggled inside.

She considered what to do next. Since she'd already entered without permission, how much more trouble could she get into by opening the envelope? It wasn't addressed and it didn't have a stamp. If she opened it, she wouldn't be breaking any federal laws.

She opened the envelope and found a flash drive.

Now her curiosity was piqued to a whole new level. She had to find out what was on the drive. She set her bag on the table, pulled out her laptop, and turned it up.

Kelly inserted the flash drive and prayed she wouldn't need a password. A file came up. No password required. She was both thrilled and appalled. She had passcodes and passwords on all of her devices.

Inside the file were three documents, and they were all photographs. She enlarged the first photo, and it appeared to be a financial spreadsheet from the Congregational Church. She studied the numbers. She had limited bookkeeping experience, but everything looked okay with the church's money.

She clicked to enlarge the second photograph and it was for another church. The Divine Charitable Spirit. She scanned the list of numbers. All deposits. All the same amounts. She clicked back to the Congregational's spreadsheet and searched the withdrawals.

Money was being moved from the Congregational Church's account to the Divine Charitable Spirit account. She shrugged. There could have been a dozen reasons for the transfers. The two churches could have been involved in relief programs together.

There was the third document, and it was another financial spreadsheet. She sighed. This was not her area of expertise, unless it had to do with calculating open-to-buy ratios for merchandise.

She reviewed the last spreadsheet for a company named The Omega Agency. It didn't take a math genius to figure out the company was hemorrhaging money.

She flipped back and forth between the photos, studying the numbers and trying to figure out what they all had in common. And why they were hidden away here in Tawny's storage unit?

Maybe there was something online that could connect the churches and the Omega Agency.

She opened her browser, searched first for the Divine Charitable Spirit, and came up with nothing. Next, she typed in The Omega Agency.

A result quickly came up. She gasped. It was an advertising agency and belonged to Jason.

It's always the husband.

What had Tawny stumbled on? What connection had she made between the Lucky Cove church, the ghost church and her husband's business?

Kelly drummed her fingers on the table. Her mind turned over theories and then it hit her. A financial fraud. Jason and Tawny had been helpers at the Congregational Church. How trusted, as a volunteer, had he been? Trusted enough to gain access to the church's finances? Had Tawny discovered the deception and planned to turn him in to the police?

Was that why he killed her? But then who killed him? A partner!

Kelly saved the file to her computer and then removed the flash drive from her computer and dropped it back into the envelope. She now had to figure out how to explain all this to Detective Wolman. Or, Detective Barber.

She turned off her computer. After closing the lid, an unsettling thought wormed its way into her head. Jason could have conspired with Serena to kill Tawny.

"No. It doesn't make sense," she whispered to no one. Serena had no motive to help Jason kill his wife. If anything, Jason probably had planned to set Serena up. Had he lured his ex-wife to Lucky Cove so he could get away with murder and all that money sitting in the Divine Charitable Spirit account?

Then who killed him?

Her phone rang, startling her. She reached into her bag. She groaned at the caller ID. She should have been at the library already.

"Hey, Ariel. I'm on my way. I just made a stop."

Kelly juggled the phone between her shoulder and ear while shoving her laptop into the tote.

"Okay. I'm in the community room."

"I'm heading out now. I'll be there soon." Kelly ended the call and slipped the phone in her tote. "Ella! That's where I saw the stationery." She fumbled for her phone to call the reporter and confirm.

When she entered Ella's cottage, she'd noticed, among the papers on the desk, were bulletins from the Congregation Church and letterhead. She couldn't recall what was included in the typed letter from the church, but it was the same paper as the one on which Jason supposedly had written his suicide note.

Her eyes widened. She knew who Jason's partner was. And she had handwriting proof back at the boutique.

"I underestimated you, Kelly."

Chapter 22

The cell phone slipped from Kelly's fingers as she swung around at the sound of Liza's voice. Panic stirred instantly at the sight of the gun in Liza's hand. It looked like she wouldn't need to confirm the handwriting of Jason's alleged suicide note now.

"What are you doing here?" Kelly tore her gaze from the gun to outside the unit, looking for any passersby. Surely, there had to be someone dropping off stuff to their storage unit.

"I knew from the beginning you were going to be trouble. It's a real shame, because I like you."

Kelly tried to find some reassurance in Liza's statement, but it was hard when she had a gun pointed at her. Her heart thumped so hard against her chest that it hurt. She forced herself to remain calm and maintain eye contact. She'd read those were two important things to do if you were ever in this situation.

"I like you too." Kelly was lying. They weren't friends. Maybe they could have been, but once a gun is pointed at you, it's hard to build a friendship. "Why don't you put that thing down and we can both walk away?"

"It's too late. Two people are dead. There's no walking away for you because if you do, I'll go to prison. I can't go to prison." Liza stepped forward. A grim expression was etched onto her face and her cold, hard stare was locked on Kelly.

"It's never too late to make things right. I promise I'll be by your side. We're friends." Kelly took a deep breath to keep her thoughts from racing. Their distraction could cause her to miss an opportunity to escape.

Liza's lips pressed into a thin line, and she shook her head. She had no intention of letting Kelly walk out of there. Her grip on the gun tightened.

"Why? Please tell me why, Liza. Why you killed Tawny and then Jason." Kelly wasn't sure she wanted to understand what was going through the woman's head, but keeping her talking bought time. Time to figure out how to get out of there alive.

"Jason and I were in love."

If her body hadn't been rigid because of the fear coursing through her, Kelly would have fallen over. Liza and Jason had an affair?

"How…how long have you two been seeing each other?"

"It doesn't matter now."

"I guess not. Did you kill Tawny so you could marry Jason? Why didn't he just get a divorce?"

"You do ask a lot of questions." Liza took a step forward. "I don't see the harm in telling you, since you won't be able to share any of it. If he divorced her, he wouldn't have gotten her life insurance policy."

"You killed her for money? Why?" Then Kelly realized the answer to her question. Jason needed money for his advertising agency. The one that was in the red according to the financial spreadsheet.

"I'd tapped out all the money I could get my hands on to help his business. He was a proud man, and you have no idea how hard it was for him to take money from me."

Kelly doubted Jason had to be forced to take the money Liza stole. He'd orchestrated everything. From the embezzlement to Serena's arrest.

"You embezzled the funds, didn't you? You're the Divine Charitable Spirit!"

Liza snickered. "Seems like you know everything."

"Your plan was to frame Serena for Tawny's murder? But why? You couldn't be sure she'd come to Lucky Cove."

Liza rolled her eyes, as if she was irritated by Kelly's naiveté. "Oh, we knew she'd come to town. She couldn't resist an opportunity to bend Jason to her will. He said she was predictable. And with her in prison, Jason would be able to sell the property."

"Sounds like he had it all planned out. Lure Serena out here, get you to kill Tawny, and he gets all the money." From her own experience, Kelly knew no man was worth stealing for and definitely not worth killing for. "He promised to marry you once his wife was dead and his ex-wife was convicted of the murder, didn't he?"

Liza chewed on her bottom lip as she broke eye contact for a second.

"He asked you for money. Money he knew you didn't have but could get. What was the promise? You'd be his partner? No longer the officer manager at a small church? No, you'd be his wife." Kelly's voice had dropped to a whisper.

A shadow crossed over Liza's face. She didn't look confident any longer. Chinks in her armor were showing. Kelly gathered her courage to keep chipping away at Liza's resolve.

"It was all a lie, wasn't it? He let you steal for him. Kill for him. Then he had no use for you. That's why you killed him. He betrayed you. You said so in the note. *The trusts I betrayed.* That was about you."

"He told me we'd leave once Serena was arrested and Tawny was buried. The money I got for him was in an overseas account. We were going to go to an island and elope. Maybe stay there forever." Liza shrugged. "Then he told me…he told me he needed more time. It wouldn't look right for him to leave so soon after his wife's death. I understood. I could wait a little longer."

Kelly had watched and read enough crime drama to know where the story was heading. "He emptied the account, didn't he?"

"I loved him!" Liza emphasized her words by jabbing the air with her gun. "I thought he loved me too!"

"He broke your heart, Liza. Don't let him ruin your life." Kelly didn't want to feel any sympathy for the killer holding her at gunpoint, but she couldn't help herself. Jason had preyed on Liza, used her insecurities to his advantage.

"It's too late!" She blinked back the tears and inhaled a shaky breath, squaring her shoulders, and reinforcing her grip on the gun. "Now, tell me what you found here."

"A flash drive." Cooperating was the last thing Kelly wanted to do, but she didn't have much of a choice. She reassured herself if she kept Liza talking then she had a better chance of getting out of there alive. "On the flash drive were photos of spreadsheets from both churches and Jason's ad agency."

"I knew it. I thought Tawny accessed my computer files the last time she was at the church office. She fled so fast, she tripped on the way out. So, she took photos of the file and then downloaded them to the flash drive? Huh. I was wondering if she saved the records she accessed and what she did with them. I thought, whatever she took, she put it in her purse."

"The Fendi purse?"

"If only you would have let me see it when I asked about it at the boutique. You left me no choice but to break-in. Sorry about the mess." There was no remorse in her voice.

No remorse, no empathy, no chance for Kelly to survive this encounter if she didn't come up with a plan. She needed to do something. Staying calm and maintaining eye contact was getting her nowhere. Her gaze darted around the space. There wasn't much to work with, and Liza still blocked her exit. The exercise bike wasn't going to be of any help unless she could magically ride it out of the unit. But…wait. On the floor was a body bar. Back in the city, she'd taken aerobic toning classes that used weighted body bars. Those classes were the bomb. She gave herself a mental shake. Now wasn't the time for a trip down memory lane. If she could get to the bar, she could have something to defend herself with. Perhaps she could do what Jason had done to Liza, manipulate her by appealing to the lonely little girl inside of her. The girl who wanted to be loved.

"You were planning a beach wedding, weren't you?" Kelly asked gingerly.

"What?" Liza snapped.

"You were planning on going to an island and eloping. So, a beach wedding? I'd love a beach wedding."

Liza nodded and her eyes went all dreamy. "At sunset. Just the two of us."

Kelly forced herself to keep a poker face. She needed to play it cool.

"Flip flops or bare feet?"

"Flip flops. The ones with sparkles. Ooh, and a big hat with a big flower on it."

With Liza daydreaming about her never-going-to-happen wedding, Kelly inched slowly toward the body bar.

"Under an arbor with the setting sun as your background." Kelly was *so* close to the bar. Ready to swoop down, grab it and come up swinging when a truck rumble interrupted Liza's fantasy. The loud, sudden noise startled Liza, leaving Kelly no choice. It was now or never. She grabbed the bar and lunged toward Liza. Swinging hard, she struck Liza, knocking her off balance. The gun went flying out of her hand.

Kelly watched, as if in slow-motion, the gun fall to the concrete floor and discharge. The loud noise made her jump. Luckily, the barrel was facing away from them.

Kelly's distraction gave Liza a small window to gain the upper hand again. With her arms stretched out, she stormed toward Kelly.

Kelly quickly reacted, raising the bar up to block Liza's attempt to grab her. With all of her strength, she rammed Liza with the bar until she pinned her against the wall. It was a swift movement that even surprised Kelly. She then boosted the bar up to Liza's neck and pressed, forcing Liza to stop resisting.

"Hey, everything okay in here?" a male voice called into the unit.

Kelly glanced over her shoulder. A short, chunky man dressed in ripped jeans and wrinkled shirt stood in the doorway with his chubby hands propped on his thick waist.

"Does everything look okay? Call the police. I need help." Kelly backed away from Liza but kept her eye on the woman while she picked up the gun. Having the weapon in her hand made her nervous but not as much as having it pointed at her.

"Sure. No problem. What should I tell them?" he asked.

"Seriously?"

He shrugged and then pulled his phone from his pants pocket.

"Killing you wasn't something I wanted to do." Liza's chin quivered and tears streamed down her cheeks.

"Could have fooled me." Kelly backed away from Liza and took in a deep breath. What had just happened was finally hitting her. The realization of how close she'd come to dying washed over her, and she fought back tears.

"The cops are on their way," the clueless guy said.

"Thanks. I'd appreciate it if you would stay until they get here." Kelly had control over the situation for now, but things could change on a dime.

"Yeah, no problem. I can go to the dump later. Hey, after the cops take her away, you wanna get a drink or something?"

Before Kelly could respond with a big, fat "No," the sound of sirens approaching caught her attention. Thank goodness.

Clueless Guy was jostled as two uniformed police officers appeared. Seeing that one of the officers was Gabe, Kelly heaved a sigh of relief.

"She killed Tawny and Jason! She confessed!" Kelly wanted to run to her friend and hug him, but the cautious look on his face had her staying where she was.

"Kell, put down the gun," Gabe instructed.

Kelly glanced at her hand and made a face. She happily did as instructed. Carefully, she set the weapon on the floor.

"Good girl," Gabe said.

"Yeah, she's hot too," Clueless Guy said, earning him a grimace from Gabe and Kelly.

"Something you want to tell me?" Gabe asked Kelly with a smirk.

Kelly rolled her eyes. "Are you going to cuff her or what?"

"Sweet. She's into cuffs," Clueless Guy said with a creepy smile.

"Ewww." Kelly moved aside as the other officer came forward and put handcuffs on Liza.

"Come on, let's go." The officer led Liza out of the storage unit, reading her her rights.

"Let me get this guy's statement. Do you want to wait in your Jeep?" Gabe asked.

"Sure." She walked out of the unit. Her legs felt like noodles. The rush of adrenaline left her unsteady and lightheaded. She breathed in a deep inhale of fresh air. And another. It helped clear her head.

With the back of her hand, she wiped away the tears that streamed down her face. But there were too many of them.

"Stupid tears."

Shoot. She'd left her bag and laptop in the storage unit. In need of a tissue, pronto, she reached into the vehicle, flipped up the top of the console between the two front seats, and found a napkin from Doug's. It would do. She blotted her face dry.

"You okay?" Gabe had come up behind Kelly, startling her.

Her nod turned into a head shake as her shoulders slumped. She wasn't okay. How could she be?

"Hey. You're safe. She's going to jail for a long time." He turned her around slowly and leveled a concerned gaze on her.

The look on his face was the final straw, and she dissolved into the hot mess she'd been trying to avoid. She collapsed against his chest, sobbing, and he wrapped his arms around her tightly and held her. He didn't say another word he just let her cry.

It took a few moments for her anxiety and fear to flush out from her body, leaving her feeling exhausted and in need of a nap.

"She'd better go away for a very long time." Kelly sniffled and then drew back. She looked up at her friend. He'd cracked a smile.

"She will. Thanks to you. But, don't take that as encouragement to do this ever again."

Kelly held her hands up in surrender. "Oh, never again."

"Are you okay enough to tell me everything that happened?"

She blew her nose and then took a deep, cleansing breath. Gabe wanted a statement from her not her sob story. Well, at least not at that moment. Later, when he was off duty as a cop but on duty as her friend. She closed the Jeep's door and began at the beginning when she'd found the key in the Fendi purse.

Chapter 23

Three weeks later Lucky Cove experienced a pleasant stretch of beautiful weather. There hadn't been a cloud in sight, just bright sunshine and mild temperatures, which made being alive even more sweet for Kelly.

The days following her showdown with Liza in the storage unit were a blur. There was a string of sleepless nights, days when her mind concocted different endings that left her panicked and doing a lot of looking over her shoulder for Liza. Just in case.

"You made a nice little commission on the purse." Ariel dipped her spoon into the sundae. The small cup of vanilla ice cream was smothered with chocolate sauce, whipped cream, nuts, and topped with a cherry. She'd stopped by the boutique with a mid-afternoon treat for them. And to check up on her friend, though she didn't come right out and say that. Kelly just knew and she was grateful for her concern. And the company.

Kelly swallowed her mouthful of ice cream. She opted for a cup of plain chocolate ice cream. No frills. Even though she was tempted to pile on the extras, she remembered that summer was coming with sundresses and shorts. So, no extra calories. At least for now. Come July 4th, who knew what she'd indulge in. And given what she'd been through, she would be indulging big-time.

"And it sold in a heartbeat. It wasn't up on the website for more than two hours when an offer came in." After Kelly turned over the flash drive and Fendi purse to the police, Tawny's brother contacted her. He gave permission to sell the purse along with all of Tawny's clothing. He planned to donate the money from the sales to a charity in his sister's name.

"Awesome!"

"It was a nice little addition to the boutique's bottom line. Now to find more designer items for consignment."

"I'm guessing Serena isn't going to be any help there. Surely, she has a closet or two of clothes and purses she doesn't wear." Ariel scooped out another heaping spoonful of ice cream dripping in chocolate sauce.

Kelly frowned at her plain ice cream, resisting the urge to plunge her spoon into Ariel's cup.

"Trust me, she does. And, no. She's not going to be any help. She's back in the city and back at work. My friend, Julie, texted me this morning. Serena is acting like nothing ever happened." Kelly scooped up another spoonful. Her last encounter with Serena was at the rental house when she was led out in handcuffs after her second arrest. It turned out that she had visited Jason's house and found him dead. Shocked, she fled. Her vehicle was spotted by a neighbor walking a dog who reported it to the police. After Liza confessed, Serena was let go and she left Lucky Cove without as much as a goodbye.

Ariel's eyes bugged out. "After what you did for her? You almost got yourself killed."

"I've learned not to expect anything from Serena Dawson. You know, like things that show she's a human being."

It was sad, really. Serena kept everyone at a distance and always seemed intent on being the one to strike the first hurtful blow. Kelly couldn't imagine living like that. Sure, there's always the risk of heartbreak and disappointment, but retreating into a self-imposed bubble seemed like it would be more damaging to a person. It was not how Kelly wanted to live her life.

And that was her choice. Just like it was her uncle's choice to live his life keeping his secret about being Ariel's biological father.

Kelly blinked. She couldn't think about that. Especially with Ariel sitting across from her at the table in the boutique's staff room.

Think about something else. Kittens. The new trends for summer. Anything!

"Hey, are you okay? You have a funny look on your face." Ariel set her sundae cup down and wiped her mouth with a napkin.

"Yeah…no…There's something…"

The door swung open and Breena popped in.

"Kell, Detective Wolman is here to see you," she said, saving Kelly from spilling her uncle's secret and possibly destroying Ariel's life. When she could afford it, Kelly needed to give Breena a raise.

"Wonder what she wants?" Ariel asked.

"Maybe she wants to tell you that you're getting a medal for helping solve the murders. I mean, the newspaper article made you sound like a hero. Which you are!" Breena flashed a proud smile.

"Ella did do a great job with her article," Ariel said after swallowing a spoonful of ice cream.

The day after Kelly's near death face-to-face with Liza, she sat down with Ella for an interview. When she arrived at the Gull Café to meet the reporter, she was nervous but by the end of their meeting, Kelly felt good about the interview. After it was published in the *Weekly*, it was picked up by other news outlets. The boutique's website had seen an increase in visitors and she had more interview requests. She'd been debating whether to do them. The bonus would be the exposure of the boutique. The downside would be the exposure of herself. She wasn't sure how she felt about being the center of attention. Especially in a murder case.

"She did. Well, I better go see what Wolman wants now." Kelly stood.

"No problem. I have to get back to the library. We can talk later." Ariel grabbed her ice cream and navigated her wheelchair from the table.

"Ah…sure." Great. Now Kelly had to come up with something to *talk* to Ariel about. Lucky for her, she just had a breakup. That was always good for heart-to-heart, soul-wrenching talks.

The three of them headed to the main sales area of the boutique, and Ariel continued out the front door, passing the detective and giving her a little wave. Wolman returned the smile and then turned her attention to Kelly. Breena dashed away, far away, into the accessory department, so Kelly was all on her own with Wolman.

Hopefully, it was business that brought Wolman to the boutique but, by the looks of her outfit—jeans, a rose-colored sweater, and drop earring dangling from her ears—the chances of her being there for work seemed low. Kelly's stomach twisted. The only other reason she could be there was because of Mark. Yep, she was there to gloat.

"I hope I'm not interrupting." Wolman stepped forward, drawing Kelly's attention to her white sneakers with splashes of rose gold. Look at the detective being all fashionable.

"Not at all. What brings you buy today? Something about Liza's case?"

Wolman shook her head. "No. It's in the hands of the district attorney now. I'm here to talk to you about Mark."

Yep, Kelly was right. "I'm sure you know we broke up." She dragged her gaze from Wolman and focused on a mannequin she just dressed in a pair of capri pants and blue button-down shirt. She didn't want the detective to see her eyes water. Shoot. She thought she was done crying over Mark Lambert.

"I know, and that's what I want to talk to you about."

"I don't understand." Kelly looked back at Wolman.

Wolman took in a deep breath and moved closer to Kelly. For the first time since meeting her, Kelly saw uncertainty on the woman's face. The nerves that had buzzed with seeing her in the boutique now morphed into a full-on anxiety. What was she going to say?

"Despite your irritating interference in my cases, you seem like a nice person."

"But I wasn't a nice enough person to date your brother."

"No. That's not true."

Kelly cocked her head sideways. Her tears had dried up. Now she was angry. "Really? You've been trying to get me to stop seeing him. Remember our conversation in December?" She sure did. "You didn't want to see him get distracted or have his reputation damaged in any way."

"I said that to try and—"

"And what? Look, it doesn't matter. We're broken up. You got what you wanted." Kelly moved away, heading to the sales counter.

"You're probably still hurting. Maybe second-guessing what could have been done differently. Wondering where you came up short."

Kelly swung around and faced Wolman. "If this is your idea of a pep talk..."

"Hear me out. This isn't easy for me."

"Me neither. Just say what you have to say." Then they could both get on with their lives.

"I love my brother."

Kelly shook her head. She had had enough. She walked behind the counter.

"You're not going to make this easy for me, are you?" Wolman followed and rested her hands on the glass countertop.

Kelly flashed a what-do-you-think look as she crossed her arms over her chest and waited for Wolman to continue with whatever she was trying to say.

"Woman-to-woman, I think you're probably better off without my brother. I love him, but he can be a...jerk."

Kelly's eyes bulged at Wolman's characterization of her brother. Maybe their talk wouldn't be a bad thing. "Go on, I'm listening."

Wolman tucked a lock of hair behind her ear. "You should know this isn't the first time he's put his career, his ambitions, ahead of a girlfriend. He can be a bit of a control freak. He also tends to have unrealistic standards of other people."

"Yeah, I noticed."

"As I said, you seem like a nice person, and I didn't want to see you get hurt, and that's why I gave you a hard time about your involvement with him. I do hope you find someone who won't have a problem with you being you."

"Wow." Kelly's hand covered her heart. She never thought Wolman cared about her. "That's a really nice thing to say to me. I appreciate it, Marcy."

Wolman's eyes narrowed.

"Just taking it for a test drive, Detective Wolman."

"We're not there." She turned and headed for the exit. She opened the door and then looked over her shoulder. "Yet."

Kelly was stunned. It seemed like they'd finally connected on some level, and there was hope that maybe someday they'd be friends. Despite her brother.

Breena reappeared as quickly as she had disappeared. "Is she gone? Was it bad?"

"Surprisingly, no." Kelly waved her employee over to her. "I think we're at a good place. Who knows? We might be friends one day."

Breena gave her a dubious look.

"It's possible." The bell over the door jingled and a deliveryman entered carrying a package. He requested Kelly's signature before handing over the box. Once he had it, he left and Kelly stared at the return address. "It's from Bishop's." She looked at Breena and they both shrugged.

"Go on, open it!" Breena handed Kelly a pair of scissors to cut through the tape.

When she got the package open, Kelly found a shoebox inside and a note card. She flipped the card open and read it.

"Out loud," Breena urged.

"You are so nosey."

"Look who's talking." Breena laughed.

"Fair enough. It says, *Thank you, best Serena*." Kelly lowered the card.

"That's all? You saved her from going to prison and you almost got yourself killed and all she said was thank you?" Breena's face scrunched up in disgust. "She should be ashamed of herself."

"No, you don't understand. This is huge for Serena. She actually said thank you and sent me a pair of Christian Louboutin shoes!" Kelly's heart raced as she pulled the cover of the shoebox off and reached in for the shoes. She could swear she heard angels singing when she touched the shoe. Serena had sent her a pair of patent leather, four-inch stilettos in the classic beige shade.

"OMG! Let me see!" Breena grabbed the shoe. "It's beautiful. Look at the red sole!"

"I know. I'm really shocked she did this." Kelly took back her shoe and set it gently in the box with its mate.

"Well, you deserve them. I am totally jealous. Too bad we don't wear the same size." Breena wrinkled her nose and smiled. "You'd let me wear them if we did, right?"

Before Kelly could answer the question, she was saved by the bell. A customer bustled in with two bags of clothes to consign. She tucked her unexpected gift away while Breena sorted through the clothes. For the rest of the afternoon they worked as a steady stream of customers came and went.

When the boutique quieted down, Kelly took a break. She wanted to check on her roof, again.

Outside, she inhaled a deep breath of fresh spring air while a warm breeze flitted by.

Out on the sidewalk, she glanced up and admired the new roof. It was the most important and expensive purchase she'd ever made, but it was well worth it. Buck had worked overtime without any additional charge to make sure she had a solid roof in time for spring and for the upcoming start of hurricane season, which was only a couple months away.

"Miss Quinn."

Kelly spun around and saw Detective Barber approaching with a coffee cup from Doug's in his hand. Unlike Wolman, he looked as if he was on duty in a lightweight sports jacket over dark gray pants.

"Good afternoon, Detective."

He slid off his sunglasses and glanced up at the roof. "Looks good."

"Thank you. It's one less thing I have to worry about. What brings you by? Or, are you just out for a stroll in this gorgeous weather?"

"I thought I'd check to see how you're doing. You got yourself into a very dangerous situation." He slipped his sunglasses back on and took a drink of his coffee.

"Yes, I did. I'm doing okay." The Louboutin shoes definitely helped boost her mood, but he wouldn't understand that. "I've had some bad dreams but they're happening less and less. And I have some really good friends to get me through this." One of them was approaching from the direction of the bakery.

"Good to hear. Well, I better get back to the PD. Hopefully, I'll see you around, but not at one of my crime scenes." He grinned before heading off. His swagger was cool and confident. Kelly tore her gaze away from his swagger and the view of his backside.

Liv hustled to Kelly and gawked at Detective Barber walking away. "Who was that?"

"Nate Barber."

Liv hit Kelly on the arm. "You didn't tell me he was cute."

"Ouch! It doesn't matter if he's cute or not. I'm not interested." No, she planned for the foreseeable future to remain unattached. Relationships were too much work, too complicated, and ultimately too painful.

"Well, then give him my number." Liv giggled.

Kelly rolled her eyes. "Will do the next time I see him. What are you up to this afternoon?"

Liv tilted her head upward. "It's so nice I'm thinking of taking a drive to the beach. How about you play hooky with me?"

Playing hooky sounded like fun and Kelly was tempted. "As much as I'd love to, I can't. I really should stay and work."

Liv pouted.

"Oh, no, that's not going to work." Kelly tried not to giggle but Liv looked so silly.

"It'll be fun. Come on. Don't forget, you were almost killed three weeks ago. Life is short. Let's go to the beach." Liv tugged at Kelly's arm. She could be such a bad influence on Kelly.

"Okay." Kelly relented. She'd call Breena from the car; make up some excuse for her sudden disappearance. "But I have to be back to close up."

Kelly had learned a few lessons over the past month, and one of those lessons was never to take anyone or anything for granted. Like her hometown.

They linked arms and walked toward Liv's car. Hanging out with her friend was a great way to spend the afternoon. Wasn't that what living at the beach was all about? Sun, sand and good friends.

ABOUT THE AUTHOR

Debra Sennefelder is an avid reader who reads across a range of genres, but mystery fiction is her obsession. Her interest in people and relationships is channeled into her novels against a backdrop of crime and mystery. When she's not reading, she enjoys cooking and baking and as a former food blogger, she is constantly taking photographs of her food. *Yeah, she's that person.* Born and raised in New York City, where she majored in her hobby of fashion buying, she now lives and writes in Connecticut with her family. She's worked in retail and publishing before becoming a full-time author. Her writing companion is her adorable and slightly spoiled Shih-Tzu, Connie.

You can learn more about Debra at www.DebraSennefelder.com

Printed in the United States
by Baker & Taylor Publisher Services